PENGUI

# DARKLANDS

Arnav Das Sharma is a New Delhi-based author and journalist. His work has appeared in publications across the country, like the *Caravan*, *Vice*, the *Indian Express*, *Outlook*, the Wire, Scroll and *Hindustan Times*. He has also held positions at Reuters and, most recently, the Quint. He's working on his second book.

## ADVANCE PRAISE FOR THE BOOK

'*Darklands* is much more than a compelling first novel; it is a creditable literary achievement in many ways—the most admirable one among them is that Arnav Das Sharma could reimagine *Wuthering Heights* with such precision and render it with amazing poise. With his selection of theme and style of storytelling, Sharma has produced a remarkable novel'—Anees Salim, author of *The Small-Town Sea* and *The Blind Lady's Descendants*

# DARK LANDS

## ARNAV DAS SHARMA

**PENGUIN BOOKS**

An imprint of Penguin Random House

PENGUIN BOOKS

USA | Canada | UK | Ireland | Australia
New Zealand | India | South Africa | China

Penguin Books is part of the Penguin Random House group of companies
whose addresses can be found at global.penguinrandomhouse.com

Published by Penguin Random House India Pvt. Ltd
7th Floor, Infinity Tower C, DLF Cyber City,
Gurgaon 122 002, Haryana, India

Penguin
Random House
India

First published in Penguin Books by Penguin Random House India 2021

Text copyright © Arnav Das Sharma 2021

ISBN 9780143439929

Typeset in Bell MT by Manipal Technologies Limited, Manipal
Printed at Replika Press Pvt. Ltd, India

www.penguin.co.in

*To my grandmother, Aparna,*
*who taught me this crucial lesson early on:*
*stories matter*

He looked at the infant and a wave of something indistinguishable swept somewhere deep inside him. *Was it sympathy*, he thought, *which made him pick up the infant from out there in the wilderness?*

Despite knowing he had nothing to do with it.

Despite knowing it wasn't his, and that survival for his own small family was getting difficult with each passing day.

Despite knowing that the five evenly placed dots tattooed on its neck indicated that the creature was not even human.

So what was it that made him pick up the infant?

# 1

They came as a herd. Those men, the marauders from the west. Their grey trucks, four in number, first seemed like little inkblots against a white sheet of paper, only to become more prominent markings, large and distinct, while the horizon receded. There was dust and ash everywhere. Multitudes of minuscule granules, the imperfect marriage of golden and black, levitating, swirling and dancing—the slow ritual of open defiance against the setting sun. And against what would come in its wake. The phantom darkness.

The trucks gathered speed. The men inside, four in each vehicle, had their heads covered in white keffiyeh and wore dust masks around their mouth. Over their shoulders hung automatics and shotguns. In the back of one of the trucks were huddled together a silver-haired man with a half-asleep infant clutched tightly in his arms and a ten-year-old boy. Pulling the boy closer, the man pressed his nose to the window, stretched his neck and looked out. His expressions, absent. Fragments of dust-ash had settled on his two-week-old beard. His lips were parched. He thought of home. He thought about the baby. He thought about his boy. He thought about the world.

The approaching darkness would soon conquer the dust-ash. Infiltrate their atoms. Make them invisible. Subjugate them to silence. And from the darkness would also come the beasts, with their prehistoric breaths. Brimstone, the colour of their eyes. Their fangs, white as chalk and sharp as cut glass. Their bodies, charred. Like the earth before them. Burnt, burning.

*It all comes back*, thought the silver-haired man. The history of Earth is forever recurring. We excavate light out of a casement of darkness, only to have the casement close up. All the time. Around his neck hangs a crucifix that he, time and again, would slowly run his finger on, muttering a little prayer underneath his dry breath.

'Does it help?' the driver, a young boy of around twenty-five years of age, asked, looking at the man through the rear-view mirror.

'No. It never helps. But it's good to hold on to something,' he replied, neatly tucking his crucifix inside his shirt.

The young boy doesn't say anything back. He understands. He looks ahead, to the vast road stretching before him. Heat and frequent earthquakes have left large cracks on it. Like the scars on the body of a man, under medieval torture. Massive dust fields lay still towards infinity. The landscape decorated only by the skeleton of trees. Apart from the low collective whine of the engines that sped on and slowly scattered the dust-ash elliptically behind them, there was a gaping silence. The scorched land lying wordless.

*It isn't the silence of the approaching darkness*, thought the man, as he drew the infant closer to his chest, trying to soothe its muffled cries. *The silence is that of a mortuary. Of unclaimed corpses, a charnel house of a country that once was and will never be again.* The infant tugged at his jacket that had now become ragged, squinted its eyes and went back to sleep. The sun sank like a pebble in a dark moonless ocean.

■ ■ ■

The infant was not his. He and his son had gone out to hunt. To cross over the perimeters of whatever remained of civilization in the city that once was. Look for food, any kind of food. When he was young, Earth was a giant cradle of abundance. A long chain of green fields everywhere. He remembered the early evenings when he would visit the garden near his house with his friends. Climb the tall mango tree. And the sourly sweet taste of unripe mangoes trickling down his throat. But all that was long ago. When Earth and its inhabitants were blessed.

If one were to ask at what point it all started going downhill and if the cracks in the bricks of civilization started tearing it asunder, he didn't think there would ever be one answer. Like a love affair gone sour, turning it into a nightmare, Earth started detesting the weight of mankind walking on its back. *There is a thin line that separates a blessing from a curse,* ruminated the man. Always scurrying behind the skein of blessing, curse lurks around. How long before then did it rear its ugly head? In other words, how long did it take to reduce the blessed Earth into a mound of cinders? The residue of centuries past staring out from the caverns of those million worn-out cracks in the road seem to offer no explanation. Only a quiet acquiescence. *No,* he thought, *mankind wasn't supposed to evolve.* It was nature's terrible mistake. And she was paying dearly for it.

He looked at the infant and a wave of something indistinguishable swept somewhere deep inside him. *Was it sympathy,* he thought, *which made him pick the infant up from out there in the wilderness?*

Despite knowing he had nothing to do with it.

Despite knowing it wasn't his, and that survival for his own small family was getting difficult with each passing day.

Despite knowing that the five evenly placed dots tattooed on its neck indicated that the creature was not even human.

So what was it that made him pick up the infant?

■ ■ ■

The road ahead had already darkened. Aakash, the young driver brought the truck to a halt, making the stream of trucks behind him halt as well.

'We need light. The more, the better,' said a tall, thin man who was wearing a dust mask that covered his face. Aakash nodded. The man came out from within the group of ragtag hunters who had stepped down from the vehicles and sparked a flint. Aakash and a few others scurried around to collect dead branches and leaves. They piled them up on a mound a few metres from the edge of the broken road and set it on fire.

The crackling fire revealed a mosaic of worn-out faces, their masks glowing yellow in the dying heat of burning embers.

'We can't stop here for the night. It won't be—it cannot be—safe,' the young driver said, his eyes fixated on the brown branches that were turning to ash in the all-consuming fire.

'There is nothing we can do apart from stopping here, Aakash,' replied the tall, thin man. Although no one really knew his real birth name, Eaklavya is what they called him. 'We have little supplies. We can cross the river and reach the city by daybreak tomorrow.'

'The streets are filled with stories about those beasts and what they do to you. Hungry. They're hungry . . . A fire burns in their belly. I want you all to shoot me if I am ever caught. I don't want to die at the hands of a beast!' an old man exclaimed. His head and mouth were covered with a black scarf. His voice was cold and distant. There were tiny flecks of dried blood splattered on the scarf, now obscured by darkness.

'Shut the fuck up, Phanai. No one is going to die. No one has to die,' Aakash replied, his eyes still glued to the fire that was now dying.

Eaklavya removed a carcass of a goat from the back of one of the trucks and carried it closer to the bonfire. He held the legs aloft and hacked them off with his kukri into precise yet inelegant pieces. He passed it on to Aakash, who cut it into further pieces and gave each piece to the men sitting alongside each other, while the fire burned out slowly. Their faces seemed lacklustre. Like the ruins of the land now obscured by darkness. The men roasted the piece in their hands before eating it ravenously. As if consumed by an antique hunger.

The silver-haired man broke his piece of mutton into smaller portions and gave them to his son, who quietly chewed on them. Aakash got up and sat near them, his bowl still full of meat.

'He doesn't seem to speak much. Just like his father.'

'There isn't much to say now, is there?'

'Back home in the village where I grew up, before the calamity, my mother would cook some delicious fish. She would, when her health allowed her, go to the pond and catch those fishes herself. Nothing stopped her; she just moved on. Kept going. From one fish curry to the next. From one day to the next.'

'It's good to keep going, when you know *where* you're going.'

'Yes, and that scares me. Mother is long dead. The dead have it easy, I guess. Not having to live this, this fucked-up life.'

They stare out in silence. In front of them, the remains of the fire heaved and sighed like the last torturous breath of a dying animal.

'She suffered, though, those last few years. Didn't have it easy. Her lungs bled. That sound of her coughing, through the nights. And I would be there, on the charpoy, lying wide awake, looking at the stars, wishing for her to die. And then, just like that, one morning, she didn't wake up. I woke up to my sister's cries; she was kneeling over that bed, and I walked over. There she was, my mother, resting peacefully. The ash had devoured her lungs to the point that she could no longer breathe.'

The silver-haired man didn't say anything and just nodded. Aakash, finishing up his meal, threw the bare bones into the fire. The fire sizzled for a second, only to quieten down.

'Did you have to pick it up?' Aakash asked, eyeing the cradling infant on the man's lap. It opened its eyes and reached for the man's coat. The man responded by gently rocking the infant sideways and then feeding it with a sliver of meat from his bowl. The infant rolled its tongue, swallowed the morsel of food and went back to sleep. The man brought the lapel of his cheap cotton coat forward and tucked the infant inside— the coat covering it up partly like a malformed blanket.

'No. I didn't have to. There was nothing that I had to do. But then I did what I did,' the man answered. His voice, the terrible tranquillity of death.

■ ■ ■

The man was named Easwaran. He had left early that April morning, on his old motorbike. His son, Harish, sat tightly behind him, holding a long-range rifle. What remained of civilization had gathered itself into collapsed adobe houses in the south, with the river dividing the city into two. When the temperature began to rise, the river slowly dried up. But that was just the beginning. The weight of the sun hanging heavily upon the earth brought with it, at first, the mosquitoes, raging and swarming, with plagues hidden in their bellies.

The man remembered it all. Him as a boy, looking down upon the almost dry river, longing to catch that lonesome fish. But by then the fish had either swam upstream to where the river was still strong or had died. He had returned home empty that evening. But his father, who worked in the mines on the outskirts of the city and who would die of the terrible mosquito plague in only a few years, quietly ruffled the boy's hair and promised he would take him fishing soon. It would be weeks, even months, perhaps, and the boy might have even forgotten about it, but his father hadn't.

When they eventually went, outside the city to the north, where the rivers emerged, the boy's father carefully ran the line through the eye of the hook, expertly tied a somewhat loose double overhand knot at the end of the line. He then tied the open edge of the loop over on to the hook and slowly pulled at it, as the loop tightened. He then cast the line over on to the water, waiting patiently for the fish to fall for the bait. The first sight of the wobbling fish as his father deftly pulled it up, woke up the boy from his torpor in that nippy morning air, and he would look wide-eyed at the small silver-bodied animal gasping for breath while splashing its tail hither and thither. Instead of fascinating him, the sight rather scared the young boy, and the memory of this nippy, dew-glistened morning would reappear years later, when in a decrepit house, the young boy, now a man, would sit beside his sister as she'd cough blood and particles of ash, thirsty for air, now being burnt by the scorching sun.

However, on that April morning, none of these thoughts bothered him. The only thing on his mind was his son and the approaching darkness. His wife had pleaded with him not to take the boy along. But he had to. Someday, the boy had to grow up, become a man and learn to hunt, to ride in the darkness, face those beasts and build a family. For when everything that was familiar, humanity itself, was breathing the last of the toxic air; when the very idea of 'tomorrow' had no meaning, the only marks of manhood lay in the ability to survive, to force that invisible tomorrow to show itself, to grasp it by its hands, to arrive at a point when the evasion of death becomes a means . . . perhaps the only means to conquer death's forever all-encompassing shadow. So Easwaran took his ten-year-old son on his sputtering Enfield into the wasted country.

They had to ride up north—the same way he had gone fishing with his own father, during a time that now seemed light years away. Once the climate became warmer, people began migrating northwards, thereby veritably splitting the region into two. Those who couldn't move out died due to the heat and ash or lived like savages, as the water flowing to the south began to dry out.

And slowly, as the years accumulated, the north became a city, a witness to mankind's arrival in the new millennium. A city of tall glass spires and plush French-windowed apartment blocks. A city owned by the global consortium called Inspire

Corporation, which traded in water from the three interlinked rivers that flowed into the areas, giving the city its opulence. A city of innovation, where science triumphed over nature and perpetuated the illusion that everything was still safe and that mankind was here to stay. Millennium City also became a testament, in a way, that it's only the fittest that survive, and those who do not meet this criteria, like the people in the south, die a painful death. But who decides the basis of being 'fit'? And to what extent? By what means? These were, of course, a few questions that were never even considered, let alone answered. As if, like species, questions too could be classified into what were fit to be asked, and what weren't.

■ ■ ■

In the makeshift camp, darkness slowly ate away the remaining tendrils of the burning fire, and with it, time became inchoate. Up in the bleak sky, the stars twinkled with their indefinite lights. Five men were asked to stand guard, while the rest of the gang slept. Somewhere from afar, echoes of shrieks, thin and faint, whistled through the silence. With each little shriek, in the arid darkness, Easwaran's son would wake up. At first, his young, grimy face would betray fear and some bafflement, as the sound of those phantom shrieks would criss-cross and overlap each other. But as they became more frequent, the boy's fear receded and habit took over. He stopped getting startled. Through the chinks in his blanket, Easwaran witnessed this entire ritual but uttered nothing. Neither did he get up to cradle the boy, knowing full well that there was no need. The only way to teach his son to conquer fear and the darkness was not to teach him resistance but acceptance. To enable him to embrace the darkness and his fear, domesticate it, make it a part of his everyday life.

Eaklavya had instructed everyone to sleep closer together to ensure no one fell behind or slept apart from the group. One could never know what the darkness contained within it. And what it gave birth to. Towards the edges of this improvised collection of slumbering men lay Phanai and his seventeen-year-old son, Kanishka. It must have been well past midnight, though one could never be sure. Kanishka got up. A slight cold breeze, with a hint of moisture, blew past his sleep-laden eyes. His soft black hair rose and fell like wavelets. He tried to brush away granules of ash from his hands and face. His throat was incredibly dry. Canisters of precious water were kept beside the men who stood guard on the other side of the camp, two of them leaning against a tree, nodding off. Kanishka decided to walk towards the canisters via the long encircled path, leading away from the group. The young lad didn't think it was necessary to wake the men up. It had been a long, tiring day after all.

As he walked two hundred yards away, he was beyond the pale light of the electric lamps the guards had set up near them. In the vast silence of the wilderness, somewhere a lonesome owl hooted. Kanishka kept walking. His boots brushed through the dust. It sounded like the muffled reverberations of teeth gnashing against each other. The echoes of shrieks carelessly punctuated, time and time again, the gentle whisper of the breeze. Kanishka, meanwhile, was lost in the thoughts of the dream he had just woken up from.

In the dream, he saw Mani, the sixteen-year-old girl from his village. She was walking towards him with a pitcher of water clutched carefully in both her hands. In the dream, he could almost feel his heart slowly climb up in his mouth as she approached. But she was only a few yards away when she stopped. Her eyes hovered around for a while and then settled on her feet when she saw a snake. Its thin, scaly body glistened in the mid-afternoon sun, as it crawled up from her fair ankles to her thighs. Mani's voice had somehow stopped in between a cry and a gasp. The snake, as it wound its way around the girl's body, began to grow, slowly enveloping her, making her a part of itself by not so much eating her as absorbing her essences into itself. As she disappeared, the snake began to grow and its green skin became paler and paler until the reptile acquired a deathly white pallor.

Kanishka woke up at this point, feeling his throat parched. As he came to his senses and began walking to quench his thirst, his mind wandered over to Mani, now a thousand miles away. He stopped midway, took out a cigarette from his pocket and lit a flint. In the darkness, his lighted cigarette looked like a small red bead of an insect's eye. Lost in his thoughts, he had walked a considerable distance away from the group. The little globules of light from the electric lamp were no longer visible. But he didn't mind. There was silence here. Eerie, but calming nevertheless. Somewhere deep inside, he felt strange. The dream, like the incantations of a demonic spell, made him think of things he didn't want to. He wasn't scared, neither for him nor for Mani. But as he remembered the fragments of his dream, especially the bit where the snake was winding itself around Mani, he felt pangs of desire rise up within the aridity of his heart. And then he made up his mind. This time, he would approach Mani, talk to her. As he puffed out ringlets of invisible smoke into the echoing darkness, he suddenly felt a foul smell invade his nostrils. *Must have stepped on something*, he thought. He decided to walk back towards the camp, drink water and just go to sleep. He turned around, only to stop short. The cigarette dangled from his half-open mouth like a pencil from the hands of a sleepy child. He turned his neck sideways to the right. His eyes widened.

All of a sudden, he heard a low growl. Then a short shriek. Eyes, glassy and pale, transfixed upon him. The sound of hooves squishing the dust underneath. Kanishka reached for the flint in his trouser pockets. He had read somewhere that the beasts were scared of fire. He lit it up and turned sideways. As the pale, flickering light of the flint pierced the fabric of darkness, like a thin needle into a blanket, Kanishka saw the beast. It was four-and-a-half-feet tall. Its face and body was covered with crisp black hair. It walked heavily in the dust, on its four sturdy legs. As it came near, Kanishka could feel the smell of sulphur emanating from his mouth. As it snickered, part of its long-pointed canines shyly protruded. Like a child peeping out of a half-closed door. Kanishka took a step back. Air wheezed slowly out of his dry mouth. *I need a sip of the water right now. I should have got my goddamn gun. What was I doing?* he berated himself with a volley of angry thoughts. Should he run? Or shout? How far had he drifted from the camp? He pondered the alternatives. A faint voice, closely resembling an inchoate cry, escaped his mouth. He turned back and decided to run. The cigarette had long since gone. He thought he would lose balance, but he didn't. He tried to sprint, but the inertia in his legs held him back for a moment. There was no sound of hooves following him. In the distance, he saw the faint familiar glow of those lamps. *I think I made it*, he thought. He was breathing heavily. He stopped to calm his nerves and his pulsating heart. He looked back.

*Nothing.* He let out a faded, uneasy laugh. *That was fucking close*, he thought. With that uneasy grin still on his face, he decided to walk the remaining distance. As he took a step forward, from the impenetrable darkness, something jumped. Before any thought could cross Kanishka's mind, the beast sank its sharp, pointed teeth into the boy's soft neck. The warm blood oozed out and fell on to the beast's thin, black, papery lips. Drop by drop. The helpless lad pushed his legs in the dust. The beast tightened its hold on the neck until the blood slowly trickled out whatever life remained in the boy.

It slowly pulled itself back. Its glassy eyes and foul breath, both devoured by the darkness that gave birth to it. And took a boy named Kanishka with it. What reigned in its stead was silence. The stars still glistened overhead. In the distance, the light still flickered from the electric lamps. The darklands still stretched out, as eternally as always. It was as if the universe remained unaltered.

## 2

He woke up, dreaming of sheep. They were everywhere. Atop a hillock, cascading down a brook, their curly white fur gleaming in the soft, wintry sun. And then, with a slight flutter of an eyelid, they were gone. What surfaced was the wasteland, corroding away in the harsh morning sun. It was still early morning, but the sun was already severe. Through his half-open eyes, still very heavy with sleep, Easwaran tried to look. The dust and ash had begun to swirl across the barren landscape. Some people were up from their sleep, while some had wrapped their tattered blankets around their heads, trying to evade the daylight. Easwaran tried to gauge what time it must have been. Probably still seven. But in the vast, desolate landscape, time and its precise classification had become vestigial rituals of an age that no longer can be. It was reduced instead to a rough probability. As was everything else. Life even. His son was still in the blanket, but Easwaran knew he was wide awake. The infant was still asleep close to him. From a bit afar, towards the edges of the makeshift camp, the lanterns were giving up the last of their flames. Set against the glowing daylight, these tiny flames seemed pathetic, like a puny space rover approaching the cosmic infinitude of Jupiter. But the flames stayed, pale and almost invisible, but intact nevertheless. No one in the camp seemed to mind.

Aakash walked softly over to Easwaran, a cold rifle gleaming in his hand. His face was taut and visible from a distance. Well, at least to Easwaran, it seemed hardened. As if laughter hadn't meandered on the soft pastures of his face for a long time now.

'There's trouble,' Aakash said, crouching unevenly near the man. 'Apparently, that Phanai's lad is missing.'

'Is it what I fear?' Easwaran remarked. He was up by now. Granules of dust and ash were on his face, but he seemed unperturbed by this.

'Could be. But no one knows. I saw him last night, quiet and all by himself, as he normally is. More than anything, he seemed safe.' Aakash regretted the moment he said this and he even anticipated what Easwaran's reply would be.

'Nothing is safe,' Easwaran replied, his eyes turning away from Aakash and towards the desert landscape that stretched before him and all around and shimmered like a hot metal freshly pulled out of industrial fire.

'I was thinking of telling Eaklavya that we need a search party. We should look for him, no?'

'Look for him *where*? Where do you think he could go? How many nooks and crannies and undiscovered lanes do you see here? It's a damned wasteland.' Easwaran tasted the bitter trickle of bile rising in his mouth. He thought he had accepted his fate and along with it, everyone's. He thought that he had stopped caring. For that was the only way he could make sense of it all. But he was clearly wrong, it seemed.

'What else are we supposed to do then?' Aakash asked. Easwaran knew he could not answer that—he didn't have an answer. He chose to keep quiet. The infant woke up crying. He picked it up and began cradling it in his arms. He recognized those to be peals of hunger. But he also knew he could do nothing about it.

Sleep, and the sweet oblivion that it brings with it, had deserted everyone now. Not that anybody noticed. Phanai had begun to rove around the camp and its vicinity, as the rifle clung to his frail, wrinkled arms. His keffiyeh and gas mask lay abandoned on the ash-ridden ground. Phanai, pale and thin, was still the best sharpshooter in the gang. Though of late, some members of the gang, which included Eaklavya, had begun to harbour the thought that he was becoming delusional. Phanai could still shoot an apple off someone's head at a distance of over five hundred yards, that too with perfectly choreographed precision. But throughout the journey, he kept complaining of ghosts. This could have been attributed to the forever parched desert and the tricks it sometimes played on one's mind, but what was actually worrying was that Phanai had started conversing with these ghosts. As if, for Phanai, the thread that bifurcates reality from its opposite had somehow begun to thin. Eaklavya didn't want to think about it now. There'd be time for that. But looking at Phanai now, adrift in a sea of pain at not finding his son, he was beginning to worry. Phanai had started shouting, first at Eaklavya and then at any member of the gang that came into sight. When he couldn't find anyone, he shouted into the wind, which only ricocheted back at him with an indifferent silence.

The men were mostly quiet. Eaklavya, when he first heard the news, immediately felt the need to send someone from the group to search for the disappeared boy. But the land lay desolate in front of them. Naked. And till the far reaches of the horizon, the furthest point of one's vision, there was no sign of any human. A quiet, dry breeze whispered over the ancient bodies of tepid cactuses and stray brambles that were as black as soot. The breeze blew particles of the dust and ash that rested upon them, into the dying air where they stood, levitating. This quiet nothingness was suddenly pierced by the undulating screams of Phanai, while the eyes of the rest of the men tried to trace the lost figure of a seventeen-year-old.

But even in the midst of such a turmoil, Easwaran was besieged by a series of thoughts, which were not quite connected to the issue at hand.

*If I were to write a memoir, I'd begin with these words: there was once a broken man from a broken country. He sat crouching on the ground, cradling the infant in his arms. His son sat beside him. Between them, not a word stirred. The breeze had gathered momentum by now. Blowing past him, across the ravaged plateau, simmering away in the morning sun, it brought with it a faint promise of rain. Rain showers had become infrequent in this part of the country. But he knew that in the other parts, like further south, the sea had eaten up large pieces of land, and along with it, whatever remained of humanity had sunk underneath the ocean. In those areas, rain and too much of it had killed the crops. In this broken planet, there was either too much or too little of something. Extremities had become the bane of humanity.*

Behind him, some of the gang members had gotten hold of an inconsolable Phanai. Eaklavya had sent two men to look around. He, like everyone else around him, knew that was futile. But some sign, even an artefact from the boy's body, could work as that elusive thing called 'closure' and allow the men to go back to their trucks and head home. In fact, as per their plans, they were supposed to have left by now.

Ravi Rajendran, a quiet boy aged twenty-five, was squatting a few yards away from Easwaran. He came up and sat beside him. He drew out a handmade cigarette from his pocket and lit it up, blowing puffs of smoke on to Easwaran's, and more directly, at the infant's face. The infant winced, opened its eyes to look around and sneezed.

'Push off! You do that again, and my hands will be wrapped around your neck,' Easwaran growls. Ravi, his mien unchanged, continued his smoke. As if the words failed to filter through his consciousness.

'I am just wondering, do these machine-made babies even feel anything? Weren't they made just to endure whatever the shit we are supposed to throw at them?' he said, assuming an air of nonchalance.

'It's none of your business the way I treat *my* kids.'

'Sure. But *this* one right here ain't yours.' He turned around to Easwaran's son, Harish, who was clearly getting alarmed by this particular exchange.

'You know, Easwaran,' Ravi continued, his nonchalance intact, 'I really wonder how the hell you will even survive. I mean you have a son right here, and he seems mighty fine to me. What the fuck will you even tell him?'

'That's not for you to know . . .'

'Damn you, it's for all of us to know. It's a *thing*, it's not even human. And you're treating it like you gave birth to it. It's fucking affecting us, man.'

Easwaran, who by now had decided enough was enough, wrapped his fingers around the rifle lying beside him.

He didn't want to fight. Not today. There'd be enough of that in the coming days that'd be filled with uncertainty. The heat was getting severe. Beads of perspiration shone like little pearls on both the men's foreheads. Ravi's finished his cigarette, but instead of stubbing it, he got up, dusted the back of his trousers and threw the cigarette butt towards Easwaran—which didn't hit him.

'Son of a . . .' Ravi muttered under his breath. Easwaran didn't get up. He didn't think there was any need to. His eyes were fixated on the discarded cigarette, now slowly being swallowed by the dust. *There'd be more to come*, he thought. Many more. He knew the choice he had made, and whatever he did, it would have repercussions. Every choice has its own comeuppance. His will too. *A broken man from a broken country. Yes*, he thought, *and a cartload of broken choices*.

■ ■ ■

Easwaran, while growing up in the thick of the changing climate, was perhaps the quietest man in Old City—the southern part inhabited mostly by the castaways and those who could not get out and into that most cherished place, Millennium City. He didn't want to get married. But love has its own agency. He ended up meeting a demure, shy woman, almost half his age, in whose eyes he found a comfort the crumbling world before him had failed to provide. In other words, fixity. They married after a year of courtship and she bore him two children—Harish, his son, and Chhaya, his daughter. Most days, he would sit on the ground that was gradually being coloured in a dreary hue and wonder about them and how what he had done would change everything for them. But if there was one thing his father ever taught him it was: a man is made not so much by the choices he makes, but the way he accepts them as choices and owns the result.

He would teach the same to his children, he resolved. And he would stick with his choice, no matter what. Broken they may be, but they're his choices and they will be treated as he treated his other choices—like staying back in Old City, even when he had begun to realize that soon things would become difficult both for him and his now growing family—with dignity. As his father had tried to teach him, he knew that things were changing, and changing fast. The world, as they knew it, was no longer to be. The sun had grown hotter by the day, and droughts had become severe and acute. Trees and animals, whichever wasn't able to live up to the changed conditions, died out. Another thing that his father taught him, which he had taken to heart, was that the zeal to survive resides within every man, and it's this zeal, if anything at all, which will see us through. It was with this thought that he joined one of the fiercest gangs operating out of Old City, knowing full well that this would be his opportunity to survive. The moment his children came into this world, he knew he had to pass on this teaching to both of them, and he had been trying to do the same ever since.

Since the construction of Millennium City and the time Inspire Corporation became the primary multinational organization controlling the region and the precious rivers, Old City had become a region shunned. And like all regions that are discarded, it had become decrepit with decaying old houses and a population both poor and living on the margins of survival. The people first tried to infiltrate Millennium City through the porous borders, hiding in the Interstate.

But then the corporation, deeming the influx of refugees as undesirable, decided to put a stop to it.

The Interstate was an in-between space between Millennium City to the north and Old City further south. A vast desert wasteland of a million charred dreams of a humanity that was now on the verge of extinction. Nothing grew here for miles—only brambles and old cactuses and a few spare prickly pears. The rest was conquered by the corpses of dead trees, serving as a stark reminder of both the past and the future, of what was and what can be. Over the years, like dust accumulates over a forgotten antique clock, the Interstate turned into a no man's land—a land of darkness and of unbearable heat, a topography of savagery and cruelty. A place devoid of rules or grammar, a place of a million possibilities and a million deaths. It had become the place swirling with gangs, most of them from Old City, like the one Easwaran and his son had joined. They would go all the way to the north to scavenge and hunt for food, but most importantly, water. In a world where water had become precious, it became the *only* currency.

And so, the Interstate endured. A notion against time, the forever expanding wasteland consumed everything as it marched on, inch by inch. And it ensured that the borders surrounding Millennium City remained obscure. At once it became a symbol of mankind's bleak future and a reminder of the eternal notion that borders like walls and every spatial marker of separation cannot endure over time.

His gang was called Madira. One of the most cruel and brutal gangs operating out of Old City. At first, when Easwaran wanted to enrol, he didn't know much about these gangs and their modus operandi. But he knew one of the leading members of the gang—Jaidev Singhla. It was Jaidev who'd recruited Easwaran. A tall and lanky man, Jaidev was about the same age as Easwaran, which was somewhere in the forties. And as Easwaran remembers, the process of recruitment had been rather easy. Jaidev had come down to his house and asked for two bowls, one white and one black, and kept them in front of him, telling him to think of them as two life choices. If Easwaran chose the white bowl, he opted for survival. If he chose the black one, he would die in a year's time; if not consumed by the ash and the poison in the air then by hunger for sure. Easwaran had peered into his wife's eyes, the same eyes that had made him marry her, the same eyes that now showed utter desperation. Later, during quiet moments in the Interstate, when his face would be obscured by the darkness all around him, he'd think to himself: he didn't have to choose anything; those eyes had already made the decision for him.

■ ■ ■

Now sitting down in the bleak nothingness of the Interstate, he imagined those eyes. But this time, he found them silent. And silence always confounded him. Harish was sitting near him, looking at the infant who had gone to sleep. The camp was quiet. He didn't stir. Easwaran stretched out his hands to draw Harish closer to him. Harish, giving in, shifted towards his father. Easwaran, thinking this would be a good time to introduce the infant to his son, tried to place the baby on the young boy's lap. Harish, however, refused any such advances and recoiled from him. Easwaran felt a tinge of fear crossing through his heart like a shard of glass piercing through one's skin. He didn't do anything more. He wanted to glare at his son, thinking that'd change things, make his son more deferential. But he knew doing so would have only hardened his son towards him. It is then that he realized something he hadn't considered till now: Harish was growing up and was learning to form his own decisions. And a man that he was, he'd only respect it. But he knew that something had changed, not just in his son, but also between them.

'There's a saying . . .' Eaklavya said, walking closer to Easwaran and squatting beside him, '. . . Sons are never one's own. Daughters, yes, but never the sons.'

'Yes, and one should just let them be. That's what my father did with me.'

'I wonder what Jaidev would say once he sees that *thing* on your lap.'

'He has nothing to do with it. It was what I had to do, so I did.'

'Yea, but that's not how things work. I saw that little thing that happened between you and that Rajendran guy over there. He's an asshole, you can ignore him. But what he said was right. There'd be a scene when we get back.'

'I am expecting it too. But I did what I had to do. And I am not turning back. Not as long as I am walking on this Earth.'

'And how do you propose to raise this thing? Have you any idea what all it entails? What it can do to Old City and our ways of life? You're not in Millennium, and you don't have the goddamn bucks and those big-ass houses. How the hell will you deal with it all?'

'Let's just leave it to time now, shall we?'

'My mother was right. You're just like your father. A stubborn piece of shit.'

'What's with Phanai over there? Any news on the boy?'

'None. But that's precisely why it's worrying. I don't know what the old man will do.'

Almost as if by instinct, the two looked towards Phanai, who was sitting on the ground, whimpering and talking to ghosts. At times he'd be quiet and not speak. But this silence would soon be disturbed by a large staccato of words addressed to the thin invisible air. Easwaran could estimate that it was almost noon, which meant they'd have to leave sooner if they wanted to reach Old City by late evening. The two men Eaklavya had sent scouting hadn't returned, but he expected them to be back soon.

'We should prepare to leave, Eaklavya. The longer we stay, the more dangerous it becomes here,' Easwaran pointed out, his eyes still fixated on Phanai. 'Gather the old man and let's leave.'

'One thing or the other, we leave once the two men are back.'

Suddenly, Phanai got up and took his rifle, slung it over his right shoulder and began to shoot at the empty horizon, the loud sounds jolting everyone in the camp.

'Kreeeeeech, I kill you all. I kill all of you, one bullet at a time,' the disorderly, disjointed voice that was Phanai's rang out in the primordial wilderness. Dust and ash whirled around him like Turkish dervishes in their garb of white and black. Easwaran had considered telling Jaidev about Phanai, long before the commencement of this part of the gang's travels. Phanai, now pushing seventy, used to work in the same coalfield as Easwaran's father. Years later, when the fields were closed, auctioned and sold off, removing an entire workforce from employment, the young Phanai had driven all the way into Millennium City on his stammering Toyota truck, tracked the old mine's general manager—who'd become an employee of Inspire Corporation—at his palatial French windowed-apartment and shot him dead. One bullet, from a range of over six hundred yards and two open windows, was all that it took. The news had travelled fast and thick through Old City, making Phanai an important person to be recruited. When asked about his shooting skills, he would always say it came naturally to him like poetry.

Easwaran remembered how his father had regarded Phanai with a degree of awe the old man hadn't reserved for anyone. For, he suspected, Phanai reminded his father of the very possibility that a man was capable of, if he only set his mind to it. The general manager and the other mining officials were all bought over by the Inspire Corporation. After buying out the properties of the older Sterling Inc, which included the mining operations, the corporation decided it needed these officers, who had important degrees in mathematics and engineering. Engineering was how Inspire thought the world, and all the things in it—once bountiful, now a mere shadow—could be remade. And like God in the Book of Genesis, the company decided to remake the world in its own image. During particularly dark days, Easwaran could still picture the scene when he was barely eighteen, waiting for his father to come home. And his father did come back but only much later. Inebriated and with a quiet anger that was slowly flowing through his intestines. When Easwaran's mother had brought his supper to him and inquired what had happened, his father, perhaps for the first time in his life, had snatched the plate only to fling it towards her, hitting her head on the way. It was also for the first time in his eighteen years of existence that he saw his father sob uncontrollably. Months later, when Phanai 'had done the job', as Easwaran's father would exclaim with glee sparkling in his eyes, he had gone to Phanai and was the first to congratulate him. When talking about what a perfect man ought to be like, he always gave Phanai's example. Now, with age, Easwaran knew deep down that his father had congratulated Phanai not because he appreciated the deed—for his father, as he knew him to be, could never condone violence—but because Phanai did what his father wanted to do that night when he was laid off from the mines but lacked the conviction to see it through. In his father's world, conviction mattered more than anything else.

Seeing the same Phanai dancing stark, raving mad and shooting at his imagined ghosts, calling out the name of his son who once was, Easwaran felt a thread of sadness coil around his throat. He knew he could do nothing. Somewhere from the horizon, a bundle of dust began to blow, as the men in the camp heard the distant sound of an engine revving. The two men, sent by Eaklavya to do a recce, were returning.

By the time the truck reached the camp, Eaklavya had managed to calm Phanai down and the old man went back to his former position: crouching in the dust and conversing aloud with people in his imagination. As the two men approached, all eyes in the camp darted in their direction.

'Doesn't look good,' Aakash whispered, facing Easwaran.

'Let's just get it over with now,' Easwaran whispered back. His eyes were on the two men and Eaklavya. The two men had taken Eaklavya aside and the three were seen whispering to each other. Easwaran saw one of the men pass something over to Eaklavya, and the changed look on the latter's face almost gave out the whole story. A few minutes later, the meeting ended and Eaklavya gathered everyone in the camp, except Phanai, near him.

'Well, none of us had any doubt in our hearts now, did we?' Seeing only silence painted on the men's faces, Eaklavya continued, 'Good. Because I see we weren't disappointed.' Slowly, he brought out, for everyone to see, a silver lighter. On one side, embossed on it in gold, was the letter 'K'. A little far away from the gathering, Phanai sat whimpering. His face became ashen. Easwaran, for some unknown reason, was reminded of his father. Around him, the vast wasteland simmered and burnt. There was nothing to do now but leave.

# 3

## Old City

The shadows of rain loomed over the afternoon like an unfulfilled promise. Chhaya, barely three, ran over the makeshift veranda right outside the house. Thin grey clouds hovered above, partly obscuring the relentless onslaught of the sun. A brittle breeze picked up, laden with moisture. It put the particles of dust and ash into a surreal dance as they pulsated over empty rooftops, swirled away into the emptiness between the buildings and finally rested on to the broken roads that were ridden with holes and inhabited by thorny climbers and moss. Sprouting from crevices, jutting out from roofs and germinating on veranda floors, moss was everywhere—another mute witness to what civilization had become.

Chhaya stopped in her tracks and looked up at the sky. Granules of ash, like snow, drifted down and fell on her large black eyes. Only, unlike the snow, it was warm, and so, it disintegrated into smaller particles as soon as she tried to touch it, leaving a thick grey trail from her right eyelid all the way to her forehead.

The buildings surrounding her were all in ruins, with naked, unpainted bricks jutting out of them. Some of these buildings had been converted into houses, mostly makeshift. As the weather changed, from the rousing summer months to the dry winter days, most people would leave their present dwellings with a hankering for places more conducive to the corresponding season. The relatively well off, which included within its ranks Chhaya and her family, occupied more staid dwellings. These were stronger, looked better and were positioned in cleaner areas. Old City, with its congregation of bare-bones buildings, was like a black hole, with its mass turned inwards. What went in never escaped. And for those who were inside, their desire to escape was higher than their collective desire to survive.

'Why doesn't it rain, Mama?' she asked her mother, who was standing a few yards away, leaning against the half-broken boundary wall and looking out on to the street.

'It'll rain soon, Chhaya. Just pray to the rain gods, like I taught you to,' she calmly replied. 'And don't look up. Haven't I told you, the ash can spoil your eyes? And where is your mask? Go inside and fetch it.'

Chhaya, visibly unmoved by these series of quiet admonitions, didn't budge. Crinkling her eyes tightly shut, she kept her face turned towards the sky. Her lips parted widely into a smile, as if she was revelling in the quiet warmth of the falling ash on her face and the cool breeze flowing over her hair and forehead. And like the wild ash, Chhaya slowly stretched out her arms and started to twirl. Enmeshed together—the ash, her white frock with grey streaks of ash particles on it and Chhaya herself—the trio resembled a part of a dance troupe, a rhythmic convergence.

Looking at her daughter, who was not even three, whirling away to madness, a sliver of fear pierced through her mother. Dayani's chest almost tightened. She didn't like what she saw. This girl, her daughter, seemingly had a mind of her own;

and what was scary was that even at a tender age, she had
somehow realized it. Girls with a mind of their own . . .
Could they survive in times like these? Moreover, Dayani
was failing to recognize her fear. Maybe all of this was to
do with Chhaya's innately irreverent nature that made her
do things such as breaking into a dance in an untimely
fashion or laughing loudly when girls ought to be subdued
and restrained, especially in troubled times like these. Dayani
brushed aside these thoughts and kept staring at her little
girl who had now gathered pace. As she twisted her legs
and contorted her body, she fell into a rhythm with the low
whisper of the breeze, which was now thrusting the dust and
ash into a performative frenzy. In that moment, her mother—
battered against the insipid wall—realized the unmistakable
contrast between this sight of her daughter and the city of
which she was an unmistakable part. The latter reminded
Dayani of one of those grainy black-and-white documentaries
of London, ravaged during the Second World War.

'Mama, I am waiting for the rain . . . I had a dream last
night that it would rain today!' Chhaya exclaimed. Although
she had stopped dancing, her hands remained outstretched.

'I am sure it will rain. Now please go inside. The ash
seems to be falling fast now. Go and fetch your mask,' Dayani
replied dourly, as she walked towards Chhaya. Kneeling beside
the little girl, holding both her hands in hers, she carefully
wiped her face with her saree. 'Look at you. What kind of girl
gets her face all dirty like you? Wait for your father, I'll tell
him to get you married or send you to Millennium City.'
The girl, wanting to escape from her mother's clutches, tried
to wriggle free by distorting her body and pushing her face
away. This only made Dayani tighten her grasp over her

daughter, yanking her forward, as she slapped her left cheek lightly but with a certain determination that made Chhaya go quiet for a little while.

'I have told you so many times to behave. Go inside. *Now.*'

Chhaya was still. Instead of crying—an effect that would have pleased her mother—the girl just stood still. Her eyes, large and seemingly vacant, were glued to her mother's face. This was another thing that frustrated Dayani. Unlike other children who would invariably break into uneven sobs after a beating, only to quieten down later, this daughter of hers just wouldn't cry. When feeling affronted, she would just stare, and piercingly at that—as if through some uncanny ability, her eyes could scan an individual for its soul and leave it bare. Dayani both dreaded and hated that look in equal measure. It was yet another symbol of what she perceived as 'unwomanly' in her daughter: the desire to see—not with borrowed eyes, but from one's own—and subsequently, to probe, to question, to struggle independently for meaning. For Dayani, it was just another unnecessary requirement. As Dayani would tell her husband, who was always so eager to take his daughter's side, that when you are pinned against a wall by a force greater than you are, you don't fight it. Instead you look for ways to wriggle free. But much like her father, Chhaya did not want to learn the subtle tricks of wriggling free—at least that's what it seemed like to her mother. Chhaya too wanted to push her way through the world. But unlike her father, who still was able to accomplish that without feeling the weight of the world crash in on him, Chhaya had all the odds stacked against her.

'Do you know what they do in Millennium City to girls like you who refuse to listen to their mama?' Chhaya didn't reply, her eyes still fixed on her mother.

'They put disobedient girls into cold prison cells without food or water, until and unless they learn to behave. They chop their hair and they are made to look ugly. Do you want that treatment, Chhaya?' her mother continued, unabated. Her daughter, unperturbed, looked at Dayani. When Dayani saw that her tactics to scare her daughter into submission wasn't producing results, she sensed the anger boiling within her. Sometimes, she wished she had another son like Harish who was responsible, orderly, understood his place in the scheme of things and acted accordingly. In other words, a survivor. Although her husband, Easwaran, thought otherwise.

Her fury rising, she pushed Chhaya away from her, and then holding her by her ears, dragged her away to another corner of the veranda where a charpoy lay resting. Her daughter did not utter a single word nor did she wail, like other kids her age would have done. Making her daughter sit on the charpoy, Dayani fetched a long, slender dead branch that she kept precisely for instances such as these, when Chhaya was being particularly unruly. Flashing the cane in front of Chhaya, Dayani caught hold of her mass of curly, uncombed hair and pulled them down forcefully. Then, yanking the girl away from the charpoy, she lifted Chhaya's frock just a bit to expose her legs. Holding the mass of hair with one hand, Dayani began to cane the girl's legs with the other hand.

The cane tore through the invisible air, carving an arc as it whistled its way from nothingness and on to Chhaya's soft, stinging flesh. It seemed like a miniature version of a missile falling over staid quarters of a town, lost in the deception of its own security, leaving behind a trail of smoke and screams as it wound its way onward to its lethal passage. Bent over the charpoy, the girl closed her eyes, fighting away the little beads of tears that had made their appearance unannounced. Dayani, in her frenzy, kept yelling, 'Will you listen to me *now*! Tell me, will you listen?' Her voice rose with each stroke of the cane and lowered as she moved the cane away from the girl's legs. Through this entire ordeal, Chhaya focused on fighting back her tears, as they burnt their way through her eyes, rather than on the even trajectory of the cane, which was stinging the girl's flesh. It lasted for a good twenty minutes, though Chhaya was sure it went on longer than that. Dayani would tighten her grip over the girl's hair, pulling the locks away, as if she were exorcising some kind of a ghost that had taken possession of her daughter. With each pull, Chhaya would clench her teeth and tightly shut her eyes. But never did she let a sound or a yelp escape her mouth. Long after the ordeal was over, Dayani, thus defeated by her own daughter and with her heart gripped in the delirium of fear about the future, would lie wide awake in her lonely bed feverishly wishing she was someplace else—and that she hadn't given birth to this daemon of a daughter at all.

■ ■ ■

# Interstate

The trucks had sped their way across the dead river. Sitting inside one of these mechanic beasts was Phanai, his eyes set on the ghosts that presented themselves only to him. Easwaran, holding the infant on his lap, and sitting near Phanai, looked out. Outside, the evening, now almost auburn, crawled away over Old City on its nimble fingers. The river, on whose dry body the vehicles now trudged, resembled the shape of a fossilized prehistoric beast whose corpse had become so dry that it had become indistinguishable from the rocks in which it lay embedded, and yet, as if by some curious magic, one could very well distinguish the finer contours of its body, and what it once was. Once, long ago, although the river was in its death throes, it still had a bit of water, especially when it rained. But as the rains became infrequent, the river, deprived of its only life force, had no choice but to silently perish. But the river and its tepid history were far from what was playing on Easwaran's mind. Old City, draped in its ancient clothes, was just a few miles ahead of the river. On the other side of Phanai sat Eaklavya, his shotgun on his lap and a cigarette burning away between his lips.

'The kid must have had it coming. Getting up in the dark, when expressly ordered not to do so, requires both balls and a cartload of stupidity,' Easwaran said. His voice was hovering somewhere between nonchalance and anger, while his eyes traced the contours of the broken river that he had known so well as a child.

'I liked that kid, you know. But I guess it's Murphy's Law. Anything that can go wrong, will. And that's what happened,' Eaklavya replied.

Phanai didn't seem to hear anything. It seemed as if his senses were attuned to a parallel dimension, far away from this world, and yet cohabiting with it. His lips quivered. But no words were formed. Only soft sounds that no one could understand. Garbled and true to its own ghostly logic. Eaklavya turned around and took a hard look at Phanai. No words were uttered. When his cigarette burnt down to its last remnant, he stubbed it on the floor of the vehicle. Phanai did not return the look.

'I suppose this old man is done for. Permanently. No questions asked. The Guides in Old City won't like it,' Easwaran said. He too had moved his eyes from the desolate landscape to that of Eaklavya's stern, unsmiling face.

'There's another thing the Guides won't like,' Eaklavya shot back, 'and questions *will* be asked. Many questions.' His eyes now lingered on the infant. 'There's going to be hell to pay, I am warning you. You better have answers.'

'There are no answers. It was a choice between what I should have done and what I shouldn't have. I made a choice, and pay for it I shall. And must.'

'Oh, you will need all that strength, and more. Sometimes, here's what I wonder about. Behind that stoic exterior you put forth, you're just soft jelly. And face it, man, you chose to do this because you felt bad. No, bad isn't the right word. Rather, you, Easwaran, you felt pity. Remember, pity is a luxury we cannot afford.'

Easwaran didn't reply. With every bump on the road, the truck would stumble and the baby would flinch. Easwaran would clasp him tightly in his arms and cradle. That's what he did now. There was nothing more that he could say. Deep down, he knew what Eaklavya said was true, albeit partly. Yes, there was pity, pity at seeing the helpless infant. But there was also shock. And there was also that other thing he was still trying to find words for. Down there, he knew something had happened to him. The growing desolation of life in Old City and the Interstate, the gradual disappearance of everything that was familiar to him as a child, had made him stronger. At least that's what he had thought. He had always maintained that there was nothing that could surprise him any more. He saw what he

had to see. And so much more. And as a man, as a survivor,
like so many others with him, he had taught himself that
emotions and romantic ideas were no longer applicable. Now
there was only one way to survive, and that was cold, hard
rationality. You make do with what you have, no questions
asked. Questions, debates and arguments were the luxury
the older generation, his father's generation, had. Not his.
And yet, he had picked up the infant. *No*, thought Easwaran,
*there was much more than just pity.* Pity, as he knew very well,
was more visceral; it was about baser instincts. You have
pity, and then you don't. You act stupid, yes, when pity
holds you in its clutches. But you still maintain a sense of
that cold rationality. Yet he gave shelter to a non-human.
That's much more than stupidity. That's potential suicide.
And he knew, back home, if he didn't play his cards well, he
and his family even risked excommunication. As the broken
spires of Old City glittered in the darkness of the evening,
Easwaran felt, perhaps for the first time during his whole
journey, the first bite of guilt as it slowly pierced his throat.

'Can I have one of those?' Easwaran asked, pointing
towards the packet of hand-rolled cigarettes that jutted
out carelessly from Eaklavya's right pocket. Eaklavya
raised an eyebrow as he took out a cigarette and handed
it over to him.

'Don't worry. I'm not with you on this, but I ain't saying
anything back there,' Eaklavya remarked.

As he lit his cigarette, Easwaran could feel the rush of
the vapours of burnt tobacco rush into his lungs. He had
quit smoking long ago, after the initial bout of cough that
had attacked him. With the tiny particles of ash seeping into
everybody's lungs, cough had become a common malady.

And Easwaran, knowing full well what was happening, had decided to stop smoking, thinking his lungs would one day bleed out anyway. At least, when that day comes, it won't be because of him. But now, feeling the rush of the recent events heavily against him, he felt a craving from somewhere deep inside for that heady raw tobacco. It was dark now, and they were still at least an hour away from the familiar main streets of Old City. Phanai, mumbling away to his ghosts, had fallen asleep. The trucks were now moving at a steady pace on the rough brick-littered edges of the road. Holding the infant tightly in his arms, Easwaran sat quietly underneath the heavy vapours of the burning cigarette. He leaned against his window and finally gave in to sleep.

• • •

They say it all began with the experiments.

Once upon a time, when Easwaran was still a child, the world was crazy over oil. It was as black as the darkness over the Interstate and would sputter uncontrollably from the unknown depths of the earth. But when the southern river, lying close to Old City, gradually disappeared, the inhabitants of Old City of course debated about what exactly caused its eventual death. While some say it was wholly because of the decreasing rains, Easwaran knew, as his father had once told him, it was not completely about the rains. Of course, the rains had become a rarity in this part of the country, but they didn't stop completely. Easwaran's father had told him, shortly before he died, about the primal desire lying latent underneath the skin of every man—self-preservation. So when water became precious, the shadowy members of the

Inspire Corporation started constructing large dams on
the northern rivers, which was the point from where the
water flowed into the southern parts. The dams enabled
Millennium City to restrict the flow of water, leading to an
increase in the price and complete closure of the southern
river. Millennium City then gained a monopoly on water
with the help of Inspire Corporation, which ran the city
effectually. Over the years, the added revenue flowing into
Millennium City by virtue of the global trade in water, not
only made Inspire Corporation into a global conglomerate
but also enabled the company to diversify its interests.

And one of the main areas they diversified in was human
engineering. As Millennium City expanded, so did the need
for cheap and intelligent labour. But, perhaps, what was most
potent of all was the basic human desire to create man in his
own likelihood. The same desire that went back thousands of
years, the same desire that kept the fire of human endeavour
burning. And this gave rise to Inspire Corporation's most
innovative investment—a technology that allowed the
creation of artificial humans in laboratories.

Zygotes were stuffed in test tubes, and genes were favourably
altered. They say the experiments were a combination of other
previously known branches of science. Long fields of inquiry,
with their devious names—nanotechnology, cybernetics, gene
engineering and artificial intelligence—were combined to
create the perfect zygote, a cell that would be superior to a
human cell born outside the laboratories. An artificial cell that
would then grow into a full-fledged human but would be devoid
of a human's limitations. During the first batch of experiments,
only artificial intelligence and robotics were used. But the
scientists soon realized that only using artificial intelligence

and robotics would be very inadequate. And that inadequacy was not so much in what they created but in the essential problem of integration. It was felt, during those early years, that mechanized robots masquerading as superior humans would in no way properly become a part of human society. Moreover, as years went on and more studies were conducted, it was felt that there was a need for something more than just artificial intelligence. There was a need to seamlessly integrate artificial intelligence with biological processes. This would do away with mechanical robots and would give rise to humans, using normal biological processes that were harvested in the laboratories, with artificial intelligence sitting comfortably close, and even aiding in normal physiological processes.

Code-named Project Meta.

This technology was what those engineers, biophysicists and molecular biologists recognized as the next big leap in human evolution. And yet, at its initial stages, there was a problem. Meta-Humans, or colloquially called Metas, thus harvested, would definitely integrate themselves into human society. But their superior intelligence and physical prowess, if not properly controlled, would give them a power, hereby unforeseen, over the humans, who are not harvested in laboratories. As the oldest trick of evolution in a mad competition, nature would select only the ablest and the fittest, which would mean the complete dominance of the Metas over humans, the eventual extinction of the latter. To combat this, two techniques were used to ensure that this radical possibility did not transpire. Every Meta came with an 'auto-termination clause' that ensured that none survive beyond the natural age of forty. Not only would this drastically reduced age make them mortally vulnerable, but it would also ensure a proper hierarchy whereby humans would maintain their dominance over the Metas, owing to their longevity.

The second, and perhaps, far more important step that the scientists at Inspire Corporation created was a test at the genetic level to ensure only those harvested Metas would be kept alive and allowed to enter the stream of human society that would showcase a remarkable potential for obedience. The harvested Metas were kept alive for a period of one to two years, and a thorough genetic mapping was carried out. The Metas, whose genes showed a tendency for submission and obedience, were automatically preserved and were either sold to the defence forces or to the larger market, where they were bought by wealthy inhabitants of Millennium City. The ones that did not pass the test were terminated with immediate effect.

■ ■ ■

In the thick blanket of darkness, as the trucks reached Old City, Easwaran opened his eyes to see that the infant Meta he was holding in his arms was wide awake and had his dark black eyes fixated on Phanai, as if the latter belonged to a different time period. The guilt that was knocking on Easwaran's heart lay still on the threshold. But waking up from that nap and looking at the infant in front of him, he felt as if somehow he could manage to live with it. His father had once told him that a man is known by the choices he accepts. He could have left the Meta there in the termination centre, from where he'd picked him up; he could have run like his other comrades did. But that was just too easy. You do what everyone else does, and you do it all your life with the sole thought that it adds a modicum of meaning to your sad, deplorable life. But what about the choices we avoid, not because they are wrong but because they are *made* to be wrong in light of the circumstances.

Looking into the infant's large black eyes, Easwaran felt a surge of thoughts rushing through his head, thoughts he had suppressed deep in the corridors of his consciousness all this while, but which now broke free as if they were no longer in his control. Thoughts that made him question the validity of everything that was taught to him, such as the basic difference between right and wrong, the normal and the abnormal, the sane and the insane—differences which we as children of society are made to imbibe and follow, differences that allowed the illusion of order to perpetuate, the same illusion that Easwaran now perceived as the false hope of everything being all right, the same illusion a parent would give to his child while feeling like a sinking ship deep inside that was unable to get away. But there was also that vision of his home, of his wife Dayani, his children Chhaya and Harish—all three ensconced together in the cathedral of well-being, a cathedral of which he was the cornerstone. And it was this vision that, more than anything, made the guilt sharper, to a point that he simultaneously felt pride and regret about his decision to save the infant Meta.

As his thoughts sunk deeper, the trucks reached the first outpost. The crumbling world of Old City rushed onward, welcoming Easwaran and the Meta infant into an uncertain future.

# 4

## Old City

To her, he was exasperating. This man that she was married to. Like all men out there. He could love, even be magnanimous enough to offer his support in reducing the countless household chores, when he would see her struggling with those. And of course, to every such offer, she would raise her eyebrows just a bit, accept with a smile as a proclamation of both happiness and concealed gratitude. And of course, he would take half an hour more than what it would normally take to wash the utensils, and those utensils would invariably have at least a sliver of stain. And yes, of course, her smile would disappear when she would carefully inspect every inch of her beloved utensils. No matter how miniscule a stain there was. And she would push him out of the kitchen. Exasperation written in big capital letters all over her face. She would fail to understand whether this occurred because he was *truly* incapable of household chores, while he went around the entire city as a prized member of the feared Madira Gang, known for their exploits across Millennium City. Or whether the act of him offering help and later botching up something as simple as washing utensils was because subconsciously, he didn't feel it was a job worthy of his stature.

But then, Easwaran was a genuine man. His love was genuine. He even made love to her in the proper and dignified manner a man should make love to a woman. Not that she didn't like any of this. He was cautious and meticulous. He never got drunk or came home late. He never said a word more than was necessary. And she liked all these things about him. It ensured that they were well fed. That the kids can have a future, or at least something to look forward to, and will not be like the hundred other urchins who scamper about the city, scavenging and living off others. And by God, this man, her husband, was devoted. And she loved that. But at the same time, a part of her pined for the unknown. Pined to be looked at, like she has never before been looked at. Pined to be touched and felt in ways other than *proper*. And she would brush aside this thought with a frown as soon as it would make its appearance on the far horizons of her imagination. These aren't thoughts a woman should have. But then, no sooner would she think something like this, a question—always uncalled for and always ridiculous—would occupy space in her mind: if these are the thoughts a woman shouldn't have, what exactly are the thoughts a woman *should* have then? And like most questions, this would stay bereft of any answer. It seemed to her as if a movie, which was really nothing but her life, was slowly playing out on a perfectly good television but with a somewhat rattled picture tube. It did not disturb the way the movie was playing out, but if seen over a period of time, the viewer would be greeted with sudden ruptures and frozen screens, thereby marring the entire experience of watching that film altogether. Though, when seen properly, the film in itself might not be *too bad*.

Deep down, in her heart of hearts, Dayani trusted her husband's decisions. She knew him to be practical, frugal and the man who always made the right decisions. Inside, Easwaran might have been solitary, the kind who enjoyed his books and his collection of old rock and roll music albums—albeit counterfeit and stolen during his journeys to Millennium City and hidden away in the attic. He belonged to a kind that was so very rare in these hard times. The kind that elicited a few jabs from others—far younger members of the gang—a fact Easwaran always concealed, but it was also a fact Dayani knew. That's the thing about marriage; it might bring two completely different people together, but it also enabled an ecosystem whereby unspoken thoughts and concealed incidents from one just seeped into the consciousness of the other, as if through osmosis. Maybe that is why it was called 'learning to live together'; you just learn to make do with the other. For instance, when Jaidev Singhla, one of the top-ranking members of Madira, sat before Easwaran on an evening like any other—his AK-47 gleaming in the soft burning embers of the timid light bulb—and offered him the terms of recruitment, she knew that although Easwaran would have condemned and never chosen this line of work had she known him in the golden past, he chose to accept it. He never offered any explanation, which was never his style anyway. She didn't ask for any either. She knew he chose what he had to choose because of just one word, a word so curiously lacking in the vocabulary of men these days: responsibility. Sometimes in marriage, words were just inadequate to paint a picture, describe a thought and express a feeling. All you needed was just a little bit of that osmosis to make it work for you.

But today, she felt different. By the time Easwaran was back, it was dark. She had heard the loud breath of the engines, as the trucks made their way through the broken roads of

Old City. When Easwaran took languid half steps, walked up to the door and knocked, Dayani knew it was him. There was a peculiarity to the way he walked, the way he spoke, the way he ran his fingers through his hair with an absent-mindedness that Dayani found attractive. There was even a certain way he'd knock the door: soft and raspy, as if he had all the time in the world. Within these mundane activities, Dayani could construe the patterns that were invisible to the naked eye but clear as day for her. As if the figure of Easwaran, if somehow disappeared from the face of the earth, could surely be manifested again by paying attention to myriad little details—and it was only known to Dayani. Having knowledge of these gave her a sense of pride in the fact that she could be one of those rare wives who truly *knew* her husband. It gave her a sense of control in a world increasingly devoid of it.

It was only after she opened the door that the anarchy of uncertainty rushed to reclaim its place in the cosy confines of her soul. At first, she didn't quite understand who or what the infant was. And long after the moment of meeting him was over, it would constantly play in her head like an old video cassette stuck inside the bowels of an ageing VCR. Did she really think *it* was someone else's baby? Like old, maudlin soap operas that were broadcast from over Millennium City and carried through to the rickety televisions of Old City, she felt she was being confronted with some old affair that Easwaran might have had during his innumerable visits to Millennium City, this infant being the product of such an illegitimate union. But then she knew Easwaran wouldn't do something like that. He didn't even know how to speak to women, considering how his monosyllabic nature would always act as a hindrance in any such endeavour. Having an affair and producing a baby out of it and keeping that a secret for nine months was so remote a possibility that Dayani didn't want to waste time pondering over it.

But when she did look at the infant and felt the warmth of its large black eyes upon her, she could do nothing but recoil in horror. The rest of the details about this encounter might be hazy in her memory, but this particular one was not. Even before she saw the tattoos on the infant's neck, she knew what it was. And whether it was out of shock or horror or a combination of these two, no words came out of her mouth. Easwaran holding the baby in his arms, and Harish following closely behind him, just nudged Dayani aside and walked right in. Outside, the darkness had grown thick and fast. There was a slight chill in the breeze, and it rattled the last remnant leaves that hung from frail, dust-laden branches. The promise of rain, of course, lay unfulfilled. But nonetheless, it levitated in the air, mocking the people below. As Dayani closed the door, a sudden yet unhurried sense of premonition went through her, something which she couldn't put her finger on, but which echoed in her ears tales of a gloomy foreboding.

The dinner was spread out neatly on the table. Chapattis, dal, a few chillies and a large tumbler of water. Easwaran pulled a chair closer to the table and broke a morsel. Dayani stood at a distance, near the makeshift plywood that separated the living room from the kitchen. Harish and Chhaya sat on the floor with a plateful of food placed in front of each of them. Inside the room, which Easwaran and Dayani shared, the infant lay sleeping. The house was silent all along, as if it was draped in a thick blanket of mourning. The only sound that stirred was the unhurried whisper of spoons, as they touched the surface of the plates. No thoughts passed through Dayani's mind either. Standing against the makeshift door, her eyes scanned the concrete floor. From time to time, she would raise them and stare at Easwaran. The man ate quietly.

'I hope the dal is all right. I made it this morning. I didn't know you were coming today. I would have cooked mutton curry instead,' she said.

'No. We had mutton on the way back. One of the guys stole cattle from Millennium City.'

'One of those urchins broke one of the windows with a ball. You have to get it repaired. I don't want dust settling in the house. I do a lot to keep it clean.'

'Maybe tomorrow.'

The more Easwaran spoke, the more he stooped. As if it was a vain attempt to escape Dayani's empty gaze. As if stooping low made him appear small, feeding him with the weird notion that he was shrinking in size. His eyes hovered over the tiny floral patterns that were embroidered on a white cloth that they used to cover the table with. Dayani had woven that a few years ago when Chhaya was still a foetus swimming inside her. This sudden image of a foetus gave way to another image of a foetus swimming in a large test tube filled with amniotic fluid. Easwaran had seen this in a large laboratory just a few miles from the Interstate. Going by the terminology used by Inspire Corporation, these labs were called warehouses where Metas were manufactured on an industrial scale. As these images flashed before him like a film projector stuck in his head and going on all on its own, Easwaran shut his eyes. The images did not cease to appear. They crept up, one after the other. Cold sweat trickled down his forehead. He kept a broken morsel of chapatti on his plate. Dayani's eyes never left him. He looked up to face them.

'I'm going to bed,' he said.

'You've barely eaten.'

'I'm not hungry any more.'

'I want to know what is wrong.' There was a certain desperation in Dayani's voice. Her heart was pounding against her chest.

'Nothing's wrong. You should rest too. We can talk in the morning.'

'No. You know very well I won't sleep. And I know you won't either.'

'I have to sleep. I had a very long, hard day.'

'No. I won't sleep there with that *thing*. I won't. What have you done? What have you brought on us?' Dayani could feel her voice echo through the air. Her hands and feet had gone numb. She walked over to Easwaran, her face flushed. She could feel it warm and throbbing like an open wound. The room swirled with the weight of unspoken words. Easwaran stood against his chair. His hands were moist with fragments of food.

'I want an answer, Easwaran. I have never asked you anything. I have been a good wife. By God, I know I am. I always stood by you, and I always will. As a wife, as a woman. But I want an answer.'

'What do you want to know?' Easwaran asked. His voice was heavy. As if a portion of lead hung from it.

'Who is that in our bedroom? Why have you brought it?'

'It's a Meta. An abandoned one. The ones they eliminate.' His eyes seemed to penetrate through Dayani's bones. She could feel her shoulders slouch. The floor, the weight of it, pushed against her feet. She could feel a sudden onslaught of a dull ache pounding against her head. Instead of answering, she only managed to grunt: 'Huh?'

'I did what I did. Consequences or no consequences.'

'But, Easwaran, do you know what . . .'

'Yes, I know,' he cut her mid-sentence. 'I know word must have reached the Guides by now and I would be summoned. I would be made to explain myself. Which I will. I'll stand my ground. By all means.'

'What do you mean "stand your ground"? Who the hell cares about your ground, Easwaran? We stand in danger of being excommunicated. Metas . . . Are you so naïve or innocent as to not know what Old City thinks of these artificial things?!'

'I am not. Like I said, it was a choice.'

'What fucked-up choice, Easwaran? A choice between having a good life and throwing it all away? A choice between life and certain death out there in the Interstate, because that's where we are headed if they kick us out of here. Have you even considered our children? Have you even considered me?'

'I have.' Easwaran knew he had considered nothing. He didn't even know if it was an impulse that made him pick up the Meta. *Or something more, much more.*

'Like hell you have.' The room vibrated. Her hair, always neatly coiled into a bun, was now dishevelled. Her body felt heavy. The bile stung her throat. The anger and desperation squirming inside her gave her a sense of energy she seldom found anywhere. The part of the sari around her shoulders was on the verge of slipping.

Easwaran didn't know what to answer. He wanted to be anywhere in the world but here right now. Even the thought of the Interstate, with the hungry beasts, was a possibility he'd have chosen if he was offered. But he brushed that thought aside. The picture of Phanai's young boy suddenly surfaced in his mind. All he wanted was to light a cigarette. He felt his hands slide into his trouser pockets. Thank God he had borrowed a couple from Eaklavya on the drive back.

'Look, that kid, that *baby*, was lying there. Somehow, something had gone wrong. The Millennium City police weren't supposed to know we were going to raid the corporation's water storage facility and get some barrels out. But they did. They gave us chase, a dirty chase. Throughout the city. Me and one other guy, we were in one truck. We were carrying a large consignment with us.' Easwaran realized he'd said more than he should have. These details, or 'business as usual', stayed only within the gang. He breathed heavily. The air seemed oppressive. To breathe was almost a chore. Only the warm fumes of tobacco could liberate him. He walked towards the broken window. Outside, darkness hung like a spider's cobweb—intricately woven, networked, with multiple tentacles spread everywhere. It seemed those tentacles had crept inside his own heart as well. He didn't know what time it was. The call of the crickets and a dank, oppressive silence reigned. The kind that presaged an event.

'And what happened?' Dayani asked.

'We drove faster than the others and were able to get away. We had almost reached the Interstate when we thought we should park the truck somewhere safe and wait for the others. We saw some buildings. Unmarked. We thought we could hide the truck there, cover it. The building seemed deserted. No one would come snooping around here. Plus it looked like the corporation's property. So we did just that. Tired of waiting alone, which would have been suspicious anyway, we thought we'd explore the building. Nothing was marked there. Just dust

and ash. So we had no idea. It was locked from the outside. One
of those heavy old iron locks. But we knew how to open them.
That's the first thing the gang drills into you. To open locks,
any lock. We opened them and snuck in. It was all dark there.
Dark as a thousand midnights. And we didn't know why. But
we went in anyway. We were carrying our torches and our
flints. So we lit them and walked through the darkness. When
we went further inside, we saw rooms. Neatly lined with each
other. With doors bolted shut. We broke one open.'

Easwaran could already see the images float before him.
Like dead bloated bodies. Long stems of those test tubes, filled
with some liquid substance. Amniotic fluid, he would later
learn from Eaklavya. And floating in them were babies. Long
ago, when books were still around, and Old City was known
by its former name—Delhi or Dilli—his father had gifted him
a series of books that were neatly bound. The golden letters
on the spine read 'encyclopaedias'. And in one of them, classed
under the category of 'science', he had come across sketches of
little babies caged inside what looked like a large sperm. This
was, of course, of a time long ago, when science was still in its
infancy, and alchemists thought every sperm contained a fully
formed human, albeit very tiny. It was called homunculus. Early
alchemists like Paracelsus—he had remembered the name—
had even written precise formulae, detailing ways to extract this
homunculus from the sperm without injecting it into any human
womb. The idea of man creating a man in his own likeness was
the very germ of humanity. The very essence of our being. And
it was all here, ingrained in our collective imagination, flushed
through countless monochromatic images of an actor with steel
rods inserted inside his neck, and his face all sewn up, rising
up from his hospital bed. And a scientist looking down at his

creation with joy as well as horror. His words—'It's alive, it's alive'—hung in the air, as if they were not words but only aerosol. Easwaran had seen those Frankenstein films as a child, on old DVDs, and had screamed in horror. What he saw in the room was no seven-feet-tall Boris Karloff rising from the dead, Lazarus-like, but countless little homunculi floating in the liquid of mankind's imagination. And he had screamed 'God!' A cry at once defiant and yet the one that contained echoes of man's collective heartbreak. A heartbreak for what? God's affirmation or its complete absence? Easwaran did not know. He was, after all, just another man. With a family.

He had walked inside the room. He went further on and saw other rooms encased within this big room. And once inside the labyrinth, he half dreamed he would encounter the monster. But instead, he encountered God. The same God who was always there and would only follow him back. An absent presence. The God that was the very spirit of history. The same God who lurked underneath mankind's very subconscious. The God that changed form, taking on the shape of the era it was in: large gas chambers constructed out of titanium. And connected to these chambers were multiple assembly lines. There was no trace of any human here. Everything was perfectly automated. Fully formed Metas lay on one side. Robotic tentacles—multiple and rhizomatic and attached to no bodies—scooped each Meta baby and lay it on the assembly line. The line would then move into the chamber where cyanide gas, percolating like water from a bathroom shower, would stream down over the rejected Meta. The body was later collected and disposed of into the vast emptiness of the Interstate. It was all too precise. Calculated. Above all, efficient. If God's eternal silence was what man had to endure, it was only necessary to invent one. And this God would be meticulous. Efficient. It would get work done. It would separate the wheat from the chaff. It would categorize. Those who were fit to last, and those who weren't. After all that's what a god should do. When a voice cried out in the wilderness, God answered. Not as a voice first but as a flaming fire.

Easwaran had stopped speaking. His eyes, wide open, seemed to stare into an abyss of darkness. The gas chambers, the automated machine arms, the test tubes, sixteenth-century sketches of homunculi, Boris Karloff rising up from his doomed bed, the voice of the children inside those gas chambers, both imagined and real, all flashed in front of his eyes. One image bled into the other, to the point that there was no difference between them, like the blood of multiple races commingling into one. They all became one large collage, the microhistory of all humanity.

Dayani didn't interrupt. She waited. Without flinching. Without even a grunt. Easwaran took out a cigarette from his pocket and lit it.

'I saw how these Metas are eliminated and I couldn't stand it. One infant, this one, lay next to me. Looking at me. I looked back. And before I knew what was happening, I was holding it in my arms and running away from that shithole. I ran out, took the other guy by his collar into the truck and drove away, like my fucking ass was on fire.'

Before Dayani could answer or even react, their front door reverberated, in the silent darkness, with four precise knocks.

# 5

## Old City

The punch landed flat on Haksh's face. His square jaw shuddered. His temples throbbed. Haksh was barely able to keep himself from hitting the ground when another punch hit him. This time, right below the chin. His skin came off like peeled rubber. Blood, warm and sticky in the afternoon sun, trickled down his neck. His fists were half-clenched and he wanted to lunge back. He knew he had enough strength. But something gave way. A familiar voice, as if from a half-remembered dream, whispered in his head. And he did nothing. He stood there, gaping in silence.

'Stay away from my sister,' Harish said forcefully. His right fist, which had landed on Haksh's chin, was red.

'I did nothing. And you're no one to say what she should or shouldn't do,' Haksh protested.

'Do you fucking think I need your filthy advice?'

Before Haksh could say anything, Harish had grabbed him by the collar.

'You keep your filthy ass mouth shut,' Harish said. His voice at once became whispery, not seeming malicious at all. It was only a matter of fact. The cold violence behind that voice pierced Haksh's heart. 'I did nothing,' he repeated.

Harish pushed him back. He lost his balance and fell to the ground. Face first. The stones scraped his lips and he bit his tongue. More oozing blood. Before he could get himself up, big and sweaty arms wrapped around his own and jerked him forward. The ground brushed against his back, opening pores on his smooth nutcracker face for more blood to flow out. And with the blood came a lot of pain. It was Abhishek. Harish's friend. *Compatriot*, thought Haksh. Easwaran had taught him that word. Words that came swirling down at him like a dream. Words that kept him awake at night. Words with smell. Words with colour. A living thing nestled inside his skin, waiting to protrude.

Abhishek grabbed him by the back collar and made him get up.

'When you are being taught a lesson, you learn. You keep your mouth shut,' he hissed.

Haksh looked on. The pain in his back had offset his tongue's dull throbbing. His white T-shirt was smeared with dust, ash and blood. As was his face. Abhishek lunged forward and pulled Haksh towards him. He felt the collar of his T-shirt tear. Abhishek held him tight, confining his hands behind him. Harish came forward to face Haksh.

'Stay away from my sister, asshole. When I tell you something, you listen, or else . . .' Two rapid punches hit Haksh on his face. Granules of ash swirled in the silent air and entered inside his mouth, making his tongue reddish grey. His head throbbed and his back stung. He knew he was bleeding there. His smooth black hair was awry, as if it were a bush that had been trampled by the hooves of an animal running wild.

Eight years had passed since that sombre evening when Easwaran had brought that boy. The same boy that now lay bleeding on the dirty flow from the darkness of the titanium can and into the darkness of Old City. Darkness was omnipresent. It lurked everywhere. It escaped from the hot breath of the smokey chimneys up in Millennium City, only to creep up between the broken buildings of Old City. It crawled away from the ground, a relic of the colour grey, and into the very pores of the people. Through nostrils, ears and assholes. It commingled with snot, sweat and semen. And in the midst of it all, countless souls hovered between the living and the dead.

Five years. And every bit of that time sank into Haksh's head like a collection of sepia-toned images. And of all the images there, there was one that he recalled time and time again: that of Chhaya. Chhaya dancing away in the quiet loneliness of the night. Chhaya sitting atop one of the broken empty buildings, her legs dangling over the edge as effortlessly as she danced. Chhaya slipping her hands into his when walking together, only to remove them soon after, engulfing Haksh in a strange concoction of bliss and a profound melancholy.

In the rustling ashes, his face bloody and blue, she was the only image Haksh wanted to conjure. And he knew, if he didn't, he would clasp his fists. He would let his anger swamp him in its ever tightening embrace. Last year, he had taken Chhaya to the Muslim Quarters to play with Abdul, Basit and Malik, his only friends. And while coming back, Harish and his gang had caught hold of them. Harish had pulled Chhaya away from Haksh and towards himself, taking her back to Dayani, leaving Abhishek and a few of his friends to deal with Haksh. But Haksh didn't flinch. He wasn't scared. Before Abhishek could do anything, Haksh had held him by his collar and had pinned him to the ground. But he didn't beat him. The blackness in his eyes burnt like coal, and he had seen fear, thick as dusk, cloud over Abhishek. Haksh walked away without doing anything more and no one followed him.

Now, as blows rained on his body, Chhaya's image hung like a cobweb over his eyes. He had realized this long ago. This ability to bring Chhaya back, even when she wasn't there. And these images weren't composed of multiple fragments—one image juxtaposed on to another—like they usually materialize with memory. For him, every image of everything that he had ever seen appeared distinct and clear. The reason why he sometimes found it hard to understand whenever he'd hear someone say 'Oh, but I forgot' was because Haksh never forgot. The images never left him. And he hated it. He knew, for instance, that long after today, he would remember every little detail of being beaten up. He would remember every little pain. And that made him angry. There was nothing more he'd like now but to rise up from the ground and tear Abhishek and Harish by their throats. But there was something else he didn't understand: why did he let Abhishek go away that day, when he could have easily beaten him to nothingness. What was in that boy, his irises fixated on him, lying helpless before Haksh like a victim before an execution? There was a part of Haksh that wanted to hold Abhishek by his hair and pound him to the ground. But he had desisted. The very thought of Abhishek pinned to the cold, hard ground thrilled him. But it also made him sad. Walking back home, with the breeze blowing flecks of dreariness against him, Haksh had felt confused. He wanted to go to Easwaran that night after dinner. But when Easwaran called him over to his side, as he did every night, and asked him about his day, Haksh had only shrugged. The words had died down somewhere in his throat.

Now pinned against the ground and unable to feel his own body, Haksh felt as if someone hiding away inside his skull was whispering to him a message of deeply entrenched sadness. But what exactly was that message, he had no way of deciphering. His hands were held behind him. He could feel Abhishek's breath brush against his skin.

'We're not letting you go away this time,' Abhishek said. His teeth clenched. Harish walked closer. He lifted Haksh's face by gently nudging his chin. Thin blue circles formed around Haksh's eyes. Apart from some dried blood sticking out of his lower lip and chin, his face was mostly fine. Harish had taken care not to hit him too much there. He'd have died at the hands of his father if he ever found out. And he hated Easwaran all the more. But that didn't mean he would leave this lab rat alone. Rats, as Harish thought, were only that—pests. And you eliminate them, without asking any questions. It was only people like his father who complicated a simple fact such as this. Metas were only parasites. You don't keep living with parasites. It was as simple as medicine. Viruses and bacteria were harmful. A fact that he learnt in school. And those that are harmful must be eliminated. That's what medicines were for. To keep you healthy, to remove these parasites from the body. It was all science. But people like his father, an ignorant gang member, foot soldier at best, can never be expected to understand this. So, for people who don't understand, it is the job of people like Harish to impart this education. And he thought that was precisely what he was doing.

'You don't learn, do you?' Harish said. He moved his fingers from Haksh's chin and over to his forehead.

'Tee-hee . . . Is the Meta scared? I bet he feels like he wants to pee,' Abhishek said, grinning. He brought his face

closer to Haksh's ears. 'Do you feel like peeing, you rat? . . .
Why don't you show us how Metas pee?'

Harish then leaned closer and opined, 'They do make
you fine and perfect. Though I could do without this black
skin.' His breath fell on Haksh's face like breeze falling on
rustling leaves.

'Hey, get him to pee. I wanna see that,' Abhishek said.
The two laughed together.

'You know you could have been useful to us, if you didn't
have those ratty eyes set on my sister,' Harish said.

Haksh only looked back at him. He said nothing.

'Say, why don't we take those ratty eyes out? Like
we did to that cat down at the Muslim Quarters on your
birthday, Harish.'

'Nah. Not till my old man's around. He likes rats.'

'Do rats get horny? I bet they do.'

'I'm sure they do.' The two laughed again.

'How do rats stick it out? I heard back in Millennium
City where they breed Metas, they use rat genes. Do you
have rat genes, Meta guy?' Abhishek sniggered.

'Just hold him tight, will you, man?' Harish said.

Haksh was breathing heavily now. His legs had grown
numb. His back ached and his hands, held tightly behind by
Abhishek, stung. He tried to move. Harish's fingers were
on his head. Haksh flinched. Holding his face by one hand,
Harish's fingers closed around his hair, yanking his head
back. He let go of his face and slid his hands in one of his
trouser pockets. When he brought them out, a blade, long
and sharp, glistened in the heat of the warm, careless sun.

'Tee-hee . . . Yea, that blade will make you pee, what say,
Meta boy? It's pee time.'

Haksh's eyes were on the blade, and they stayed there, unmoved. Harish inched forward and brought the blade closer to Haksh's face.

'You know, if you see a bit closely, you can see blood stains on the tip. I sliced off a cat's eyes with this. It was my birthday present to me.' Haksh didn't react. He knew Harish would not do the same to him. Easwaran was home and if there was anyone Harish still feared, it was his father. But at the same time, Haksh felt uneasy. Harish took the blade away from Haksh's face and moved it towards his chest. He ran the tip on Haksh's chest, towards his stomach and onwards to his crotch.

'Does it tingle when I bring this thing here?' Harish said. He received no answer. 'Does it tingle when you look at my sister?' The blade pressed against his crotch. Haksh slithered. His legs pushed against the hard ground. His eyes stayed frozen on Harish's face, which betrayed no signs that he was in any way joking.

Before Harish could do anything, however, a voice called out his name from behind.

The voice that caught Harish, and Haksh, off guard, belonged to Latif. Harish and Abhishek had caught Haksh as he was walking away from the Muslim Quarters towards home. They had dragged him around a corner, thinking it would keep them away from prying eyes. But Latif appearing before them, like a daemon materializing from thin air, wasn't something they thought they would encounter.

Growing up in the crumbling Old City, Haksh had found company with the Muslims. The Muslim Quarters was a large area that once boasted some of the finest architecture, when the city was still thriving and culture existed. The centre had a grand mosque, which, as the years accumulated like sand on a beach, had fallen into disrepair. And it was in the Muslim Quarters and with the Muslims that Haksh found company. Lonely and unable to understand the strong hatred everyone seemed to exhibit around him, he found in Abdul and his older brother, Latif, a warmth he never found elsewhere.

'Go the fuck away,' Harish said.

'Why? Scared I'd spoil your two-boy party?' Latif said. If the ash had swirled in the opposite direction and away from Latif's face, the boys would have seen a smile playing there. Barely perceptible.

'Ha ha ha, you can join the party. This blade is enough for the two of you,' Harish said.

'Don't worry, rug rat, I am enough for an asshole like you.'

'Ha ha ha . . . Says who?'

'You should learn numbers. You're two, we are three,' Abdul said, walking towards them.

'Actually, I won't be gracious enough to count that guy who laughs like a fox and stinks like a hyena. You're better off yourself, Harish,' Latif said.

'Who do you think is a fox, you rag?' Abhishek shot back. He had loosened his grip on Haksh and his eyes were on Latif and Abdul.

'Shut up, Abhishek,' Harish said, 'And hold the guy tighter, will you?' He had removed the blade away from Haksh's crotch and had turned to face Latif.

'Hey Harish, do you think I laugh like a fox? You surely don't, right?' Abhishek whispered. His eyes, large and round, seemed as if they had suddenly grown by a few inches in their sockets. Perturbation was written in clear indelible ink over his smooth, round face.

'Shut the fuck up, Abhishek. Do the job you're asked to do!'

'But if I laugh like a fox and if I stink, I won't get any girls, man.' Abhishek had dropped Haksh. He stretched his right armpit before his nose, trying to sniff out the truth.

Harish slowly turned around to face Abhishek.

'You get girls, you don't get girls. Whether you laugh like a fox or a faggot monkey . . . when you're asked to do a job, you fucking do the job!' Harish shouted.

'What happened, rug rat? Your boyfriend scolded you?' Latif said. The boys had walked closer to where Harish and Haksh were.

Ignoring the heckle, Abhishek slowly said to Harish, 'Hey man, I don't have a nice feeling about this. I mean hitting this Meta is all right, but I don't want to be a part of a war, man.'

'What are you talking about? They're two, we're two. I have the blade. We'll trample them in no time,' Harish said.

'Yea, but I dunno. I mean, what if they all start charging after us? We're still technically in *their* area, man.'

Harish scanned his surroundings. His eyebrows, furrowed. His irises, large. He convulsed for a moment, gave Haksh a long, hard look and turned around to face Latif and Abdul.

'You can do nothing. One day we're going to show you who is really the boss.' Turning back to face Haksh, who was crouching on the ground and trying to get up, Harish said, 'Stay away from my sister. You won't be spared next time even if your Muslim brothers come to save you.'

'Yea, and remember, I don't laugh like a fox. And fuck you,' Abhishek said, as he walked past Latif.

'Let's go, faggot,' Harish said.

'Hey, Harish, why are you calling me a faggot? I am not a faggot.'

'Let's go, Abhishek.'

As Harish and Abhishek walked away, Latif walked over to Haksh. His feet fell heavy on the ash-covered ground.

'Are you all right, man?' Latif asked, offering his hand to Haksh.

'Yea, I am all right. I am not hurt badly. Just bruised a little,' Haksh said. He grasped Latif's arm and got up. His back had gone numb and the skin around his legs, scraped off by the little invisible stones buried in the grey ground, throbbed with a dull pain.

'Don't let these guys get to you, Haksh. You should fight and you *can* fight. Why didn't you?' Abdul said.

Haksh scanned their faces with a blank expression and just managed to nod.

'Hey, enough,' Latif said. He held one of Haksh's arms and asked Abdul to hold the other.

'Guys, I am all right. I can walk,' Haksh said.

'C'mon, let's go to the Old Masjid and get you all tidied up,' Latif said. Haksh protested for a bit, wanting to head back to Easwaran's. A faint whisper of sadness still hung over Haksh as he limped back with Latif and Abdul. The answers that he sought to so many questions were hard to come by.

■ ■ ■

Haksh was tall for a boy of five years and owing to his increased metabolism (something that characterized every Meta), he grew faster than the others around him. Both physically and mentally. From the outside, the circumstances of his birth notwithstanding, Haksh resembled any other boy of about eleven or twelve years. Yet, he had always found himself different from the rest. As he was growing up, he used to think that the world's indifference, bordering on hostility, was because there was something inherently wrong with him. When he couldn't figure out exactly what it was, Haksh would get angry. Angry at both the world for rejecting him without offering an explanation of any kind and himself for not being good enough. It was this same anger that made him, as if by instinct, clench his fists with a want to lunge at the world at any given instant.

With age, the anger stayed dormant within him, but he also knew that the years, however few, also brought with them a sense of sadness. A feeling, which no matter how hard he tried, would never leave him. And for him, at that age, happiness meant being the way people saw Harish. For Dayani, Harish was the world, a boy who could do no wrong. Although Haksh knew how foul Harish's temper could sometimes be. How behind her back, Harish hated his mother and the way she constantly tried to clutch him to herself, how he taunted her mannerisms in front of his friends. But Haksh never did such a thing and yet, Dayani never treated him with the same affection she lavished on her elder son. Haksh was always an irritant, an unrequired burden Dayani had to shoulder through no fault of her own—this was something she never got tired of expressing to Haksh. Despite all the unbridled anger in him, he never went out of his way to show his displeasure to Dayani. During the thick of the night, when he would lie awake trying to hear the sound of the cicadas as they made love in the ever-thickening ash, he would ponder over this mixed bag of emotions that he always carried on his back.

As a boy, quietly removed from the world, Haksh liked to think. He liked taking things apart in his head to try and understand each part as a thing in itself. But unlike his memories that always ran as clear as daylight streaming through his windows, his thoughts were mostly in lumps, entangled with each other in such a way that instead of giving him the clarity he so desperately needed, they made him more troubled. And the more troubled he felt inside, the more he retreated into the confines of his thoughts. He would return again and again to that one question that bothered him constantly: was he happy? And if he wasn't, was it because of someone else, or was it because he didn't have it in himself to be happy? He'd think of one of those innumerable evenings spent with Abdul, who he counted as his best friend. The boys would run around with a stick as a makeshift bat and a ball made out of road tar.

Ever since the Guides came in, the old ways of gang wars steadily gave way to systemic development. Roads were being constructed anew. And the tars, still wet and warm, would always be found lying on a street corner. The boys would scoop out a bit of fresh tar, roll it in their hands into a ball, which was good enough to last for several cricket matches once it had dried down and settled. Long after, while oscillating between sleep and wakefulness, Haksh would think and come to the conclusion that if an average day from his life was taken into consideration, then it could be said that he was happy. A faint glimmer of smile would play over his lips as images of him with Abdul and the black tar ball rolling in between them would float across his mind.

All these were indeed *nice* things, happy things. And then of course, there would be Chhaya who would join the boys on

and off and who would always side with Haksh in the event of
an argument with Abdul. Times when an electricity of ecstasy,
warm as fresh blood, would flow through his being. Or the
times when Chhaya, joined by her other friends from the nearby
Hindu areas, would wander around in the Muslim Quarters to
watch an ongoing cricket match. During those days, Haksh
would take extra care to play well, aware that Chhaya's eyes
would be on him, or at least he imagined them to be on him.
These were the times that can be counted as when he was happy.
But he also wondered if that was all that people meant when
they said they were *happy*. If that was all there was to happiness,
Haksh's young mind would try to reason why he should feel this
overwhelming sadness. It was a sadness, dense as a fog, which
never left him. As time went by, he had learnt to live with it, as
he had learnt to live with that cloud of anger. Realizing quite
early on that the more he grew angry with the world, the sadder
he became, he was able to control that anger. But as the anger
receded inside, albeit never dying down, the sadness acquired a
different shape. It had stopped being this overwhelming burden
that would haze around him from time to time and had acquired
the quieter hues of a certain melancholic longing. A longing for
what, he didn't know. Maybe answers, his young mind would
deduce in times to come. But to arrive at them, you need to
ask the correct questions. But his young mind, curious as it was
with the world, didn't know what questions he should ask to
the confused mass of feelings that swayed back and forth in his
heart, like a treetop in the midst of a powerful wind.

As he would also struggle to understand Dayani's apathy
towards him, Haksh would do what he thought then was the
only way to *correct* himself. If Dayani's apathy was because
there was something inherently amiss with himself, Haksh

would have to forego himself. And the only way to do so would be to imitate Harish. He would copy the way Harish walked—fast with long strides. He would copy the way Harish furrowed his thick eyebrows when he was displeased with something. Or the way he styled his hair, allowing it to grow long so he could comb them back and settle them with a thick dollop of coconut oil. The more he imitated Harish, the more Dayani became irritated, which just pushed young Haksh into a whirlpool of frenzied confusion, confronted with strange questions. For instance, Harish hated insects and showed a strong distaste for animal life. Out in the open, he would catch hold of a dragonfly—so many of them in Old City—only to pry open the creature's wings, one after the other. And he would also devise newer, more creative ways to kill the insects. Harish would catch butterflies and dragonflies, trap them inside jars while leaving a hole to ensure the insect did not die at once. He enjoyed the initial fluttering, when the creature, deprived of its freedom, would first look for a way out—its wings displaying the maddening fear that must have clutched at the creature's heart. Having grown tired of this, after a while, he would slowly squeeze the air out the jar by closing off the tiny hole. Haksh, seeing all of this, would try doing the same. But no sooner would he catch hold of a dragonfly, feeling its tiny legs buzz around the inside of his palms, a strange indescribable feeling would clutch at his heart. And he would let the creature go. Defeated in his attempt to transform fully into Harish, he would retreat more into himself. And to the company of those myriad voices that spoke simultaneously in his head.

■ ■ ■

The masjid was a large, bleak and dilapidated structure that still retained around it an air of regal authority. Half the structure was buried under the ever-thickening haze of dust and ash. Steep stairs wound themselves around the masjid, leading one to the topmost dome. The rest of the area lay in shambles. A cemetery lay behind, dating back thousands of years. Holding Haksh from both sides, Latif and Abdul climbed the stairs to reach up near the topmost dome. A large courtyard lay adjacent to it, bounded off by low-lying walls, which also served as balconies. The masjid was where Latif and Abdul lived. Their father was the imam here and the family enjoyed the respect of the other Muslims living in the nearby areas.

'Hey Abdul, carry Haksh over to the charpoy and have him lie down,' Latif said. While Abdul did so, Latif walked straight across from one side of the courtyard to the other, where under a small brick structure—a shack made of concrete—the family of three lived. Their mother had died when Abdul was still a year old.

'Isn't your father home?' Haksh asked.

'No. After the prayers, he must have gone over to Hussein Darji's place,' Abdul replied. Hussein Darji and his small house, only a few blocks away from the masjid, was the proverbial social centre in the neighbourhood. Old men, like Latif's father, gathered together around an ancient television, devouring an endless number of samosas and cups of tea.

'You'll be all right very soon. If I were you, I would just lie still and not worry a bit,' Latif said. He came out of the shack, bearing a small tray that contained a bottle of iodine, bandages, a small ball of cotton and hot water.

'I am not afraid. Not even one bit,' Haksh said.

Latif dipped the cotton into the iodine bottle. Haksh opened his shirt and lay down on his chest. His bare back had distinct marks upon it. In a corner, the skin had come off, and a black patch on his shoulder blades screamed of what he'd just gone through. Latif removed the cotton ball from the iodine bottle and placed it on Haksh's shoulder blades. As soon as the wet iodized cotton touched his skin, he flinched in pain, as the exposed skin stung terribly.

'Easy,' Latif said.

'You should have done something to those punks. You so should have, man,' Abdul said. He was standing in front of Haksh, trying to look him in the eye.

'It's all right, Haksh. You do what you think is right, okay?' Latif said. 'And Abdul, stop bothering the kid. He's had a bad day as it is. He could do without your stupid comments.'

'But—'

'No, Abdul. It's his life, he has to figure out what he needs to do,' Latif said.

'For now, all I want is for this pain to go away. Owwww! Can you please do it quick, Latif? It freaking hurts,' Haksh said through clenched teeth. His eyes were shut tight, and his face, contorted.

When Latif was done tending to Haksh's wounds, the two brothers pushed the charpoy from the centre of the courtyard to rest near one of the boundary walls. From here, the boys could see the entire district spread out before them, flat as a slice of bread. The masjid, despite having shrunk in size, could still be used as a vantage point to see Old City stretch out till the river. The breeze, warm in the setting sun, had picked up. The boys sat on the charpoy and looked out.

Latif removed a packet of tobacco from his pocket and some cigarette papers.

'It was about Chhaya, wasn't it?' he asked. His hands were busy squashing the rough lump of tobacco into finer grains. He would then put them on the paper, before rolling it.

'Yes. What else can it be about?' Haksh replied. He did not look at Latif. His eyes were set on to the distant horizon, as thick breeze blew against his long black hair.

'He came pretty close to hurting you today. I've known Harish for very long. I seriously thought him to be a bully, yes. But you know you cannot take a bully seriously,' Latif said.

'But he seemed dead serious today,' Abdul said. 'Also, I hear he is going to start working with the Guides.'

Latif, who was about to roll the second cigarette, paused. 'Who told you?'

'I hang out with that slimeball Abhishek's kid brother. He's unlike his brother, you know. We were out hunting for dead branches to make a bat with. That's when he mentioned both Abhishek and Harish.'

As Abdul was speaking, Latif brought the rolled cigarette, thick with tobacco, up to his lips. Using a bit of saliva, he stuck the loosened ends of the paper together.

'All the more reason why Haksh should stay away. You really don't want any trouble.' Latif said.

'How exactly do I stay away, Latif?' Haksh said, turning around. His voice betrayed a certain desperation. 'Staying away would mean staying away from Chhaya. How do I *do* that? Besides, Easwaran is still here. Harish won't do anything as long as his father's around.'

'Yea, but for how long?' Abdul asked. The boy, although only ten years of age, had an innate sense of realism. Haksh found this quality of his equally puzzling and endearing. In the earlier days, when Haksh would imitate everything Harish did, it was Abdul who first saw through what Haksh was doing and warned him that copying Harish would only get him into trouble and reduce him to a joke. Haksh didn't accept the fact that he was actually imitating Harish, something he wouldn't accept even now. He had fought with Abdul then and called him names, only to apologize much later. And Abdul, being the person that he is, had forgiven him without asking any questions. This was a trait that made Latif worry about his younger brother—the boy's forthrightness, the fact that he never really cared either about the circumstances or surroundings before blurting out what was in his mind. His mind seemed to lack the filtering process that was so necessary.

'I don't agree with my younger brother most of the time. But you'd know yourself that he is right this time,' Latif said. Once he had finished rolling up the three cigarettes and lighting them one by one, he offered them to Haksh and Abdul. 'I mean you're a Meta and Metas grow fast. For how long would you stay with Harish and the family? You're slaving away down there. High time you find your kind, man. You gotta think for yourself.'

Haksh didn't say anything. He took a puff from the cigarette, feeling the tobacco vapours fill up his lungs. His head felt light. The breeze blew through his ears and he swayed in the collective rhythm of it all.

'I'll think about it when the time comes. Let's not talk about this any more. Chuck it,' Haksh said.

'Escapist. Always an escapist,' Latif said with a smile. He stretched his legs forward, easing his back on the charpoy and resting his head against the wall. 'Soon the stars would be out. You should stay, have dinner with us.'

'It'd be killer to see them once actually. Anyway, no. Gotta go back. Easwaran would ask for me.'

'Hey, Latif, tell us a story,' Abdul said. Although the younger one, he never referred to Latif by the Urdu honorific *bhaijaan*, meant for elder brother. Latif, lying down on the charpoy, just shrugged in response.

'Do you plan to tell Ruby that you have feelings for her?' Haksh asked all of a sudden. Latif was just gearing up to form rings through the smoke he had exhaled, puffing it out in short easy bursts. But when Haksh referred to Ruby, the unformed smoke rings broke down prematurely in his mouth, resulting in bouts of cough.

'Where did that come from?' Latif asked, getting up.

'Ha ha ha ha,' Abdul sniggered. 'Haksh knows how to take your case.'

'No, seriously. I wasn't being funny,' Haksh replied, embarrassed.

'I dunno . . .' Latif shrugged. He could say nothing else. It seemed that along with the smoke, he had swallowed half his words as well. All that came out was nothing but a half-baked rendering of his feelings.

'You know what you should do—write her a letter or something. A poem, or a song or a story. You write so well,' Haksh looked at him.

'Maybe.'

Although Latif claimed there was nothing of the sort, the truth was that he had loved Ruby Prasad since he was seven years old. In fact, it was an open secret amongst his friends. Ruby was the daughter of Rajaji Prasad, one of the Guides. She lived in one of the finest houses, somewhere in the southern part of the city, which was predominantly the Hindu Quarters. Latif was sixteen years old now, and for years, he had been jotting down all that he felt in a diary hidden away in the darkness of his trunk. He had taken care to remember how Ruby looked when he'd first seen her, which seemed like a thousand light years away. She had worn a light green summer dress and was walking with her mother to the Muslim Quarters. A servant who followed them was carrying boxes of sweets. They had come to distribute these to the homeless, who squatted their lives away in the dark dampness of the streets. He didn't know what the occasion was, but he was right there all right, with a tennis ball in hand. And he had stopped in his tracks, as something warm and fuzzy and eerily indescribable crept into his heart. Latif would not sleep that day. Turning over in his bed, he would try to form words to describe his feelings. And he had been trying to do that ever since.

'Leave it,' Latif said. His face was flushed and lovelorn. 'It's not going to happen. She's from *up there*. I don't have the means to reach there.'

Guilt, sharp as a needle, pierced through Haksh's skin for bringing Ruby out in the open. The three friends silently sat on the charpoy. Not a word passed between them for a good fifteen minutes. Smoke slithered from their mouths and dangled in the almost impenetrable air before it dissipated.

'Tell us a story, Latif,' Abdul said, breaking the silence.

'Yea, the story about the Weaver,' Haksh added.

'How many times would you guys hear that same story?' Latif failed to understand.

'But it's a lovely story. C'mon! Tell us that story, Latif,' Abdul pushed.

'All right.' Stubbing his cigarette on the wall, Latif got up. 'The story is narrated by a magical pen with a golden nib. So, imagine I am that pen. Let me act it out for you.'

*The garbage stinks.*

*These fractured-faced cats hover all around me, sniffing my odour. Do I smell like a mouse? Why cannot you cats use Listerine mouthwash for Pete's sake? Your mouth stinks just like the garbage that I am in. I just wonder how you kiss your partners. Don't they run away from you? But then I suppose it's a mutual thing. Moreover, you wouldn't know about the life that I've lived. I am a pen and I'm proud of it. Oh! Please do not brush your dirty whiskers against my nib. Can't you see it's made of gold? Doesn't the gold fascinate you? But I presume it doesn't. So where was I before you miserable cats spoiled my tale? Hmm . . . yes . . . I was telling my listeners that I am a pen with a golden nib. Do not get fooled by this garbage. I have seen better days and have known great people, besides these wretched feline filth-manufacturing beings who are my only companions now. So should I begin my story then? Have you all settled down? I see some of you sitting on the couch . . . good. There is nothing like sitting or reclining on the couch and listening to a story. My master used to do it . . . Ah! Those were the days! However, I should not digress as I see you, my dear listeners, are very eager to hear my tale. Therefore, this is my story and mind you, every word of it is true.*

*My master was a tall man aged twenty-four whose facial features were blurred by a yellowish purple veneer that never left him. I could, however, still trace a thin contour of joined eyebrows and languid eyes iridescent with a colourless gaze.*

*When we'd arrived, Chungwa was a small town of tall glass buildings, rickety bamboo hovels and ragged plastic lanes shining in the dark haze of the burning sun. The place, however, gave me the creeps. Almost every corner of the town was plastered with huge saffron hoardings. They were of a stubby moustachioed man, his bony index finger pointing to a burning skirt. The message written below was clear and simple: 'CHUNGWAN GIRLS DON'T WEAR SKIRTS'.*

*As we reached another street, I saw an elfish eatery painted in yellow chromatic hues, jam-packed with young couples; some girls wearing jeans and T-shirts while some were sporting their newly bought skirts (perhaps unaware of the Divine Command of Posters), snuggling up to their sticky-haired, broad-chested, clean-shaven, musk cologne-smeared boyfriends, smoking chocolate hookahs. The other end of the street was filled with some fruit hawkers selling oranges, which I later learnt was the national fruit of Chungwa.*

*Our residence was amidst thick hedges of lantana shrubs and gooseberry bushes, consisting of four rooms evenly distributed in the two stories. The main bedroom (which would soon be rechristened as the Weaving Room) was wrapped in the thick sugary, grimy and humid scent of the gooseberries, and adjacent to it was the kitchen.*

*'So here we are, home at last,' my master said.*

*'Yes . . . The house is quite nice,' I answered, 'but master, this place is quite queer, not that I don't like it, but it's very strange.'*

*'Every place looks strange when you're a stranger.'*

*I would have asked him to elaborate on this enigmatic statement but seeing an odd puzzlement on his face, I refrained from doing so. Regardless of my excellent erudition in comprehending human nature, I always found it quite difficult to understand my master. Many a times I was enticed to ask him to reveal himself but always desisted from doing so, lest he should flame up and hurt my nib, which I am afraid wasn't infrequent.*

*Even though our abode was quite modest, this fact never dissuaded the natives from prying into our lives. We had hardly settled when a throng of people gathered on our porch, staring at my master and trying futilely to penetrate his misty face. They just stood there whispering and making gestures while their snotty little kids ran around, playing hide-and-seek, crushing the melancholic shrubs and stealing gooseberries. His blurry face shining in the stardust of the crowd's awe, my master only smiled.*

*'Did you see his face?'*

*'Yes. He is so beautiful.'*

*'How come you know that? I could barely make out his visage.'*

*'But he is so tall and well built.'*

*'I know . . . I just wish our husbands would have a body like that.'*

*'What does he do anyway?'*

*'Just look at his attire. I think he is a businessman.'*

*'No . . . He can't be a trader. I suppose he is an engineer.'*

*'And how can you be so sure that he is an engineer?'*

*'Because only engineers can look so good.'*

*I was so beguiled by these bits of conversation that I barely noticed him. He was an old man draped in ancient clothes with his once-deep-but-now-hollow marble eyes staring fixedly at the crowd with neither repugnance nor hatred. Instead, I think I saw in those eyes a sense of incomprehensibility, much like a weary sailor contemplating his state by gazing at the indifferent ocean. In a faint voice that carried in it a lost baritone of yesteryears, he said:*

*'He is not what you think he is.'*

*But this emphatic interjection only evoked frustrated grunts from the crowd and the old man was anything but amazed at the crowd's evident display of silent hostility mingled with indifference at his remarks, as if he had foreseen all this before. With an annoying drawl, someone in the crowd shouted:*

*'Why don't you shut up, old man?'*

*But the old man was hardly perturbed. Instead, his baggy toothless face contorted into a wry smile and his eyes lit up for a second, only to diminish an instant later.*

*'You don't believe me . . . Why don't you ask him who he is?'*

*My master, slowly coming down on the granite portico and staring intently at the old man's hollow antique eyes, murmured:*

*'You sure you want to do this?'*

*'The people should know it,' the old man answered.*

*'Well then, let the truth be told.'*

*'Dear people,' my master addressed the crowd, 'the old man here is correct in his surmise. I am not what you think. Neither am I a corporate biggie nor an IT professional. I am . . . ahem . . . a Weaver.'*

*My master looked at the crowd and sensed their disbelief merged with incomprehension.*

*'Yes, I am a Weaver and have come here for a very special purpose.'*

*'Don't keep us in unnecessary suspense . . . Blurt out what you have come here for . . .'*

*'Yea . . . We are already loaded with clothes to keep us cold in this hot place. We don't want anything from you!'*

*'Maybe you don't,' my master said, concealing his wolfish smile beneath the protective façade of the veneer, 'but I don't weave clothes. I weave something else, which I think you're very much in need of and which I can provide.'*

*'Go ahead . . . Tell us what you weave. Tell us your specialty,' the crowd shouted in unison.*

*With his blurry face glowing even more than before and that wolfish smile slowly turning into a hyena's laugh, my master answered, in his typically laconic style, of course:*

'I weave stories.'

The effect of this particular disclosure wasn't electric. Perhaps using the simile 'akin to a silent supernova explosion' would be more apt and fitting rather than hyperbolic.

'And,' my master continued, 'that I suppose you people are in dire need of.'

'So does that mean,' an emaciated but nonetheless proud middle-aged man, who silently emerged from the interior of that human jungle, shouted, 'you will weave a story about us?'

'Yes, my dear friend . . . a story about you.'

'No one has ever woven a story around us . . . We don't exist.'

'That is wrong to say, you know. Sure, you exist . . . You are standing right there.'

'But to weave stories, don't you need Voice? We don't have one.'

'Don't worry . . . I'll lend you mine.'

Amidst sounds of unified euphoria thumping my eardrums, I managed to catch a passing glimpse of the old man whose eyes were very strange, but as strange eyes don't bother me, I chose to overlook him. But I couldn't help but notice that these strange eyes were constantly fixed on my master's foggy face with a sense of resignation and defeat in the place of incomprehensibility, as if he had given up on something or someone. Later, as the ocean of the voiceless Chungwans enveloped my master and me, the old man and his antique eyes drowned in the crowd's elation.

For the next couple of days, following the aforementioned incident, my master, much against his wish of course, became something of a medicine man. With the Chungwans coming to him with their afflictions, our meek residence that was in perpetual disarray from then on turned into some sort of a charitable hospital. Perched comfortably on my velvet stand and with nothing in

*immediate sight to kill my boredom, I began to watch the long line
of diseased Chungwans. Among them was a dead farmer who was
suffering from acute depression. He had gone on a short vacation
to Kifo, the land where all the dead lived, and had come here with
the desire to pay his bank loan, wishing not to trouble the poor bank
manager further. However, he misplaced his travelling permit
and the Kifo authorities wouldn't let him enter as they demanded
documental proof of his death.*

*As my master was busy jotting down his complaint, someone
arrived. This was a woman aged somewhere between 150 and
200 years. She was suffering from a bad case of insomnia as the
broken, tuneless songs of her past wouldn't let her sleep. Another
individual to arrive was a young man of twenty years with thin
hair and watery bones. He was suffering from a congenital disease
of stealing people's dreams, pruning them and stuffing them up in
neat glass satchels, to form a library of dreams. The next to arrive
was a man who had lost his shadow somewhere, due to which
he was fast losing weight, a matter that seriously threatened his
married life. For the next week or so, these and several others
with their diverse maladies kept frequenting our humble quarters,
hoping to share their afflictions to help my master in completing
his task of creating a story. Patiently and without uttering a single
frustrated syllable, my master carefully examined the various
maladies, assuring them of his gratefulness and their worth.*

*'So, master,' I asked him one day, 'when do you think we should
start weaving?'*

*'There is a right time for everything.'*

*'But don't we have enough material already? Those ailing
Chungwans . . . Didn't they provide everything we need?'*

*'You are uneducated in the ways of the world . . . We don't
have any raw material to weave a story yet.'*

'But what about those ailing Chungwans?' I repeated, perplexed.

'You sure don't want to weave a story out of those materials . . . No one would read it.'

'So, what should we do in your opinion?'

'Nothing . . . I've ordered the raw materials from somewhere else. They will be here soon.'

Six long months drowsily passed by since that distant morning when my master first walked on the half-mud half-concrete roads of Chungwa with that singular vision of weaving a story about this alien place, but apart from rearranging our quarters, no breakthrough was accomplished. Near the boredom-wrapped windowsill, perched upon my velvet stand, I saw winter descend on Chungwa as the sky shed ominous, yellow, pearly tears that metamorphosed into yellow snow, sucking Chungwa into a wormhole of thick, impenetrable, yellowish gloom. Watching the translucent snow lazily float, my master would slouch on a couch and either read his curious book, 'The Book of Countless Fables' or put on his father's blue sailor hat and sing about the wild roses that grew near the lemonade sea.

'That's a good song,' I quietly said one day.

'Yes . . .' He almost whispered. I waited for him to continue, but he didn't. He stopped, as if he was lost in the distant greasy scent of the irretrievable past.

'Master?'

'Yes?'

'Weren't you saying something?'

'Someone I once knew loved this song . . . Life is funny . . . How quickly everything changes . . .'

As always, my master did not wait to elucidate his statements and walked inside without casting a second glance.

On a dusty morning, two days after this incident, they finally came.

With an annual turnover of over forty billion dollars and a workforce of 50,000 people, Inspire Corporation was one of the largest manufacturers of dreams, memories, shadows and words on the other side of the hemisphere. Covering a little above 10,000 miles in just twelve hours, their Boeing, smeared with the pulpy yellow snow, landed on our porch that morning. Soon the workers, dressed in blue overalls, began to unload the cargo, which to my slight surprise wasn't much. Some, perhaps due its volatile nature, contained ice trays neatly packed with cubic memories at a temperature of -10 degrees, while in eight medium-sized boxes were enclosed syrupy, peach-scented reddish dreams at room temperature. One box was stuffed with a pair of carefully folded papery white shadows and the last two contained about 10,000 sachets of words. All these cartons were brought down from the plane and as per my master's desire were kept in the bedroom.

The next day onwards, my master stopped all his social activities and locked us in the newly christened Weaving Room. Since our arrival, due to the lack of work, my nib had lost its earlier sheen and thick green moss were seen sprouting from its temporal end. So before joining my master in his work, I, with utmost care, performed my ablutions and cleaned my nib thoroughly, polishing it gently with silicone paper. Only when I was assured that my nib had not only surpassed its earlier glimmer but also looked more beautiful than ever before did I venture into the presence of my master.

He was a meticulous worker, my master. But he didn't start work right way. Instead, for a whole hour, he just sat on his cracked chocolaty chair, gazing at the empty gooseberry-scented ceiling with a vacant fuzzy look. At times he would rise, pace around a bit, hum a song and return to his seat, only to resume his gazing.

*There were instances when he'd be deeply engrossed in his weaving but he would suddenly drop me aside and, through empty eyes, gape at the vacuum of his half-finished story.*

*As the crystal nights crept in, flushed with the day's tiring work, I'd slump upon my velvet stand and instantly fall asleep. But many a times my master's gloomy moans would wake me up and stealthily, I'd sneak into his quarters to find his dreams hovering over his closed eyes. They were mostly about a large white snake swallowing a wrinkled brown tortoise that had stars on its shell.*

*I sometimes felt a strong inescapable urge to ask my master about his nocturnal dreams. But I somehow had to stifle it inside as I knew that such an inquiry would only incur one of his cold dreaded stares, freezing my beloved nib that I had spent so much time cleaning.*

*Soon the yellow winter lost its colour and slowly faded away. With the passing of winter, Chungwa was back to its old dusty self. Lonesome fruit hawkers returned to their reserved places, selling oranges under the dark crackling of the neon lamps, yelping in the doleful dirge of the dead dour lanes that wafted leisurely in the thick rickety air through the sad cobwebby shanties of crushed bamboos and forlorn defeat.*

*After fourteen months of arduous knuckle-cracking work, the story was finally woven. The next day, a thick crowd of Chungwans gathered on our granite portico and patiently waited to catch a glimpse of the story. But unlike last time, the crowd now was more orderly. Among those numerous faces, I tried to look for Phanai, but he was nowhere to be seen. Anyway, dressed in a sparkling robe that beautifully complemented his shiny, foggy face, my master came out and stood on the staircase, which was at an elevated level than the portico, like some uncrowned king of the ancient days addressing his subjects, holding a* notebook wrapped neatly with a yellow cloth. Soon the crowd begin chanting my master's name, begging him not to keep them in suspense any longer.

The story was woven on a peach-coloured notebook with embroidered edges. He slowly unwrapped the notebook, gesturing to the crowd to calm down and finally began to read the story aloud.

He must have been reading for quite some time when some restless sounds from the crowd made him stop. He scanned the starchy faces of the people, and to his ghastly stupefaction, realized that no one could understand the story. It was too alien and too outworldish for them, but he continued unabated.

Suddenly, the restless sounds gave rise to cruel grumbles and gasps of surprise, compelling my master to stop. At first, he took those sounds to be the expression of people's incomprehension, but this surmise could not last for long and gradually evaporated. It was then that he realized that something was wrong with his face. As he was reading the story, the veneer that blurred his face slowly began to thin out, and within minutes, disappeared, as if it never existed.

He looked strange. His sombre face was embedded with two pale round eyes encircled by a pair of disjointed dark bushy eyebrows, while his shrivelled lips were dry and colourless. His nose was stubby and appeared deflated, the only beautiful spot on his face being those two dimples on his cheeks. The failure of the story was only an incident in the minds of the perpetually dejected Chungwans. But the disappearance of the veneer was a catalyst. Soon livid grumbles gave way to irate shouts entwined with the constant refrain: 'DOWN WITH THE WEAVER'. They began closing in and even blocked the entrance to our house. But somehow, my master forced himself through the crowd and scurried into the house, bolting the door from inside. The angry crowd of

*Chungwans banged the door for some time and even tried breaking in. The door, however, was strong and did not give way. They lingered on the portico for a few more hours and left only when they realized that banging on the door was useless.*

*In slow, languid steps, the muddy evening descended and everything was calm again. But the sweet sickly aroma of the gooseberries became faint and crumbled into dust, leaving us in perpetual loneliness.*

*So this was my story.*

*My master never wove any story from then on and left Chungwa the very next day, never to return. I, being of no use to him hereon, was carefully dumped in a garbage tank through which I made my way here to be among these feline friends of mine. Since garbage tanks are usually devoid of any postal facility, I never found out what became of my master. My memory of late has been growing weak, and like all memories, will soon die away. Even then, during the cold wintry evenings, with the garbage stench overpowering my olfactory faculties, I cannot help but reminisce about that fading sickly-sweet smell of the gooseberry-wrapped ghost-ridden town of Chungwa.*

# 6

## Old City

As Haksh walked back home by traversing the ancient, dusty streets of his crumbling town, he thought about Latif's story. *Latif was a born performer*, thought Haksh. The kind who immerse themselves in the story, becoming something else entirely. The way he narrated the story of a pen playing the protagonist's role left Haksh and Abdul in splits. Haksh had heard the story innumerable times and every time Latif would change the protagonist. If it was the pen today, a month before, it was a donkey. And Latif had gone down on all fours, enacting the donkey, making faces, braying and modulating his tone of voice. But beyond the fact that it was fun and Latif was funny, there was something else that drew Haksh into the story every time he heard it. It was the character of the Weaver.

How sad someone must be, Haksh would reflect, to be without a face and to not be who the world thinks you to be. The weight of that thought, and the sheer idea that one day you might just be discovered for what you are not, both frightened and intrigued him. He imagined if one day, Harish would wake up to find that his mother and his friends did not love him any more, without offering any explanation, how horribly sad would Harish become. The thought of Harish being sad made him smile. That also meant that someday he would wake up to find that Dayani and all the others, who looked at him as if he was some kind of freak, would wake up to see that his face had changed with the lifting of the veneer. And he would become one of their own.

He had crossed the Muslim Quarters, and the breeze had picked up even more. It was not warm any more, but there was a hint of moisture that made it cool, and he felt it across his face. He loved walking when the breeze was cold. It was not every day that it happened. And he thought he was lucky enough to be in the streets at this moment. The darkness had set in. The sound of the azan from the masjid, now far behind him, wafted through the breeze. A faint, distant echo throbbed through his heart. *Such a lonely sound*, he thought. He imagined Abdul and Latif and scores of other Muslims now down on a mat, praying with their faces turned towards Mecca—the holiest city, as Latif had explained to him long ago.

Haksh himself never understood the concept of God. Latif, Abdul, their father, Dayani and even Harish spoke of God so many times that it seemed like God was a flesh-and-blood entity standing right in front of him. But God was also invisible at the same time. It was as if God was like the Weaver in Latif's story—hidden behind a veneer. So that would mean God could be loved today and hated tomorrow. More than anything else, what confused Haksh was the *way* his friends explained God's strength—that it was all-knowing and all-powerful. When Haksh would despair, Abdul would comfort him by saying that he ought to have faith in God, for it is watching everything, and that one day, everything would be all right. Until a few years earlier, Haksh would even pray. Not knowing which god to pray to, he would pray to *everyone* and in different ways—sometimes like a Muslim with his palms outstretched, facing the Mecca—although he always got the direction wrong, for he didn't know which side Mecca was on. On some other days, he would sit near the small idol of Ganesha, the elephant-headed god, which Dayani would keep in the house. At first, praying to Ganesha appealed to Haksh, not only because he was able to see the idol but also because the idol did not look like a *human* at all. It was as if, like him, this god did not fit in as well. And he had always imagined the laboratory to be the place where Ganesha was made, for only such a place can stitch an elephant's head on to a human's body. Elephants were extinct by then. And Haksh had seen photographs in one of those big books that Easwaran always kept in his room. Day after day, Easwaran would sit him down and teach him the names of animals and plants, teach him how to read while showing him photographs.

But he never received a reply, either from Latif's faceless God or from the elephant-headed deity. This just made him all the more angry. If there was a god, why didn't things become better? He had asked Latif the duration it normally took for God to reply, and Latif had only laughed. If he didn't know the time it would take for even one reply—for he thought a reply wasn't such a big deal—then what's the point of praying anyway? Either God was grossly rude for not respecting his prayers, or God too thought it shouldn't respond because Haksh was a Meta. In either of the cases, there was no point. Much like there was no point in explaining to Harish what he felt for Chhaya, as he knew

Harish would never understand. So that meant, like Harish, God wasn't this all-seeing being after all. It also indicated that it only answered the prayers of humans. The only one that mattered, that ever mattered, was Chhaya. The girl who was constantly berated by Dayani for spending too much time with Haksh. And yet, she never gave in. The more Dayani forbade Chhaya, the more closely she clung to Haksh, and in the process, shooting through his heart a thousand echoes of man's lonesome call to God.

As he reached home, Haksh thought about how the house resembled an old lady, her body bent with age. Bereft dead trees with bare-bone branches surrounded it. The boundary wall—broken earlier but subsequently mended by Easwaran—was low. A half-broken gate was attached to it. Haksh jumped over it. If the house was to be reduced to a particular smell, Haksh thought, it could very well be that of death. Not that he knew what death smelt like, but he was sure it would smell something like this house. Dank, musty, draped with cobwebs and nests of various insects. *So lifeless*, thought Haksh. The courtyard leading to the front door was long and spacious. If one could go around the courtyard to the backside of the house, one would find two different outhouses, lying adjacent to each other. Separated from each other by about three hundred feet and another hundred from the main house. One shack was where Haksh lived. In the other shack was a bathroom, which was only used by Haksh. The house itself was two-storeyed. Chhaya, Harish and Dayani lived on the ground floor. Easwaran lived upstairs. Earlier, the house had only two rooms. But since bringing in Haksh from the Interstate on that distant day, Easwaran used whatever money he had saved and constructed an extra room for Haksh inside the house. Dayani had insisted that Haksh could not stay anywhere close to where she was, and so that room had been given to Harish. A couple of years later, Easwaran built an attic upstairs, where he began to spend more and more of his time.

Instead of going around his house, Haksh opened the front door and walked inside. In the centre of the room was a large circular table and four chairs. Seated on a chair with Chhaya on her lap, Dayani was braiding and combing Chhaya's dark, dense and curly hair. She looked up and saw Haksh. She didn't flinch or react in any way.

'Sit still, Chhaya. You're not helping matters by fidgeting constantly,' Dayani said. Chhaya did not answer but jumped lightly on Dayani's lap. The woman pulled Chhaya down. Her movement was stern and firm.

'I *said* sit still.'

'You do it so hard. My head hurts. Why should I always comb my hair, Ma?' Chhaya asked. She did not look at Haksh, but something in the way she moved her body to escape from Dayani's clutches told Haksh that she was aware of his presence. Haksh would have greeted Dayani, but he knew that Dayani would either nod or not respond altogether. He did not say a single word. His eyes scanned the room. A few feet from the table, there was a large sofa, of which one of the legs was broken and had been saved from collapsing altogether by placing beneath it a somewhat large chip of wood to give the sofa some sort of balance. A television set stood in front of it.

Usually, the TV would be on and either Harish or Dayani would be watching it. Chhaya did not enjoy watching television all that much, although she had her favourite channels. Harish was nowhere around at the moment and

Haksh deduced that he must be at Abhishek's. He probably must have thought he should avoid the house, in case Haksh said anything to Easwaran. Although, Haksh thought that Harish must also be equally sure that Haksh would say nothing. Over the last so many years, Haksh had never said a word about Harish to Easwaran. It was a fact that both bothered and made him proud. Easwaran had always tried to teach the boys about the need to rise up to one's own shit, to deal with it. And going up to Easwaran wouldn't have made Harish better. It would have only made Haksh look weak—something he didn't think he was. He could have been born in a laboratory but he'd never been weak. Haksh walked up to the kitchen, washed his face, opened the back door and walked out.

His room was a dismal grey. The steel that was used to keep the wood in place had grown rusty. The bed, covered with a light blue bed sheet, creaked. The bed overlooked a window with a large ledge. A little table was near it. The only graceful thing in the room was a large leather chair. Easwaran had given it to him last year. That day, Dayani had threatened him, perhaps for the umpteenth time, to die starving if something was not done to get Haksh out. By nightfall, she had quietened down. It was evident that Easwaran had stopped caring a long time ago.

Haksh walked over to the window and opened it. The window shook for a split second and then stood still. He looked out. Like a thick, black thread, darkness wove around him everywhere he looked. Not a soul stirred. Echoes of insects, weeping through their lonesome little lives, could be heard. *Necropolis*, thought Haksh. It was another one of those big words Easwaran had taught him.

And with the word, he would conjure up images of sleepy, ancient cities and their collapsing architecture. Athens, Rome, Alhambra—these were exotic names that drove through him a sense of ecstasy and dread, both in equal measure. Maybe there still are people there, hoped Haksh, who'd be different from those that are here. Maybe these are places he'd visit one day and end up finding a home. But another thought would come to him and send a shiver down his spine: what if the people there are the same as here? What if there is *nowhere* to go? The handle of his door turned. Haksh moved away from the window. Chhaya walked in. Her feet were bare and her hair was tied in a single tight plait at the back of her head. She closed the door behind her, walked up over to Haksh's bed and sat down. Haksh did not move an inch away from the window, but his eyes followed Chhaya through every inch of her movements.

'You came in late today. Ma was wondering where you were. I think she was worried,' Chhaya said.

'You lie through your teeth. And you're not even ashamed of it.'

'I don't lie. I never lie,' Chhaya's hands—nimble yet firm—moved to her hair as she began to twirl her plait. Haksh knew she hated tying her hair.

'Why does your hair always have to be . . . unkempt?' Haksh asked. His face was sombre, although Chhaya knew he was trying to suppress a smile, an act he did particularly well.

'Unkempt . . . What does that mean . . . Gosh! Sometimes I feel proud of the fact that you know so many words.'

'Only sometimes?'

'Yes. Mostly, I feel irritated.'

'Because I know too many words? That's a strange thing to be irritated about, you know.'

'Maybe I am strange. But no, I look like an idiot when you use such words. I don't know too many words, and you do. And that's really not fair, if you ask me.'

'But you're really not an idiot.'

'I think I am. I was playing with Ruby di and her sister the other day, and I fell down. Ruby said I was an idiot and her sister laughed.'

'Did you cry?'

Chhaya did not reply. She had managed to remove the rubber band and loosen her hair. The hair—long and curly—fell across her face. She moved the loose strands and stood up.

'Your room is as miserable as you are,' she said. Her eyes were scanning the room as she spoke. Haksh did not reply. His eyes remained fixed on Chhaya. She walked close to where he was standing and went past him. Standing very close to the window, she looked out.

'Did you feel bad?' she asked, not facing him.

'No,' Haksh replied. He turned to look at her and noticed the way Chhaya's hair obscured her features. He always noticed such minute details about her. The way her wayward hair bounced when she walked; the little mole underneath her chin; the somewhat large eyebrows, which he loved and she hated; even how she took small, even steps that always made her come last on those innumerable walking races they used to have with the children in the Muslim Quarters.

'Your hair looks like Medusa's,' Haksh said. Chhaya turned around.

'Who in god's name is that?' She had a puzzled expression on her face.

'Some woman,' Haksh uttered.

'Is she pretty?'

'Maybe.'

'What does she look like?'

'She had snakes in her hair, and you'd turn to stone if you looked at her.'

'Huh? How on earth is that pretty? Are you pulling my leg?'

'No. I never pull anyone's legs. Besides if I did, it would have made you taller. Which you're clearly not.'

'You're making fun of me!'

'No, I am not. Medusa was quite pretty despite the snakes.'

Chhaya scanned Haksh's face for a trace of irony, but his face was straight as a die. But Chhaya knew the boy could crack a joke or tease someone with the straightest face possible. You probably would even accept the fact that he isn't joking. But she knew him better than most. And she knew that deep inside, he must be having a laugh riot.

Haksh walked closer to where Chhaya was standing. The two sat on the ledge, their feet dangling down. The breeze, now cooler than what it was earlier, blew against their backs. Chhaya moved her face closer to Haksh's shirt. She wrinkled her nose as if she was sniffing something.

'Did you smoke?' she exclaimed.

'Yes. I was at Latif's place. He rolled a few cigarettes. He also told us a story.'

'Oh, the one about the Weaver. What did he become this time? Last time I heard it, he was talking in a cat's voice.'

'No. He was a pen this time.'

'Crazy guy he is.'

'Yes. But he also knows so much.'

'Is that why you spend so much time with him?'

'Yes.'

'Ruby di thinks he looks good too. I think she likes him.'

Haksh looked at Chhaya. His face brightened, and he asked, 'What did she say?'

'That he has a really straight nose.'

'And?'

'And what? Nothing.'

'Nothing? That's all she said?'

'Yep.'

'So how does she like him, duffer? I can say the stone has shiny surface. Does that mean I am in love with the stone?'

'Oh, she does. You're just plain stupid. All your big words still means you're stupid.'

'Okay, tell me this. What makes you think she likes him?'

'Because she is a woman.'

'Huh?' Haksh's face betrayed complete perplexity.

'Yep. She's a woman and I am a woman. I know what a woman should feel.'

Haksh laughed out loud. 'You're not a woman yet. Ha ha!'

'Well, I am,' Chhaya said, her face straight. Then she looked down at her chest. After a brief pause, with a slight frown on her face, added: 'Well, sort of a woman.'

Chhaya moved sideways to face Haksh. Then she straddled the window ledge and dangled both legs, giving the impression that she was riding a motorbike. Haksh laughed quietly to himself.

'I think we should do something for those two, Latif and Ruby di,' Chhaya said.

Haksh stopped laughing. 'Are you serious? We could get into trouble.'

'You get scared very easily. Nothing will happen.'

Chhaya put her hands in her jumpsuit pockets and retrieved a box-like object.

'You're never going to get rid of that, will you?' Haksh said, pointing to the thin box Chhaya was holding. Easwaran had given this to Chhaya a year ago. He had called it an MP3 player and had found it during one of his innumerable trips to the Millennium City. It was old and obsolete technology that was used to listen to music and had fallen into disrepair. He had loaded songs on it and given it to Chhaya. For Chhaya, of course, this was to be the best gift because finally, she could listen to her favourite songs whenever she wanted. The television music channels weren't enough and most played the same numbers on repeat, as if somehow, just like water, music had also dried up and become inadequate. Although, of course, she was too young to understand that music was tightly regulated in Old City and only those songs that were allowed by the Guides were played on television.

'Do you ever go *anywhere* without those wires dangling from your pockets?' Haksh asked again. Chhaya untangled the earphones and put them on.

'Shut up. Listen to music with me,' Chhaya said, as she inserted one earphone into Haksh's ear and the other into hers. It was a song that began with the quiet grace of the sound of the piano. It was a calm, sombre tune with no other instrument playing in the background. From within the

phantom notes of the lonely piano, the singer's silky voice
began to croon:

> *You may tire of me as our December sun is setting*
> *Cause I'm not who I used to be.*

Haksh and Chhaya sat close together on the ledge, as the song
coursed through the soft stillness of the evening. Chhaya had
stopped dangling her legs and had instead curled them up
near her, as her back rested against the side of the ledge. She
looked out. There was something in the way she responded
to music that always caught Haksh off guard. It was as if
music was a safety blanket inside which Chhaya would curl
up—warm and fuzzy as against a harsh December night. Lost
in the world, she was drawing unknown shapes in the dark
invisible air. Thick curls wound around her face like waves
engulfing a lonesome rock adrift at sea. And Haksh could do
nothing but look on while feeling an emotional turmoil.

'Let's run away from here,' Chhaya said suddenly, her
words breaking Haksh's silent reverie into a thousand
unrecognizable shards.

'And go where?'

'Oh, anywhere. I was looking at pictures from one of
Easwaran's books. One of those places where it rains all
the time.'

'I don't know if I would like it, with water pouring down
all the time.'

'You're just boring. Rain's awesome.'

'Yea, like you've seen it. Duh.'

'No, but Easwaran has. He told me what it's like when it
rains. You feel cold, and you feel water flowing everywhere.

He also told me rain has a smell to it. And that he'd do anything to smell it again.'

'So how do we go to this place where it rains? Does it even have a name?'

'I dunno. I mean, gosh, you think so much.'

'Nope. I don't think at all.'

'Who cares about the name of the place? You don't require names for *everything*. I think I'd love rain. I wouldn't want to go back home at all.'

'What would you do then?'

'I don't know. I haven't thought of that yet.'

'You're so stupid.'

The song was long over, and Chhaya stood up to face Haksh. Bringing her face close, she scanned the contours of his face, as if there was something amiss. Haksh looked away.

'What's wrong with your face?' Chhaya asked. Her eyebrows were furrowed, but her voice betrayed not concern but curiosity. Haksh turned around to face her again.

'Nothing. I fell down.'

'Oh.'

'Are you worried?'

Chhaya did not answer. She walked over to the ledge again. The MP3 player shuffling in her hands, while the earphones rolled on the floor as carelessly as the person to whom it belonged.

'Did you cry?' she asked. Haksh flinched for a moment. It wasn't as much about what Chhaya asked as the manner in which she did so. Her voice was barely able to conceal the cold nonchalance, although with the way she moved her mouth, there was a certain playfulness to it as well.

The detachment broke his heart and he couldn't help but wonder what exactly it was that made him feel terrible—as though all his unarticulated desires were nothing but an illusion altogether.

'No. Did you cry when you fell down earlier today?'

'No. I never cry. By the way, that makes two of us. The falling down. I wonder if we did it at the same time. Wouldn't that be cool?'

'Yea. I guess,' Haksh said, as a faint, withering smile played on his lips.

'Harish can be mean sometimes, I think,' Chhaya uttered after a moment's silence. She was now away from Haksh, hovering near his bed.

'Huh? Where did he come from?' Haksh asked. The smile was long gone, and the very mention of Harish brought with it the sensation of the strange way he was holding the knife against him, earlier in the day. He hadn't thought of it since, but now the images came back to him. He felt queasy.

'Nowhere. I'm just saying. But he loves me. Just so you know,' Chhaya said. Her back was turned towards Haksh, and she seemed to be inspecting the wooden table that stood near the bed, her fingers gliding along its edges.

'Yea, I know that,' Haksh managed to say. He felt as if he wanted to smoke so terribly, as if that was somehow the panacea for everything, a momentary relief. The breeze had only grown stronger and colder. It blew the ash inside through the open window, and in the faint yellow light of the room, it glimmered like millions of all-seeing eyes merging in the finitude of space. The figure of Chhaya, when seen through the thick fog of the ashes, appeared both grey and yellow, making it seem like her figure did not possess any inherent colour but acquired it from the surroundings.

'Weren't you telling me the other day that you so wanted to go to the Eastern Side of the city and see the Old Man Who Spoke to Ghosts?' Haksh asked. Chhaya turned around and walked back towards him.

'Uh-huh. What about it?' she said.

'Let's go tomorrow. Dayani would have gone to visit the gurus. And Harish anyway is mostly at Abhishek's. We can sneak out and come back by evening. I'll ask Abdul and Latif too.'

'Wow. You remembered *and* you made a plan. I thought you were the boring types. Not that I am wrong, mostly.'

'Ha ha . . . So, are you in?'

'I don't see why not. Besides, even when Ma is around, do you think I'm scared of her?'

'No. You're not scared of anyone. That's why I . . .' He stopped mid-sentence.

'I what? Gosh, despite knowing so many words, you're so stupid.'

Haksh said nothing but smiled. After what seemed like an eternal pause, Chhaya came closer to him and patted his right arm. Then she carefully put the MP3 player and the earphones inside her pocket and walked towards the door. She opened it and looked at Haksh for a split second. She then turned around and walked away into the unquiet darkness. Haksh's unfinished sentence remained on tenterhooks. He sat still on the window ledge for a long time, allowing the ash to enter freely through the half-open door. The breeze gained force and transformed into a wind. It seemed it would rain. But for as long as Haksh could remember, the wind only promised rain, it never delivered. He got down from the ledge, closed the door and walked back towards the window. His heart beat through its walls, and for a moment there, he thought it would burst. Placing his forehead against the wall, he closed his eyes. Ash particles impinged on his face. His palms trembled. Haksh knew that this unquiet evening would play out in his dreams in times to come.

# 7

The harsh morning sunlight streamed through the window Haksh had kept open before falling asleep. Easwaran stood in the crumbling lonesome outhouse, looking at the sleeping boy. *Does he dream like us people, and if he does, does he remember them? Or do they fade away in the waking light of the morning?* Since the time Haksh was brought home, so much had changed. Sure, he'd anticipated some changes. Like Dayani's hostility. But he had also hoped that that early glimmer of hatred—both for his decision of bringing Haksh and towards Haksh himself—would eventually fade away, and that Dayani would come to love the boy. But he was wrong. The years only saw Dayani's feelings alternate between complete indifference towards Haksh—even to the extent of not acknowledging his existence in the family—and hatred. Love, maternal instinct, motherhood—the ideals which he'd taken for granted earlier—proved to be non-existent. And with that failure, Easwaran and Dayani drifted away from each other.

During the first year of Haksh's arrival, Easwaran and Dayani fought almost every single day. And most of those fights had a similar trajectory. It would begin over a mundane matter, like Easwaran feeding Haksh or playing with him and not with his own children, and would escalate as minutes bled into hours. And Easwaran would storm out of the house. The door would be subjected to the force of his anger and disappointment, while the furniture inside the room bore witness to Dayani's muffled sobs. In the intervening days, no words would flow between the couple. After a few days, Dayani would make overtures, or on some days, Easwaran would make the attempt. Each time, either of the two would eventually give in. A feeble hope of a new beginning would linger on as an unexpected guest in the house. But after a couple of weeks, the cycle would start again. The fights would begin, and the unnurtured hope would be deferred. Again.

The morning sunk its teeth into the room of the boy who had altered their lives forever. Easwaran hated being in this outhouse, although he had it built himself for Haksh. It was dank, and the uncontrollably swirling ash scared him. But nothing happened to Haksh. He never coughed, unlike boys and girls of his age who carried a cough somewhere in their throats that refused to die down—some were even born with it. And Haksh was seldom tired. The more Easwaran saw the boy, the more his curiosity was piqued.

During Haksh's growing years, Easwaran would make it a point to sit with him and ask him important questions. Questions like, does he know who his mother or father were? Does he carry a picture of them in his head? Haksh would reply in the negative. Easwaran would probe further. Does he remember where he was born, what his first thoughts were, does he feel curious about the world he is living in? Haksh would just look on at Easwaran, his large, round, black eyes examining the contours of Easwaran's face, saying nothing. And Easwaran would give in. Time and time again, he would feel the weight of those eyes—shining with the soft glimmer of innocence—hang around his neck. If he was unable to understand Haksh's world, he made sure he would do everything within his power to make Haksh understand the world Easwaran came from.

As part of the Madira Gang, during those numerous trips to the Millennium City, long before he found Haksh, Easwaran would always come back home with antiquities. On some days, it would be old books or music players, and on other days, it would be movies—things whose forms had changed over time. These days, whether in Millennium City or Old City ruled by the Guides, music, movies and books had changed considerably. Only those that espoused strong moral content were allowed to be circulated, for if there was one thing that the Inspire Corporation and the Assembly of Guides both agreed upon, it was the belief that the citizens' easily corruptible souls needed to be saved. The Guides took it upon themselves to ensure that only those forms of entertainment and knowledge will be allowed that bore a strong congruity with the ideals of the Guides themselves, upheld the sacred history of the Old City and chose the principles of tradition over those heinous forces that threatened to corrupt it. For in an increasingly dark world, the only source of light came from these traditions— ancient and unchanged through the centuries. Of course, what these traditions were long before today, no one knew. And because no one knew, it was all the more important to emphasize their existence, their moral superiority.

But for Easwaran, who grew up during an era long before the Guides, things weren't always this clear; morals and traditions weren't always this certain. When he was growing up, his father, although only a miner, had ensured his son got a proper education. As a bookish boy, he would find comfort in stories and books with a thousand pictures. And movies. The stories in these books and movies were never one-sided. The characters chose to lead complicated lives. They loved, they hated and they always asked questions. Like that young boy—Easwaran's favourite character—who grew up in a warehouse and who thought that the overbearing lord of the warehouse hadn't served him enough food—chose to get up on his feeble legs, hold out his little bowl and humbly ask: 'Please, sir, I want some more.' Easwaran had always imagined that boy's voice to be shaky, quivering with fear. But the boy *chose* to rise anyway, to ask for more.

If there was one thing he remembered from his time, it was that convictions are seldom desirable. It was in the grey improbability of uncertainness and ambiguity that we as humans choose our actions, and bear the consequences they'd give rise to. And this was where he found himself at sea, in the present world. Where certitudes, almost always of one kind, are decided upon by those in power, and the rest are made to follow. And that's when he understood the undeniable power the idea of choice possessed. If left uncontained, such a power could break boundaries, flatten borders and give rise to newer alignments. As the years passed, and the earlier way of life became unrecognizable, it became much more imperative for Easwaran to preserve it. And he did so by collecting the desideratum of that life. These discarded objects—movie discs gone out of fashion, books that no one would read, music that no one cared about any more—became the footprints of a life that no longer was. Like an obsessed historian, he collected these footprints.

Harish never showed an interest in his father's odd ways of collecting things, the ways that led to some people in the Old City even calling him mad. Chhaya, owing to the fact that she loved music, only took interest in Easwaran's old music collection. The rest she didn't bother with. When Haksh was dropped into their lives, Easwaran took to educating him. And unlike his offspring, Haksh genuinely took to his collection. Easwaran found that old stories of kings and queens; faded photographs of ancient, faraway places; and movies in their time-worn scratchy prints intrigued Haksh. He would spend hours with Easwaran, listening and watching and always asking questions—some pointed, some naïve and some that didn't make any sense.

For instance, one of the preeminent elements of fascination for Haksh were ants. The house, especially the attic when it was built, was filled with ants that walked in a straight line towards some invisible source of food. Haksh would take the large magnifying glass from Easwaran's table, walk up to the large window ledge, focus the glass on the stream of ants and peer at them, like an explorer in the midst of a jungle. And he would wonder and ask Easwaran, why did the ants always walk in a straight line, one after the other, each ant not deviating from its own proper place? And he'd wonder what if one ant broke the line and got away. In such a case, would it be punished? What would the other ants do? Easwaran would be bereft of any answer, and he'd only grunt and encourage the young boy to ask more questions.

Sitting now, looking at the boy, all these thoughts came flooding into Easwaran's mind. He slowly placed his hand on Haksh's forehead, which was glistening with sweat. His eyes moved behind his closed eyelids. *The boy is surely dreaming,* thought Easwaran. This made him wince. *What would become of the boy*, he wondered, *once he passed on?* There was no way Dayani or Harish would ever ensure the boy is taken care of, at least the way things stood today. Only a divine miracle could make Dayani love the boy. But even if Dayani did love the boy, sooner or later, she would also decease. Easwaran could feel the cough tingling in his throat. It was dry and foreboding. He ran his hand across the boy's forehead. Haksh slightly recoiled. He shifted a little and then slowly opened his eyes. Easwaran had removed his hand by then, and he was sitting, unmoved, on the iron chair beside the bed. As soon as Haksh's eyes rested on Easwaran's face, he got up with a start.

'I didn't see you there,' Haksh said.

'You were sleeping. You couldn't have even if you wanted to,' Easwaran replied.

'Uh-huh.'

The light was sharp and his eyes were still minutes away from getting used to the morning. Easwaran's gaze stayed unmoved.

'Am I late? Did I sleep too much?' Haksh asked.

'No. In fact, it's quite early in the day. Chhaya is still sleeping.'

'Oh.'

'Your door was not locked. The wind broke it open when you were asleep.'

Haksh looked at the door flapping in the wind. His face flushed.

'It's all right. But don't keep the door unlocked at night. This city isn't a safe place. Far from it in fact.'

'I won't,' Haksh said, almost in a whisper.

Easwaran got up from his chair and started pacing around the room. He stopped near the windowsill and traced the wood with his forefinger, brushing aside a thick sludge of ash. He turned around to face the boy.

'Your mother was talking with me last night, about you,' Easwaran said.

'My mother? But I don't have one.'

Easwaran's eyebrows twitched a bit at hearing this. Sensing the awkwardness, he cleared his throat.

'*She* does love you, you know.'

'Then why does she not talk to me? Why does she scold me or frown at me when I am around? I never did anything to her, or to Harish. Why does he . . .' Haksh stopped himself from completing the sentence.

'Why does he what? What did Harish do?' Easwaran asked. His voice was still calm, almost matter-of-fact. When he was in the gang, he had learnt that one should keep their voice unwavering when asking someone something important. He had suspected something was amiss when Harish did not turn up yesterday and sent word that he'd be staying with Abhishek. And not to mention, the blue bruise on Haksh's forehead. 'How did you get that wound on your forehead, Haksh?'

Haksh's eyes were lowered, hovering on the door knob and the door flapping in the light morning breeze like a bird's wings.

'I fell down yesterday while playing with Abdul and Latif,' he said.

'You hang around a lot with them. You should be careful. I've told you this before.'

'They're my friends, Easwaran.'

Haksh always referred to everyone by their names, even Easwaran. A trait he'd learnt from Chhaya. Although Easwaran never articulated it, Haksh had an inkling that the old man might be pleased if he were to call him 'Father' or 'Dad', as Harish did. But he was never able to bring himself to call him that. The reason for not doing so, of course, was beyond him. It was one of the several questions he carried within him—the answers to which always eluded him.

'So you got that wound from falling down. Hmmm,' Easwaran repeated to himself. His eyebrows were furrowed. He suspected that Haksh might have been trying to hide something, or he was not being entirely truthful. But unless the boy came to him to confide, he could do nothing. But no matter what, he must have a word with Harish, Easwaran resolved.

Haksh was still sitting on the bed, looking at Easwaran's pensive face. He felt bad and immediately regretted being rude to him. A part of him wanted him to get up from the bed, walk up to Easwaran and apologize. But another part of him blamed Easwaran for bringing him to Old City in the first place. Did he not foresee what might happen all because of that one decision? On those numerous occasions that Easwaran sat down with him, poring over books and movies, he wanted to ask Easwaran two questions: Why did he choose to bring him to Old City, a place where he did not belong? And what would have happened to him, if he'd stayed back in Millennium City?

Easwaran had never really told him about the circumstances that had led him to make the decision of picking him up in his arms that day. And whenever Haksh would try to ask anything about Millennium City, Easwaran would only repeat what everyone knew—about where the city was, about laboratories that produced hundreds of Metas, about Inspire Corporation. And Easwaran had an uncanny ability to gauge the trajectory Haksh's line of questions would follow; for after repeating what Haksh already knew, he would always change the topic or refuse to entertain him further. The questions about Haksh almost always remained unfinished business. This was the reason why, of late, Haksh chose to spend more time outside, hanging out in the Muslim Quarters than with Easwaran. Although, he still enjoyed the numerous conversations with Easwaran. Sometimes, he would sneak into the attic, rummage through Easwaran's antiques and take a book or a movie disc from the shelves.

'We ... we should get this door of yours fixed. I think ... I think it's not locking properly. I'll get a spare lock from the house, and we'll ... we'll get to work,' Easwaran said. He wasn't looking at the door in particular, and his words came out in mumbles, as if he was masticating the sound of those words. Haksh, now sitting cross-legged on the edge of the bed, nodded in agreement. Both seemed lost in their own unbridgeable worlds.

The day seemed to have moved on rather quickly. As all days usually were in these troubled times, it was rather warm and dry, with spells of hot breeze blowing in from the south. As the sun would set, so would the heat, and the same breeze would grow cooler. Haksh's mornings usually involved doing odd jobs around the house. Dayani had reluctantly agreed to have him sweep and clean the large open veranda, and sprinkle a little water on the shrivelling shrubs that had sprung up around the house. When something needed repairing, Haksh would do it. He had learnt it all from

Easwaran. But Easwaran was careful to not overburden
the boy with too much work, and he'd almost always allow
him to go out after lunch or during late afternoons when
Dayani would have her siesta. The boy would then loiter,
play with Chhaya or just play by himself. On many occasions,
he would dress up, remove a few branches from the dead tree
near the house and play by enacting one of the stories he
had read with Easwaran. Perhaps in that regard, he wasn't
too different from Latif. But the stories that Haksh would
enact were taken entirely from the books. On other days,
he'd sneak out to the Muslim Quarters and play with Abdul.

The sound of the hammer hitting the disjointed door
jolted the quiet morning air. As Haksh welded the door,
Easwaran stood behind him and supervised, while passing
him nails from a box. They had removed the door from its
hinges and had brought it out to the courtyard.

'Hit it right there,' Easwaran instructed. His voice
was calm but loud enough to reverberate in Haksh's ears.

'I know. I have done it before,' Haksh said, turning
around. Little chunks of wood tore open from the door and
became anonymous amidst the thickening ash.

'That's it. God knows how many times I have told
Harish to learn a bit of work from you. He doesn't listen.
I must tell him again, I think,' Easwaran said. Haksh paused
for a moment and looked at the empty courtyard. He didn't
say anything. The small lane, which connected the house to
the main street a few blocks away, was lined with similar
half-decrepit houses that resembled something between
respectability and abject poverty. A few people passed by,
greeting Easwaran on their way. Easwaran waved back.
Haksh did not turn.

A few hours must have gone by like this. Easwaran lifted his eyes from the work Haksh was doing and towards the street. That's when he saw Harish walking towards the house with Abhishek in tow.

'There he is, my good-for-nothing son,' Easwaran murmured to himself. Haksh kept working. But as Harish opened the front gate to walk inside the courtyard, Haksh could hear his own heart beating. How he wished to be anywhere but here, how he wished to be invisible. More than anything else, he wished Easwaran would stay quiet. Although he never told Easwaran anything, he often times fervently wished for the old man to just *get* things without him having to voice anything. Haksh remembered the earlier days, when he very small, when Easwaran would just pick him up and place him in front of Harish, to which Harish would just frown, roll his eyes and walk away. However, the circumstances were different when Easwaran would take Harish's plaything and give it to Haksh. At first, Harish would not protest, which Easwaran would construe as Harish warming towards Haksh—thereby encouraging the old man to only make more efforts to bring the two closer. Only then would Harish disappoint him by either hitting Haksh on his cheeks or even kicking him. And not playfully, but with a certain vengeance. When this would not work, he would purposely stay away from Haksh, and this would lead to fights between father and son. If the fight escalated, Easwaran would hit Harish, and that would lead to a parallel fight with Dayani. As Haksh grew up, Harish drifted away from his father and reached a point where he openly began to express his disapproval in front of his friends. And yet, Easwaran persisted. This was something that now bothered Haksh. The more Easwaran tried, the more Haksh had to bear the brunt of everything. Dejected, and mumbling about the inequality of the world, Easwaran would walk away to the quiet seclusion of the attic and his books. Haksh would be left behind, scorched and scarred by reality.

Harish walked up behind Easwaran and glanced slyly at Haksh. Haksh did not look up but was acutely aware of Harish's eyes on him. He could even sense the torrent of thoughts going on in his head, the jubilation that he must be feeling. Haksh felt embarrassed. At his own weakness, for not doing anything. Haksh increased his pace. The hammer went loudly against the door, and big blocks of wood escaped from its body.

'Hey, take it easy. We have plenty of time here, Haksh,' Easwaran said. His hands were on Haksh's shoulders. Harish stopped for a second to look, though he tried to conceal that he was doing anything of the sort. Easwaran turned around to face Harish.

'Stayed there all night, eh? Try working and helping me out sometimes instead of loitering around with that loser,' Easwaran said, his eyes moving to Abhishek. Harish stared back, a thin smile playing on his parched lips.

'Why? Don't you have anything to say?' Easwaran continued.

'No, I don't,' Harish said with his usual nonchalance.

'How long before you get to work in the Citadel?'

'About a few weeks. I don't remember the exact date. Will ask his father,' Harish replied, signalling Abhishek.

'Do you ever take anything seriously, Harish?' Easwaran said with palpable disappointment in his voice. 'Don't think I don't know how you feel about me. You think I am bad and all, don't you? But really, do you ever do *anything* with all your heart?'

'Well, I certainly hate *him* with all my heart,' Harish said, gesturing towards Haksh. Haksh paused and turned around.

'Yes, but he does his work, and he does it diligently. He's far better than you are, Harish. And I'll vouch for it.'

'Of course, you will. You always did show your displeasure towards me. Do you think I don't know that?'

'God! Since when, and from whom, do you have all these misconceptions, Harish? You were never like this, child,' Easwaran said. He was standing very close to Harish, and Haksh, who had been observing this exchange, was scared whether Easwaran might just hit Harish in a fit of rage. Although a part of Haksh longed for such an eventuality, another part of him dreaded it. And this duality, these conflicting desires, and its cause, posed another set of questions for Haksh.

'I don't wanna do this, Dad, I don't. I have had enough of it. Please don't ruin my happiness,' Harish said and walked through the front door.

Abhishek followed suit.

Easwaran muttered something inaudible under his breath, then turned around and motioned Haksh to finish the work. All the while, Easwaran remained oblivious to the fact that Chhaya, standing at the open window of the attic, was a silent witness to the whole incident. Haksh, however, had noticed her but only from the corner of his eye. He knew Chhaya had crept inside Easwaran's room in search of music records. He also knew that Chhaya would bring those records down to her room without letting Easwaran know, close her door, play the music and dance. Dayani would be in the kitchen, either cleaning or preparing to make the morning meal. And faint echoes of Chhaya's music would bleed through the walls and into her ears.

She would frown at Chhaya's utter irresponsibility and lament over her fate, but will do nothing and let these thoughts drive her through the task at hand. And perhaps, in that regard, there was something similar between Easwaran and Dayani: both disapproved each of the children and thought they were both headed towards certain disaster.

By the time evening fell, the door was repaired and fixed to its proper place. Haksh was tired after doing all that work, and now that it was over, it was all too late to go out and meet Abdul. So he just stood outside in the courtyard, his back against the big leafless tree. 'Neem', he remembered Easwaran telling him about it. One of those trees that lived for hundreds of years. He ran his fingers across its rough, dark bark. The thought that people were around this tree, long before his time and now long since gone, touching the very bark his hands were on, sent a chill down his spine. He couldn't help but notice that although he was not related to Easwaran, somehow he was able to understand the old man's obsession with the past. It was as if the past was an exotic country he so wanted to escape to. A place where everything was all right, and things could not go wrong. Easwaran always spoke so fondly of it. Maybe at that time, things were better; maybe, if he had been born then, he would have been treated differently than what he has to go through now. But you could never say for sure. All that he knew about the past were only through books and music and movies. Was that all there was to it? And what if there was more, or what if they weren't all true? He closed his eyes and rested his forehead against the bark. It felt cool, the contours of the tree brushing against his forehead. Haksh felt sleepy.

'Have you gone mad?' Chhaya's voice called from somewhere behind him. She walked towards him, her mouth slightly open, while looking at Haksh as if he was from some other planet altogether. Haksh turned around to face her. Visibly embarrassed.

'Were you just kissing the tree? Rolling around it with your eyes closed. God, you're so weird,' she said.

Haksh didn't reply at first, trying to avert Chhaya's gaze, which seemed fixated on him.

'I so was not,' he managed to answer. Chhaya looked up at the tree, then placed her fingers on its dried-up skin.

'I dreamt about the tree, you know. I don't remember exactly when, but it must have only been a dream and nothing more,' she said. Her eyes were carefully scanning the bark, as if some hidden message must have been inscribed there.

'What did you dream about?' Haksh asked, resting his body against the tree in order to look at Chhaya.

'Nothing. You'll laugh and make fun of me, and I'd only get angry.'

'Tell me.' The force in Haksh's voice surprised Chhaya. She turned away from him and did not say anything for what seemed like eternity, while the silence was filled by the echoes of the dust and ash billowing past them. The empty branches heaved and sighed in the unquiet breeze.

'I dreamt that I had grown old. And you hadn't. And I was standing near here, like I am standing now, under this same tree. And you were near me, and yet I could remember nothing. I felt like dying when I saw this dream. It was horrible. Do you think it's possible for something like that to happen?'

Although Chhaya's face was turned away from him, Haksh could make out that she was going to cry. But she did not. Her voice quivered, but her eyes were dry. Chhaya would never cry—Haksh knew this. He had no idea how he knew this, but he just *knew*. Haksh wanted to reach out his hands to touch her, but he didn't. He stood against the tree, frozen.

'No, it's not possible. You really think too much sometimes,' he said. His voice, matter-of-fact.

'Who, me? Ha! Yea, right.'

'I saw you peeping from the attic in the morning, when I was working.'

'Yes. Harish can be an ass sometimes. But he isn't bad, if you ask me. I mean he loves me a lot.'

'Hmm. But does *that* mean he can do anything he wants to other people?' Haksh said. Chhaya saw that his face bore a grave expression, verging on anger.

'What has gotten into you today? First you kiss trees, next you scold me.'

Haksh smiled. But Chhaya could see there was something not real about that smile—not only was it forced but also seemed like it was a chore for him to smile.

'Ha ha . . . I am not scolding you. I am just . . . you know . . . pointing out some things. Anyway, never mind.'

'You don't have to laugh or smile if you don't want to, you know. Besides, I am really mad at you.'

'What did I do *now*?'

'Nothing.'

'C'mon, tell me. I am sorry for being salty. I just feel weird, truth be told.'

'About Harish?'

'No. About everything. This place, me.'

'We were supposed to go to the Eastern Side. I never brought it up. You promised, and you didn't fulfil.'

Haksh stopped short of whatever he was about to say. He looked sheepishly at Chhaya, his face flushed.

'I am sorry about that. Easwaran came in and told me the door needed repairing. I had to do it.'

'Excuses. Ruby di is right. She told me that despite you being a Meta and all, you're still a guy. And in that, you're just like everyone else.'

'What else did she say?'

'That all boys are weird and sad and idiotic. They make tall promises, but they don't keep 'em. I can understand now, you know.'

'But the repairing work took me the whole day. You saw that yourself.'

'Yes, but if you had told Easwaran you didn't feel like working today, he would have let you off. Besides, it was your own door that needed repairing. Easwaran always lets you off. It's me and Harish he doesn't.'

'When do you think you can go? Tomorrow?'

'No. I can't tomorrow. Ma will be here the whole day. Do you think she'd let me be out of her sight?'

Haksh walked over to the boundary wall that separated the house from the small lane in front of it, climbed it and sat down. Chhaya followed him. The sun had set long ago. It was all inky black now. The many light bulbs lit inside the houses did nothing to dissipate the darkness. The two sat still, wordlessly.

'So why do you feel weird?' Chhaya asked, finally breaking the silence.

'I don't know. I just don't feel good. I mean I don't know. I guess I'm just confused about a lot of things,' Haksh answered.

'We're all confused. You're not alone in this.'

'Please don't make fun of me. *Your* confusion is not the same. Mine is a different thing altogether. Let's not talk about this now. I am tired of thinking.'

'Then don't think,' Chhaya said, shrugging.

'When do you think is the right time to go? When can you go?'

'I don't wanna go alone. I met Ruby di today, by the way.'

'When did you even leave? I was right here.'

'I sneaked out when you were having lunch in your stinky room.'

'Hmm.'

'I am going to ask Ruby di to accompany us. I hate this suspense.'

'Suspense? What are you talking about? Accompany us *where*?' Haksh's voice reflected his sense of anxiety, which was rooted not so much in what Chhaya was asking, but that he hadn't even anticipated Chhaya could think of something like this. Sitting close to her, as the day waned into nothingness, it was as if the raucous, trembling thoughts that ran through Chhaya's head were making their way from there to his head. But he feigned ignorance anyway. Chhaya did not face him as she spoke, but it was evident that she was visibly annoyed by this—that this telepathic connection between them was a fact she was aware of and wanted Haksh to admit that as well.

'To see the Old Man Who Spoke to Ghosts. I want to set up Ruby di and Latif. I think we should do it.'

'Are you out of your mind? It's impossible and we don't know what might happen, Chhaya.'

'What might happen? They'll fall in love. That's what'll happen.'

'You're so naïve, so foolish, Chhaya. So very foolish. It's a very bad and stupid idea. It's also dangerous.'

'Why?'

'Because . . .' Haksh didn't finish and only wrung his hands in a mock display of frustration.

'I am waiting. Because?' Chhaya said, looking at Haksh. She had raised her left eyebrow in response.

'Because those two are from *different* families, even different quarters. It could just be bad. I don't know. Let's not do it, please.'

'You're a sissy. Really. You just don't want to take an initiative. Don't you want to do something for your friends? For love?'

'I don't know what love is. If I knew, I don't think I would have been *here*, in this place, suffering.'

'Whiner, you are. Just a whiner. How much do you whine, really?!'

'Shut up, Chhaya! Just shut up, please,' Haksh said. He could feel his voice rising. Only Chhaya was capable of increasing his heartbeat to unbearable heights and plunging him into the deepest levels of frustration. And he loved and hated Chhaya equally now.

'I don't know anything. Either we do it as *I* say, or we don't do it at all.'

'Fine, we won't do it. Let's chuck the plan, that's it.'

'Fine. Also, I will not talk to you. You can just wallow in your loneliness. And if you think it makes you look good, with your long face that you sport all the time as if you're carrying all the world's woes on your shoulders, guess what, you look disgusting!'

He did not reply. He just looked around, his heart beating way faster. He felt a craving to light up a cigarette, but he then remembered that he had left the packet in his room. Haksh wanted to walk away from this conversation right this minute. But something held him back. He thought it was the thought of losing Chhaya that must have made him sit still, while the girl huffed and puffed. In reality, it was fear. Fear of the unknown, of what lay beyond this crumbling Old City and this decrepit house. Of what he couldn't fathom, he was blocked by fear. The breeze was far lighter today than it was the previous day. But it was cool nevertheless. Even though he did not agree with Chhaya, he knew he stood no chance of ever making her listen. The girl—adamant and frustrating—listened to no one. He also knew that if ever the girl decided to walk through the dark pavements that led to hell, despite knowing where it led to, she wouldn't care a dime about anything and would continue walking anyway. And he also knew, he'd have followed her.

'Fine. Tell your Ruby di, I'll tell Latif. And Abdul. When do you want to go?'

'Few days later? I'll tell Ruby di tomorrow itself. Okay?' A smile played on her lips, and unlike Haksh's, it was neither forced nor did it seem as if she had to endure the weight of the world in order to do so.

'Okay.' Haksh did not smile nor did he pretend to do so, unlike before. He just sat there, defeated.

# 8

The Old Man Who Spoke to Ghosts was called various things by various people. To Haksh and Chhaya and Abdul, and even Latif, the storyteller, he was known as the Mad Baba of the Dead Forest. To some, he was not a man made from flesh and blood, but some sort of a genie unleashed upon the world. To some others, he was a sage, a sadhu from ancient history. To Easwaran and a few more, he had a name, and it was Phanai.

More than Haksh, it was Chhaya who was interested in the Mad Baba; and more than the Mad Baba, it was the place that seemed to have fuelled her imagination. The Eastern Side of Old City was an area people did not venture into. While the river was one side that opened on to the Interstate, the Eastern Side was another. Because this area was poorly manned by the Guides and the Citadel, it was one of the entryways for smugglers and human traffickers, looking to get into Old City to pick up the women and men born in the teeming poverty of the place, lure them into dreams of a bright future in Millennium City, only to have them sold off to the highest bidder. The Eastern Side was also deadly dangerous because of the Dead Forest. The Dead Forest was where the old mines—now long closed— lay. Now, the coal-black ground was a slush of dead leaves, grass, brambles and cactuses. And the ubiquitous concoction of mud and ash.

Chhaya had first heard about the Mad Baba from Easwaran. It was a tale she was fond of, a tale she would often listen to before going to bed. Tales of his skills with the gun, his bravery and his eventual madness upon learning of the death of his only son. She pieced together the missing details, which Easwaran would not tell her, either through her imagination or by discussing them with the few friends she had, Haksh being the closest among them. And in her imagination, the Old Man Who Spoke to Ghosts appeared to take different shapes each time she thought about him or dared to imagine him. Some days, he was the harbinger of the evil spirit that swam through her house and took possession of it. The force that robbed it of all that was good and peaceful. When Old City was rife with daily stories of murders, the dead, communal riots and killings and vice versa, and those stories would circulate through the town and penetrate the walls of her house, it would take the image of the Mad Baba, the face behind her fears. The face of the evil that lurked and coursed through those dozen filthy streets of Old City. And on some days, the Mad Baba did not have a face at all. He was the mystery man who had inhabited her dreams from early on, the mystery whose true face she could never solve, and which only appeared as fragments to her alert, waking mind.

One day, cooped up in the attic, she and Haksh were going through some of Easwaran's collection of music records, while Easwaran sat on his rocking chair, immersed in a book. In her conversation with Haksh, one thing had led to another, and suddenly a reference to the Mad Baba was dropped. Easwaran had looked up from his book, and Chhaya had gathered the courage to walk up to him and ask where the Mad Baba stayed, whether it was correct that he had retreated into the Dead Forest, and if so, was he safe there. Easwaran neither confirmed nor denied, but had only been his own ambiguous self. He retold the story of how the Mad Baba, whose real name was Phanai, was a friend of his father, and how when the mines had closed down and people were beginning to lose their job by the hundreds, it was Phanai who had shot the general manager and as a result had gained the respect of the place and the people. This, of course, was a story Easwaran had repeated hundreds of times already, so much so that both Haksh and Chhaya could even anticipate the words Easwaran would use, long before he had used them. They had rolled their eyes, as they knew Easwaran would never tell them where the Mad Baba lived. And it only strengthened Chhaya's resolve to find out for herself.

■ ■ ■

The preparation for the journey took time. Haksh had tried talking Chhaya out of including Ruby in their journey, but she was adamant. And getting Ruby to agree took a while. But, eventually, Chhaya prevailed upon her. Although it took innumerable trips to Ruby's place, Chhaya persisted. She wasn't particularly fond of Ruby or her younger sister, or of going to the grand house of the powerful Guide Rajaji Prasad. The only reason why Ruby's family allowed the girls to mix with Chhaya was Easwaran, given that he was one of the former members of the Madira Gang. The Gang still commanded considerable influence in the city and enjoyed a reputation for being honest and upright. A fact that he himself was aware of and took equal pride in. Besides, Easwaran and his family had all the right blood, and that fact alone determined their position in the city. However, Ruby's mother, who was very religious, did not like Chhaya. According to her, the girl was too forthright, held a clear disregard for rules and never took care to dress carefully. Not to mention, she had seen Chhaya play around in the Muslim Quarters, and with that boy, the Meta, who in fact lived with them. On the other hand, to Chhaya's mother, the company of the Prasads was a welcome move. Dayani knew of Ruby's mother's opinion of her daughter—the trifling details of which were communicated by Chhaya herself and which was a constant source of tension between mother and daughter. Dayani, of course, hadn't had any luck in all her attempts to make a lady out of Chhaya. However, the sight of her daughter playing with Ruby and her sister was a source of solace to her aggrieved heart. If she was unable to reform her, at least being in the right company would have its necessary effect on her daughter.

Ruby, however, liked Chhaya. Although she had a very different temperament from her friend, she admired the fact that Chhaya, despite the opposition from her own mother, was still able to do what she wanted to do. And so effortlessly too. The plush decency of her own household in one of the best neighbourhoods, the fact that there was so little anyone could say to her father who always had the last word, was something that had increasingly begun to affect her. Not that she didn't love her father—she did, very much so. She knew she would never even think of doing anything that would in any way cause him pain. And it was something that she was proud of. The idea of family, she felt, was the most sacrosanct, and it always came first. And yet, the way Chhaya careened through life, without thinking about the world, was also something Ruby craved. The monotony of her life, of being locked up in the house, of trying to be a good daughter to her parents, of dressing up the right way, of walking the right way—all these unwritten rules that made up her life was also what she wanted to escape from. *There had to be a life beyond that,* she'd often thought. Even if that meant for a day.

And so, when Chhaya told her the idea of travelling to the Eastern Side, to the old mines, she gave in. Not that she wasn't aghast at first. But then, she had slowly started warming to the possibility of venturing out. Besides, Chhaya insisted it would only be for one day, and one day could do no harm. *One day would not make her a bad daughter,* she had thought to herself.

There was also another detail that may have contributed in getting her excited about the journey. The Eastern Side, and those old mines, with ages of dirt clocked up in the place, wasn't particularly her idea of adventure. But Chhaya had only casually mentioned that Haksh would be bringing Latif and his brother along. She had met Latif long ago and had noticed the way he had looked at her. She didn't like that at first. And her mother had always warned her of the boys from that neighbourhood. There were horror stories she had heard from some of her other friends, about the general licentious nature of those boys who were living without any proper upbringing or care. They didn't even know how to dress themselves!

But then, she had seen Latif again, a couple more times. Once, Chhaya had brought her along to the Muslim Quarters without her mother knowing about it. She had gone out with Chhaya to buy colourful bangles from the street market in the area. And Latif was there, playing cricket with that rickety tar ball. Haksh was around too. This time, they had both looked carefully at each other. Latif had smiled. And there was something effortless, almost childlike, in that smile, and the next thing she knew, she was returning it with one of hers. She had walked ahead, barely uttering a word. It could have, of course, meant nothing. After all, what could be wrong with exchanging smiles? It was just that and nothing more. A few days later, she had casually mentioned this little fact to Chhaya that she liked Latif's nose. It was straight and was a perfect fit for his face, giving it a square, chiselled look. Unlike her own nose, which was small and a little stubby. What could a general fact like that do? People like other people's noses all the time. But what she did not tell Chhaya was the way she had smiled to herself, without any provocation whatsoever, in the dead of the night, as she lay down on her bed. The darkness had ensured the invisibility of that smile. And if no one ever saw her smile, could it even exist? Later in the morning, she had forgotten all about it. When she learnt that Latif would be coming for the trip to the mines, she had shown no emotion, and had said no. It was the third time she had said no to Chhaya about the trip. But this time, she knew her rejection had neither the vigour nor the assertion of the previous instances. When Chhaya asked her the fourth time, she said yes.

■ ■ ■

Up on the terrace of the masjid, on a quiet lonely afternoon, Latif sat looking down at the world below. From up here, everything looked even, the houses and the streets and the faraway horizon all packed together in one big lump. Latif's father had told him that that was what the earth looked like through God's eyes. Everything even and equal, with no shred of distinction. Distinctions arose as one came down and became a part of the vast world below. Latif was with Haksh a while ago and had learnt about the trip Chhaya was contemplating. Not that he did not like the mines, but he knew this trip could lead to trouble. The Eastern Side was off limits. Abdul, of course, had no issues. He ideally did what Haksh did and believed that if it was a decision made by Haksh, there ought to be some merit in it. Of course, Abdul seldom communicated this to Haksh, which had often led to innumerable fights, but none that a night's sleep did not resolve. At first, Latif had declined going on the trip, thinking it would not be proper to accompany them. Being the eldest, he had to mind the restrictions. But then Haksh told him that Chhaya wanted to bring along Ruby, and she, apparently, had agreed.

Now, as he saw the sun dip aimlessly into the horizon, he could not help but think of Ruby. His heart was unquiet, and he felt as if some kind of storm was raging there. Or a battle, perhaps. And he knew, it was a battle he was not going to win. There was no way. He knew where Ruby came from, he knew who her father was. And yet, he felt like he was in front of a quagmire, diving in. The worst part of it was that it was all volitional.

The shops and houses below started being illuminated. His cigarette dangled uneasily from his mouth. The smoke

drifted away in uneven shapes and mingled with the falling
ash. Soon, his father would rush up and give the call for
the evening prayer. Dusk was Latif's favourite time of day.
Everything seemed so ambiguous, without a particular shape
or form. It was neither dark nor was it entirely light. And the
many electric bulbs from the shops did nothing to dissipate
the oncoming onslaught of darkness. But there was time
for that yet. If only there was a way to escape from it all.
His father had plans of making him the muezzin someday,
of leading the faithful to a life of piety. But all Latif could
ever think of was the possibility of becoming an actor. He
knew there was no way he could work for the local television
studio. The rules strictly forbade that. But if only there was
a way to reach Millennium City. He had heard stories about
how people there could be anything they wanted. He could
work odd jobs, save enough money and start auditioning.
And maybe, if he could one day become a rich and famous
actor, he would be able to come back to Old City. And then
all these restrictions and rules would never apply to him.
He could even marry Ruby. Anything is possible if you are
rich and famous. But there was another reason, far deeper,
which lay behind his love for acting. It was only acting that
gave him—even for a few minutes—an entry into a different
sort of life. Where he didn't have to be Latif, the son of a
poor muezzin, living in a broken-down mosque. He could be
Alexander, if he wanted to. All he had to do was to concoct
a story and imagine him as one of the characters. He and
Haksh loved playing this way. And he thought he saw in
Haksh this innate talent for acting. Besides, Haksh read a lot
and he always brought to him stories that had been written
hundreds of years ago. Like that young man, Romeo, who

stood below Juliet's balcony, under an ever-darkening moon, singing paeans of his undying love. Or the young Sohrab, who wrestled with Rostam, the great hero of Khorasan, only to be defeated until his death. And Rostam subsequently realizing that the boy who fell on his sword was his son, as he notices a necklace he had once given to Sohrab's mother, Tahmina. The more stories he heard, the more Latif grew obsessed. The stories and the characters inhabiting these long-lost worlds would wound themselves around the young boy's head, and he would lie wide awake dreaming about escaping and becoming one with these.

With each story Latif read, he would imagine himself in it. And that would only make him act it out. He had considered telling Haksh, about his idea of running away to the Millennium City someday. Maybe there, where Haksh actually came from, Metas and Muslims have a life better than what Old City provided.

His cigarette had long since burnt out, but it still dangled from his half-closed lips. The sound of footsteps on the stairs broke his reverie. He then immediately made up his mind. He would meet Haksh tomorrow and tell him he was going to go to the Eastern Side. But he would also tell Haksh about his idea of running away to Millennium City. The thought itself brought a faint smile to his face. And then the image of Ruby floated in front of him again. His hands quivered and his heart pounded against the walls of his chest, as if those walls were some kind of dam waiting to burst open with an undeniable force. As his father came up to offer the evening prayer, Latif threw away the cigarette butt and walked up to him.

■ ■ ■

For the journey, each of them were carrying the bare necessities. Chhaya had an old rucksack, which incidentally belonged to Easwaran. It had food, a spare mattress, masks and a large bottle of water. Haksh carried a satchel that contained some more food, a bed sheet, his cigarettes and a bottle of water. They had all gathered on the street that led to the Muslim Quarters. Ruby, however, came without food. She stood there in their midst, her hands on her hips, feeling profoundly out of place.

'That's a lot of stuff you guys are carrying. I thought we would be gone for less than half a day,' Ruby said.

'But what if we are not? We have to be prepared,' Haksh answered. His voice was nonchalant, yet Chhaya knew he still felt salty about her decision to include Ruby on this trip. She glared at him in response. And Haksh only managed a weak smile to sweeten the tone he'd used. Ruby said nothing, but only felt like she was sinking deeper into a bottomless pit of her own creation. She shouldn't have come here, and the minute she arrived, she wanted to head back.

'Listen, if it will take longer than half a day, I am going back home. Father will be around, and if he doesn't see me . . .' Ruby said.

'Don't worry. It's not very far from here. And we won't be gone long. See, even I am not carrying anything. Except a bottle of water,' Latif intervened, while avoiding to look at Ruby directly. His voice was soft. Whenever their eyes did meet, he would barely glance at her and then quickly look down at his feet.

'Why do we have to go there anyway? I mean who cares if there is a mad man living there or not?' Ruby said.

'I heard the Mad Baba can grant wishes,' Abdul interjected. They had taken the road that led them through the Muslim Quarters. They were now walking through the narrow gullies from which the main road forked. Everywhere they looked, these narrow streets were filled with little shops. This area was a narrow subsection of the Muslim Quarters, known for garment and clothing shops. As they would walk, Ruby would stop by at every other shop, casually window shopping.

'If one wants to come back soon, one needs to hurry—not stop at every shop,' Haksh remarked. This time his voice could barely conceal his irritation. Ruby blushed.

'Hey, let her be. It's not every day she sees these things. Besides, she loves clothes,' Chhaya said. She walked over to Ruby and stood by her side. Ruby, who was holding a silk dupatta and running the fabric through her fingers, let go of it. She looked up at Haksh and started walking.

'Does anyone here know exactly where we are going?' Haksh asked. The endless shops and the teeming gullies only led to more shops and more bifurcated, and narrower, lanes. It seemed more like a maze than anything else to Haksh.

'Yes. We cross this area and we take the next main road that lies just outside of this place. That would lead us to the train tracks, and we just follow those tracks to the Eastern Side,' Latif answered. They all looked back at him.

'I knew it was a good idea to ask you to come,' Chhaya said, smiling. 'Haksh here has no sense of direction.'

'Nothing like that. I know this area can be a bit mad, but I have lived here all my life. I know where it begins and where it ends,' Latif said.

'Some of these shops here are so pretty,' Ruby said. Her voice was faint and it seemed as if she was terribly smitten by the plethora of sights and colours all around her.

'Does anyone know anything about the Mad Baba?' Abdul asked. He was quiet all along, and when they had started off earlier in the day, he didn't want to come, for he hadn't slept properly the previous night. Latif had to drag him from his bed and get him dressed. And Haksh knew quite well how cranky Abdul could be without his quota of proper sleep.

'We have only heard stories. From Easwaran,' Haksh said.

'Yes. The same stories, told over and over a hundred times. I know them by heart now,' Chhaya added.

'What are those stories?' Ruby asked.

'Haven't you heard of them? Your father is as old as Easwaran. He must know the Mad Baba,' Chhaya said.

'No. My father doesn't tell stories,' Ruby answered. Her face was still flushed, and although by now she had gotten used to the others, a part of her still wasn't sure what exactly she was doing in this place that still did not cease to surprise her. It was all a bit surreal for her. It was only a day ago that she was thinking how stupid an idea it was—and not to mention, dangerous—to step out like this and go to a place she could never explain to her parents. But here she was, with a ragtag bunch. A part of her still wanted to leave and go back home, abandon it all. But that part became less vocal as the day wore on. And not to mention, she was enjoying it. She felt relieved, and happy, and was not bored for even one bit.

'Well, Easwaran had told us how, when the mines had closed, the Mad Baba went and shot the general manager of the company. That apparently made him a hero of sorts here,' Chhaya said.

'So how did he go mad?' Ruby asked.

'That I don't know. Easwaran never said that. I guess he went mad, like other people go mad. Just like that.'

'No. I heard his son was eaten alive by the beasts. Out in the Interstate,' Abdul said. All eyes turned towards him.

'How do you know?' Haksh asked.

'He must have heard it at Hussein Darji's place,' Latif answered.

'Who's Hussein Darji?' Ruby asked.

'Just a popular shopkeeper in our mohalla. He is the king of gossip around where we live, and our father usually hangs out with him,' Latif answered. Although they had almost reached the end of the Muslim Quarters, with the main road coming into view, Latif was still finding it difficult to speak to Ruby. Ruby walked slower than the rest, and hence, she was always trying to catch up. At first, Chhaya would deliberately slow her pace to ensure Ruby is not left out. But as the hours passed by, she, Abdul and Haksh were far ahead. It was Latif who lingered between the former three and Ruby, who was walking behind them all. Sometimes, deliberately, he would slow down, to walk beside her; and at other times, he would increase his pace just so that he would be ahead of Ruby but not too far.

By the time they reached the main road, Ruby's awkwardness begun to lessen. She spoke more and asked more questions, and Chhaya could see that she was opening up. While earlier there was a certain hesitancy with which she approached this unfamiliar world, Chhaya was able to see that Ruby had now grown more accepting. Haksh, on the other hand, was not sure. He still found Ruby distant and was not enjoying her company. But then, seeing them all together, walking onwards on a journey none of them had any idea about, Haksh felt a wave of something closely resembling happiness pass through him. The sun shone down upon them, and beads of perspiration integrated with particles of ash and trickled down their foreheads. The main road outside the Muslim Quarters was mostly an abandoned area. The road itself here was broken up and uneven. Other roads deep inside the Old City still bore signs of people working towards repairing them. Here, one could only spot thorny brambles sticking out from the crevices of the road and some grass, which increased in number even when one walked about a mile ahead.

'It seems so quiet down here. What a change from what we saw just a while ago,' Ruby exclaimed.

'Yes, it's strange how this area is still abandoned,' Latif said.

'What do you think must have happened here?' Ruby asked. She spoke almost in a whisper. There were a few broken-down buildings at a distance, but they appeared to be empty. As they continued walking, those buildings began to fade away into the horizon. What became apparent, however, were train tracks that were buried deep within nettles and shrubs.

'I wonder what happened to these train tracks,' Ruby said, seemingly to herself.

'These train tracks were meant for the mines. The coal and minerals that came out of the mines were transported back into the city through the trains running on these tracks. When the mines became defunct, so did the trains,' Haksh said, standing beside Ruby.

'How do you know all that?' Ruby asked.

'Easwaran told me.'

'What else did he tell you?'

'He says what he wants to say. He doesn't explain things that he doesn't want to explain. But he is quite open about most topics.'

'Does he love you?' Ruby asked all of a sudden.

That question seemed innocuous, and it even came out as if it wasn't something Ruby deliberately thought about, but as if it just emerged from her subconscious without her will or knowledge. Nonetheless, it managed to throw Haksh off guard for a split second. He didn't immediately answer. He drew a blank. He looked around and evaded Ruby's eyes, which he could feel to be resting on his face. Seeing Haksh's discomfort, Ruby felt embarrassed, but she also felt confused because a part of her did not know why or what was wrong with what she'd asked. But nevertheless, she too looked away. The question, however, stayed suspended in mid-air. Latif, who was a few steps behind and had witnessed this little exchange, came up, patted Haksh on his back and asked him to keep walking.

The question also managed to burrow into Haksh's mind. *Indeed, Easwaran had always been kind to him,* Haksh thought, *and unlike others, he always took care of him.* But is that love? Does it mean that Easwaran considers Haksh to be his son, like Harish? But he looked so different from the rest of them. Moreover, there was the other big question that Haksh had thought of time after time. Now, walking through the ancient train tracks, in a place that increasingly looked surreal to him, that question again made its presence felt. If he was so different, why would Easwaran pick him up and bring him to Old City? He had wanted to ask Easwaran this but had felt it would sound rude or disingenuous. He had tried asking it, of course, in myriad other ways. But Easwaran, the man that he was, never gave a straightforward response. And Haksh, being who he is, never tried to press further.

The tracks were long and seemed to go on forever. Ruby walked away from the tracks and on to the wide open field. She went over to a large stone and sat down on it.

'Let's take a break, guys. We've been walking forever. I am done,' she said. The others walked over to her side and sat down on the field. Even though the sun was overhead and bearing down on them, it being an open field, the breeze was stronger and surprisingly cooler here. It blew past them and drove the ash particles into a frenzy.

'Tell me more about this Mad Baba,' Ruby asked. Although she looked at no one in particular when she spoke, it was Latif who answered.

'It is said he lives deep inside one of the mine caves.'

'But why particularly there? I mean, what about his family?'

'I heard he had no family,' Abdul said. 'What was that story Hussein Darji told us, Latif?'

'Apparently, the Mad Baba had a wife. And when he came back after his son died, it is believed that he locked himself and his wife inside their house. And didn't open it for many months,' Latif said.

'Then what?' Ruby asked.

'Well, later, the neighbours complained about it and they had to break open up the door. They found the Mad Baba there, all right. But they also found the body of his wife in a room. Rotting away,' Abdul said.

'What the! Shut up! That's not true!' Ruby exclaimed. 'Latif, is this true? I think your brother is scaring me for no reason.'

Latif's skin flared with goosebumps when he heard Ruby call him by name. He looked at her askance. He wanted to say something but only managed a weak smile.

'I don't know how far this story is true. But I remember that one day, I heard Harish talk about the Mad Baba with his friends. And he told them that he was arrested for killing his wife,' Chhaya said.

'Then what happened?' Ruby asked.

'If he was arrested, I don't think he'd be in the mines now, would he?' Haksh said.

'Even I don't think he is in those mines,' Latif said, shrugging.

'Oh please, he's there all right. I know,' Chhaya said. Everyone looked at Chhaya. In her voice, there was a sense of certainty that Haksh both loved and was frightened by. He'd just be glad if they were able to go inside those mines, see the Mad Baba and come back safely by nightfall. Though he also knew that expecting to be back by nightfall wasn't particularly practical—the reason why he insisted on packing food and water for their journey. Chhaya had initially resisted, but when she saw that Haksh didn't mean to budge at all, she had relented. Haksh now opened his bottle of water and drank straight from it, careful about not spilling a single drop on the ground. Their family, being somewhat well off, was able to buy water from the marketplace and store it in big steel jugs in the house. Dayani was extremely particular about their daily consumption and kept a tight watch on the jugs. In order to bring some for their journey, Chhaya had sneaked into the kitchen late last night, filled two bottles and hid them in her room. In the morning, Dayani had stepped out to visit the Guru. The Guru resided somewhere in the Hindu Quarters, and the organization that he ran commanded a large following. Dayani was one of them.

'If you would have told me that we had to walk so much, I would have decided not to come. Also, I think I am hungry,' Ruby said. Chhaya looked at Haksh, and he knew that look was a signal for him to open his packet of food. Haksh hesitated for a bit but then gave in. He opened his bag and took out a stainless steel tiffin carrier. He opened the box and passed it on to Ruby. Feeling embarrassed, Ruby refused at first. But her hunger got the better of her, and she reluctantly accepted the food.

The ground where they sat was soft with grass and the shrubs here weren't as thorny as they were near the tracks. Haksh ran his hands on the ground, stretched his legs and lay down. He tried to see the sky through the ash, but it only appeared grey and smudged. He could make out the thin contours of the clouds floating past, but when seen through the ash, they seemed not white but as if they were sketched out with a thick dark pencil. Chhaya, meanwhile, had put on her earplugs, and as the music ran through her ears, she seemed to be in a different time and place.

They started walking again after a while. The indistinct railway tracks led them deeper into the forest, and as they kept walking, they could see the grass becoming thicker and longer. Buildings that were distant, just a while ago, had suddenly grown bigger and more prominent. The ground beneath their feet was more uncertain now, slushy. The buildings appeared half sunk in the slush of ancient water. Some broken, some bent. Vegetation grew through the innumerable cracks. Ruby looked scared as they walked.

She kept turning back, as if troubled by an unseen presence. Latif, who was beside her, did not fail to notice this.

'Those buildings that you see out there,' Latif said, pointing at them, 'used to be the living quarters of scores of labourers when the mines were operational.'

'Why did the mines close, Latif?' Ruby asked.

'No one knows why exactly. Easwaran only told me that they were running in massive losses and were bought by the company that now runs Millennium City,' Haksh answered. He was walking behind them. Ruby looked back to face him.

'But that's not the only reason. Haksh is right; no one knows the exact reason. My father told me the time when the mines closed wasn't a particularly good time,' Latif said.

'What do you mean?' Ruby asked.

'Lots of labourers lost their jobs and their daily livelihoods. They then protested and the company brought in police. Things apparently got violent and several protesting labourers were shot.'

'Abba says this place was filled with bodies of rotting labourers,' Abdul interjected.

As they walked on, Ruby could conjure images of rotting bodies floating in the primordial slush they were now almost wading through. The slush was green, and as they went on, she imagined restless spirits around those sad, empty concrete shanties, thick as smoke. She shuddered.

When Ruby was eight years old, her father, Rajaji Prasad, got elected as a permanent member of the Elected Assembly. In the political structure of the Citadel, the Assembly was the innermost chamber with which resided the right to formulate laws. The Guides, who made up the Assembly, numbered fifteen. Rajaji Prasad was the youngest.

As she walked through the slush, her fair ankles deep inside—deep enough for her to feel as if unknown creatures were crawling around her feet—she pictured her eight-year-old self, perched on the lap of her father. Why this particular image came to her mind, she wasn't able to understand. The mind thinks what it wants to think. She remembered how happy she was sitting there on his lap. Her father's dearest daughter, the centre of his being. But then her moment in the spotlight was interrupted that day. A few men, dressed in black suits and crisp ironed shirts, had come down to visit her father. She had never seen them before and assumed they worked for her father. She didn't want to get up from his lap, but her father had promptly removed young Ruby and handed her over to her mother. Instead of going back into his large study where he usually met people from work, he had stuck around in the living room. And Ruby did too. She had caught snippets of their conversations. It revolved around buying something, and involved money and water. The information being exchanged between her father and the men then was too much for Ruby's young mind to comprehend, but had the same scene unfolded now, Ruby would have learnt that the men were talking about a plan to build a large water reservoir in the centre of Old City. The men who visited Rajaji were representatives from Millennium City's Inspire Corporation and had come down with the desire to negotiate a deal with the Guides. Rajaji was young and dynamic, and he harboured dreams of making Old City shine again, to bring back the lost glory of the place, to make Old City great again—and in this ensuing greatness, inscribe his own name on it. He knew very well that the future was commerce. He realized that the only way to succeed in commerce was not by bulldozing one's way in but by negotiating. He realized that men of singular character, which most of the Guides were, were wedded to the age-old idea of Old City's past greatness and about its ancient heritage, but they failed to realize that a sense of the past is nothing without money. And money required you to bend the rules, to talk to people you did not like, to compromise, to affect a resolution. And in this fractured world, only Inspire Corporation had money.

Ruby still did not fully understand what her father was discussing with those strange men that day. But somehow, looking at the floating shanties of concrete around her, in this surreal world of swamp and dead trees, it struck her that Inspire Corporation was the lowest common denominator, that small detail that was deep-seated within years and years of events, like a fossil buried in sediments. Now, years later, in a faraway place that seemed like a page out of a nightmare she was getting sucked into, fragmented words that had long settled down into the bed of her unconscious mind, emerged in full force.

'Years ago, I remember how some men from what I now think was Inspire Corporation came to visit my dad,' Ruby said. This was the first time Ruby brought up the topic of her father and Latif clutched at this tiny detail as if his life depended on it. All this while, in all the hours that he had spent with Ruby, he found her reticent. She was interested, yes, and she did ask questions from time to time. But there was something that was almost distant about her. The more he'd talk, the more Ruby silently listened. At first, Latif thought Ruby was cagey because she was shy and it was all new to her. And she was taking it in, at her own slow pace. But as time went by, his patience turned into despair. He began to get the sense that Ruby was one of those girls who kept their world closely guarded, as though, if it leaked out into the open, their world would somehow lose its value. And the more Latif thought this, the deeper he felt sucked into that warm, mysterious world. He longed to know more about her; render her transparent if need be. Uncover everyday mundane details about her, like the exact symmetry of the sunlight that illuminated her rooms and the soft whisper of darkness as it wrapped its tentacles around her every night.

But in his heart of hearts, Latif also knew that the more deeply he sank into that world of hers, the more dangerous life would be. And it sent a faint cold fear through his skin. But at the same time, there was a sense of thrill, as if he was in the throes of something much beyond him, and he had to give in. Long ago, Haksh had read out a story of ancient Greece from an old book of Easwaran's. It was about a father and son—Daedalus and Icarus—who made wings out of feathers and used them to fly out of captivity. Before flying out, Daedalus had instructed his son to neither fly too high, for the sun will melt the wax that was keeping the feathers glued together, nor fly too low, as the sea foam would soak the feathers. But Icarus, having found this freedom, flew too high, only to have the sun melt the wax, making him fall into the ocean and die. As Latif walked closer to Ruby and felt her warm hands brush against his, he felt as though he was Icarus, flying closer and closer to the sun, as if emboldened by this new-found freedom. And he felt the heat flow through his bones, commingling with his blood till it became an inescapable part of his own self.

'Inspire Corporation owns Millennium City. I have heard Easwaran speak about it many times,' Haksh said.

'Yes, but what were men from there doing with my father? This was so long ago,' Ruby said.

'How long ago do you think it was?' Chhaya asked. She was behind Haksh and had come up near them now. Abdul still trailed behind.

'I was eight, I think. It was my birthday and I was sitting with my dad when those men came in.'

'Was your father in the Assembly then?' Haksh asked. On hearing such a direct question about her father's political career, Ruby suddenly blushed. It wasn't always that she had people to whom she could speak about her family life. Although she knew she had said nothing extraordinary, whatever came out of her mouth was surprising even to her.

'No. He was elected a year later, I think. He was still at his old job.'

'And what was that?' Latif asked, not so much because he particularly cared about her father but because he thought it would help Ruby to finally open up.

'My mother told me my father was then working in the water division of the Citadel.'

'What's a water division?' Abdul asked.

'Well, it's the main part that deals with Old City's water issues. It buys water, sells it and controls it fully,' Latif explained.

'Yea, and my father was responsible for making it efficient. I have heard stories of how he was so hard-working and all. Within a few years, he made the department profitable.'

Haksh, who wanted to say something, decided to swallow his words. Everyone knew about Ruby's father. To Harish and Dayani, he was even a person of influence. And somewhere, Haksh suspected that Dayani saw in Rajaji Prasad the possibility of what Easwaran could have been. But he had no way of answering why she thought so.

The swampy ground was slowly becoming harder as they walked on. The bent and broken buildings were far away. They were now deep inside the Dead Forest. Skeletons of long dead trees floated around, some sticking out from the ground. It was littered with leaves that were blackened with dust, and the moment their feet fell on them, the leaves would disintegrate into ashes. In the distance, they saw the mines. Dark and cavernous. Black as the darkest midnight. Coal and time had given the ground strange hues. Hints of moss lay stuffed here and there.

'The mines,' Latif said. Ruby was transfixed. The rays of the setting sun filtering through the haze of dead trees made the place seem like it was stuck inside the centre of Earth.

'This place is so weird, so creepy,' Ruby exclaimed. She had wrapped her hands around her body.

'I don't think there's anyone here, and it will take forever to explore those mines. Just look at them,' Haksh said. Chhaya, looking at him, made a face of annoyance.

'Exploring won't be a problem when we have light. Look up, it's fading,' Latif said. They all looked up. It was indeed getting dark.

'God, is it this late already?!' Ruby exclaimed. Latif could discern that she was worried, although she tried not to show it.

'How long do you think it would take to go up there to the mines, explore and go back?' Chhaya asked.

'Impossible. We don't know what's in those mines. Just look at them. They look old as hell. And dank,' Haksh said.

'Yes, and by the time we explore one and come back, it will be pitch-dark. I think we should rest here now. And maybe do some quick exploring early in the morning,' Latif said.

Ruby did not like the sound of it. She had thought it would take less than a day and she would be back home by night. At least then she could make up an excuse and hope for her mother and father to understand and even buy into it. But spending the night was a proposition she hadn't even considered. But at the same time, standing here in this strange parched land, with these new friends, she felt free. There was no one to tell her what to do, what to wear, how to speak, how to behave. She was under no constraints to act a certain way. She could walk anywhere she liked, speak whatever came to her mind. It's another matter that she didn't. The point wasn't that. The point here was that, in this surreal land, she had a choice.

As darkness fell, unspoken and unheard, they huddled together under a large, leafless tree. Latif gathered dead sticks from fallen trees and lit them on fire with a matchstick. As the embers of the fire glowed softly, each of them sat in silence for a while, consumed with their own thoughts. Much later—maybe after twenty minutes or an hour or even a minute stretched to infinity, as there was no way to tell— Latif broke the silence.

'I forgot to get the prayer mat,' Latif said absent-mindedly. Everyone stared at him. Abdul got up and went around Latif. He knelt down to feel the ground with his bare hands.

'The ground is soft enough. We can pray here itself,' Abdul said. Latif looked at his younger brother and nodded in agreement. Latif then took out his only bottle from his satchel. He used the water to clean himself and his brother. Then, standing solemnly and facing the Kaaba, the two recited the opening verse from the Quran, the Surah Al-Fatihah.

While the two kneeled and prayed, keeping their eyes closed and hands raised with palms open in the form of a book, the remaining three sat in silence. Haksh and Chhaya had seen this many times, but for Ruby it was something of a novelty. Her eyes were on Latif. Grazing every contour of his being. Something in her stirred, something she tried to brush away but which nevertheless persisted. There was something calm, almost peaceful in the way Latif articulated the prayer. The syllables, in a language she did not understand, touched her with their poetic beauty and simplicity. She had no way to articulate this, especially the simplicity aspect. *How can she be touched by something she didn't even understand?* she thought. And yet, the fact that she was touched, that she felt something move and slide inside of her, was also irrefutable. She was also unsure whether it was just the beautiful alien words that came out of Latif's mouth, or whether it was *something* about Latif or whether it was a strange concoction of everything that moved her in a way she couldn't even articulate. And there she sat, silent, her strange thoughts whirling around her head. Her cheeks felt warm and her heart beat faster. She looked around and her eyes met Chhaya's. She quickly averted her eyes. Chhaya looked away too.

Soon the prayers ended and Latif and Abdul came and took their places around the fire. Apart from the slow crackle of fire and the soft whispery conversations, not a soul stirred.

At times, the black dead leaves rustled on the ground, as the wind caressed their surfaces.

'What language was it in which you prayed?' Ruby asked. Latif opened his mouth to speak, but Abdul answered first.

'Arabic,' he said.

'What does it mean?' Ruby asked.

'It's from the Surah Al-Fatihah,' Latif answered this time, 'It's the opening verse from the Quran. It says: "In the name of God, the infinitely Compassionate and Merciful. Praise be to God, Lord of all the worlds. The Compassionate, the Merciful. Ruler on the Day of Reckoning".'

'Are you religious?' Ruby asked.

'I was, when I was young. Now, not so much. I have not become an atheist yet and I still pray whenever I can, though not strictly. What about you, Ruby?'

This was the first time Latif had taken Ruby's name, and he felt a warm sensation pass through his body, as his cheeks flushed. Ruby smiled.

'Yes, I am. I come from a religious family. My mother especially is very religious and she drilled it into us from the very beginning. Chhaya would know.'

'My mother is religious too. Baba tells me that she wasn't earlier. But now, very much so,' Chhaya said.

'Yes. Both our mothers happen to be devotees of Guru Maharaj at the temple. I used to go there a lot earlier. Now, I mostly pray at home,' Ruby said.

The more Ruby spoke about the little elements of her mundane life, the more it thrilled Latif. His head was brimming with questions, but at the same time, he was unable to give form to them. Haksh, who was silent all this while—quietly allowing the place and the situation to seep into him—stared at the bristling fire. His eyes a mixture of vacuity and fear. Years later, when this day would become just a memory, he would remember the light from the fire as it played on Latif's face, accentuating his awkwardness and happiness.

'You don't step out often from your house, do you?' Latif asked.

'No, I like home. I have everything there. Sometimes Chhaya comes over. We talk, play.'

'But then you did come here today. You agreed to,' Haksh interrupted. Although he spoke calmly, he was barely able to conceal a tinge of bitterness that the words revealed. Ruby bristled. Latif looked at Haksh.

'Yes, I did come. But if you'd ask me why, I wouldn't have an answer.'

'What do you mean?' Chhaya asked.

'I mean when you initially mentioned this trip, I told you no and I meant it. But at the same time, I guess I wanted to come . . . God, I am such a disappointment,' Ruby said. No sooner did the words come out than she felt a hint of embarrassment.

'You think too much, Ruby,' Chhaya exclaimed.

'No, I don't . . . I have to think about certain things, be mindful . . .'

'There's a song, Ruby . . . I listen to it every now and then . . . There's a line in it that goes: "Hey Jude, refrain. Don't carry the world upon your shoulders . . ." It especially applies to you,' Chhaya said.

Ruby went quiet, and along with her, so did the rest. Latif's eyes were on Haksh and could see that he looked annoyed.

'You know when I was a kid,' Ruby said, 'my father would always buy me amazing clothes. Everything that I *needed*, it was provided. Clothes, shoes, so many things. All imported from Millennium City or elsewhere far beyond. And I would always be all decked out.'

'Like a doll. Ugh . . . I'd hate that,' Chhaya said. 'I guess we're different that way.'

'It's not about being different, Chhaya. My point is I was given all that luxury, but no one ever asked me what I *wanted*. Whether I wanted those clothes and glass shoes or not. I am not complaining. I mean, I love my parents. But there are times when I feel as if I don't even belong there.'

'Then why don't you go out more often?' Haksh asked.

'Because it's easier said than done, Haksh. Because my father would never allow it. Old City isn't particularly safe either, you know. I didn't even ask permission for today. Chhaya knows. I sneaked out.'

'Will you be punished if they found out?' Abdul asked.

'I dunno. Maybe yes, maybe no. My father loves me. I guess I'll make something up.' Ruby turned towards Haksh and suddenly asked, 'What about you? What's your story?'

Haksh didn't answer for a good few seconds, then just shrugged and said, 'My story is weird. If you think your life sucks, you should come live mine for a day.'

'I wish. I have wondered, you know; call it curiosity, but I've wondered what it'd be like to be you. Not like us. But different. And yet, so much like us.'

'What do you mean?'

'I mean, you talk like us, walk like us, even look like us. But you're not one of us.'

'I don't know what I am.'

'Do you want to live in Old City forever? Don't you want to find out where you came from? What's it like there?'

'Sometimes.'

'And you don't dream?'

'Dream about what?'

'Of doing something. We all have our dreams. I'm just trying to understand yours.'

'I don't know what I want. Not like I've not thought about it. But I don't know.'

'Don't you guys think we're in this phase, this scary phase, where our lives could become anything? A host of possibilities,' Chhaya said.

'Things are changing so fast. Sometimes I wonder whether we'd even be around each other for long. That scares me,' Latif said, his voice imbued with melancholy.

'Do you fear the future?' Chhaya asked. She didn't look at Haksh. Her eyes hadn't left the little embers emanating from the crackling fire. But Haksh knew she was addressing him.

'I fear we won't be the same ever again. I fear the future, yes. But I also fear the present,' he answered with a heightened sombreness.

'Why the present? This is all that we have, don't we? This present that we're living in?' Chhaya said.

'But the future is built upon the present,' Haksh said.

'Easwaran has gone too much in your head,' Chhaya retorted. Haksh sniggered.

'I like the present,' Ruby said. Everyone looked at her. 'It's beautiful. And today has been beautiful. I'll revisit this day often.'

'So would I,' Latif said.

'What Latif means is that you're welcome to hang out with us more. We might be this gang of nobodies, but we can be fun,' Abdul said.

'You haven't told me much about yourself, Latif,' Ruby said. His face flushed again.

'What about me? I guess I am this normal guy who's always loved stories,' Latif answered.

'I've heard about you and your stories from Chhaya. I must see you enact them one day.'

'Stories are everything that we have. Tomorrow, when we'd all be on our way, far away from Old City and these decaying buildings, we'll remember these days as stories.'

'You should work in the Citadel, you know. For their TV department,' Ruby said. Immediately, a wave of regret hit her hard. How could she overlook the simple fact that Old City's segregated rules did not allow any other religious community, except the Hindus, from working in the Citadel. She bit her tongue and went quiet again. An awkward silence enveloped them.

'I want to get out of this place, this Old City,' Latif spoke up.

'We all do,' Chhaya said.

'But breaking away isn't easy. Millennium City is out of bounds for most . . . Unless you're one of *them*,' Haksh said. His face was pointed towards Ruby. Ruby, looking back at him, felt out of place for the umpteenth time.

'One day I will. Go to Millennium City, become an actor. I always believed these divisions are just superficial. If you make something great out of yourself, any kind of division wouldn't matter then,' Latif exclaimed.

'Do you feel angry at all this? I've wondered, you know, what'd it be like outside. In the Muslim Quarters and in the Christian Quarters. Outside of all those endless parade of clothes and shoes and little soirees,' Ruby said, her voice almost a whisper.

'It's beautiful. I sleep in the masjid, and when I wake up, my head is mostly overflowing with ash particles. On days when the sky is a bit clear and the ash fall isn't heavy, I see the stars, burning away. Far away from the world, I stay up and imagine other worlds. What it'd be like . . .'

Something tugged at Ruby's heart as she absorbed Latif's words one after the other. He was poetic. Quite unlike anyone she had ever seen or met. And then she remembered how many times her mother had warned her to stay away from 'them'. She remembered the stories of how the men do nothing but spend their time in coming up with schemes to abduct Hindu women and marry them. Looking at Latif, she realized how different the truth was from what it was inside the closed confines of her house. If only people would go out more. Talk to others more. *If only*, she thought. Perhaps that was the way out after all, from all the world's problems. Lock people who hate each other inside a room and throw away the key. Let them spend time with each other. Only then would they realize how superficial their differences were. It was that easy.

The embers were slowly dying, and Latif and Haksh got up to collect more wood to add to the fire. By the time they got back, Chhaya, Abdul and Ruby had dozed off, huddled together. Wind rustled through the mines and the sunken shanties. Haksh decided to keep guard for a few hours and Latif would take over later. In the darkness, sitting a few feet away from the rest. Haksh lit up his cigarette. The day finally began to sink in. He feared, of course, of how Dayani or how Ruby's mother would react when they would return. Maybe it won't be a big deal. At the most, they'd be grounded. And Haksh would receive a mouthful. It's not like that was anything new. Haksh felt a sense of hope, but he was still unable to shake off the faint niggling fear that came knocking. The smoke from his cigarette joined the falling ash, falling faintly into nowhere. He looked up. The stars were visible but not very clearly. He continued smoking.

*Footsteps*, thought Haksh, suddenly wide awake. While giving guard, he had dozed off without realizing. He had no idea how long he had slept off or what the time was. He woke up thinking it was day, but it was still dark. Everything remained the same. The fire gave off the last of its embers. Beyond it lay a bundled mass of sleeping figures. The only difference in this familiar tableau was the faint noise from afar, which had woken him up. It was as if something or someone was trying to wade through the slush that Haksh and the others had passed on their way to the mines. At first, he thought he was dreaming. But then a few minutes later, he heard the noise again. This was immediately followed by a low sound of splash. The sound grew more prominent. Haksh realized they were footsteps beating against the slush, as if someone was in a hurry. He grew alarmed. Fear now knocked harder against the walls of his chest. He got up and tried to look in the direction of the sound. He saw nothing. Only the endless fabric of darkness. He walked around the fire and woke Latif up, ensuring not to disturb the others. Somewhere in his heart a hope held out that all of this could just be a red herring. Latif got up with a start. It took a while for his eyes to register to the new waking reality, but as soon as it did, it fell on Haksh's face. He had a ghostlike pallor.

'Whaa . . . what happened?' Latif asked.

'I heard something . . . A splash . . . Footsteps.'

'What footsteps? Where?'

'Out there,' Haksh said.

Latif was on his feet now, and the two walked away from the rest. Haksh picked up a piece of dead wood lying around, lit it using the already burning fire and made a makeshift torch out of it. The sound of someone drudging through the slush came again. This time, it was unmistakable. Haksh and Latif pointed the torch in its direction. They still saw nothing. The torch only shone feebly through the long dead caverns around them.

The sound grew and it was coming towards them. Louder. Faster. There were several footsteps now. Haksh realized that whoever it was must have seen the burning torch or the fire they had lit up near them. The sounds soon metamorphosed into voices. Faceless voices ringing through the thick blanket of darkness. Haksh and Latif stared at each other wordlessly. Both in the throes of fear and confusion. The voices grew louder. All coming towards them. Like an onward rush of a wave from which they had no way to escape. The voices soon became prominent enough to pierce through the sleep of the remaining three. Before they could do anything, the voices metamorphosed into faces and bodies of men. There must have been at least fifteen. Haksh saw they were from the Citadel's police.

# 9

It was all dank and dark. The cell. Haksh had no way of knowing how small the cell was. But he felt it wouldn't be much. A thin line of light slithered in through a small window, higher up. Haksh heard nothing. No sound. The only thing he heard was his heart beating loudly, as if any moment now, it would burst out from the bony cage it was encased in.

It was all so fast. All that happened. The images filtered through his mind. The long walk. The sun-drenched fields with the ancient railway tracks going away into eternity. The sunken buildings. The forest of endless dead trees. The antique mines bathed in their infinite clothing of black soot. Abdul. Latif. Ruby. And Chhaya.

Then there were those faces. *At least ten*, Haksh thought. The footsteps in the darkness. Wading through the slush. And then, there was light.

Khaki uniforms. Sunburnt faces. Warm, tough hands. Torchlights that had penetrated the cobwebby darkness. Ruby and Chhaya, crouching near the foot of that large dead tree. Their faces, pale. Fear shining through them. As if they had seen a ghost.

From the forest, a sudden transition to this new reality. Cells. *Prison*, thought Haksh. He heard the scurrying sound of rats from somewhere. The place stank of urine and faeces. He looked up at the window. All he could see was the head of a street lamp. And the light, as it shone through a million minuscule fragments of ash, which had been falling rapidly since time immemorial.

There was a rather strange similarity between these enclosed prison walls and the world outside, realized Haksh. It incarcerated time to a point where it didn't matter at all. Everything remained static. Inert. He was sitting with his back against the wall. He felt sleepy. But the moment he tried to close his eyes, the images from the forest came gushing in. He had no way of knowing how long had it been since their trip. One day? Ten days? A year? Where would Chhaya, Ruby, Latif and Abdul be? Were they kept in a similar cell but away? The door had a small keyhole. He tried to look through it. Focus on the world outside. There was nothing there. His throat felt parched. He had tried shouting earlier. Banged endlessly on the door. Trying to make it give way. But nothing had happened. No one came. He didn't even know how long they'd be here. Would Easwaran know? Would they send word? Did they think we were trespassers? Did Ruby's father call the police? Where did the police materialize from, and how—it seemed as though from thin air. Daemon-like. Khaki-drenched phantoms. *And why did they keep us in prison? As if we were fugitives?* Questions led to more questions, to a point where Haksh thought he was trapped in a maze that just led to more and more mazes. His head hurt. He knew he had a bad feeling about the trip. He knew Ruby would be trouble. But Chhaya. Impetuous Chhaya. Stubborn Chhaya. Chhaya whose face glittered like the sea on a full moon night.

Where was he anyway? The vehicles they were shoved into were armoured. They were separated right from the very beginning. He had no way of knowing what must be going on in Chhaya's mind. Would she be scared? The Chhaya he knew was never scared. But the situation, *this* situation, demanded fear. And one only had to capitulate. Earlier, the vehicle he was thrown into, he was sandwiched between two burly men. He remembered trying to talk to them. No, that's not quite right. He had first screamed. Although his screams elicited no response whatsoever from the men who bundled him and the others in, separately, Haksh hadn't stopped. Only when he had stopped screaming—his heart beating away relentlessly, so much so that he could even feel the dull throbbing move away from his heart to his mouth, head, hands and limbs—did one of the policemen look at him and murmur.

'No one told you to go that far,' he had said. His words coming out in a slow drawl. As though it wasn't something extraordinary that had just happened. Commonplace. Business as usual.

'Metas are dumb. Why would you drag the others with you?' said another.

Haksh had quietened down by now. Black curtains covered the windows of the vehicle. There was no way of knowing where they were going. And all questions regarding that fell on deaf ears.

■ ■ ■

When Jaideep Singhla walked into the police headquarters, an inscrutable sense of worry painted his face. The police

headquarters was located in Old City's Administrative
Quarters, the centre of political power in the region. The
central building in the Administrative Quarters was the
Citadel, flanked on all sides by other subsidiary arms of
administration, such as law enforcement and the media
division. As one of the high-ranking officers in the police,
Jaideep was in a long meeting at the Citadel the previous
day with members of Inspire Corporation. And Jaideep could
see, there was finally movement in the relations between
the two cities. This meeting was one of the several that
took place over the last one year. Although, he realized, the
old guards in the Citadel still harboured a strong resentment
towards Inspire Corporation, and Millennium City by
extension. Yet, with the influx of new members, and the fact
that a churn amongst the Guides was imminent, and also
openly visible, that earlier resentment was giving way.

   *Raj, that goddamn smart bugger,* Jaideep thought. And
indeed, he wasn't wrong. A lot of the changes taking place
presently in Old City were a result of people like Rajaji
Prasad. When Rajaji Prasad had become the youngest
Guide, Jaideep knew a change was in the offing. Before he
was elevated, Rajaji had successfully closed the deal for the
construction of a water reservoir—deep in the very centre
of Old City—by making Inspire Corporation invest in the
venture. But, perhaps, that wasn't a big problem. The problem
was making the other Guides see the fact that the future
lay not so much on older, ancient hostilities but in building
bridges. And Rajaji, with his practical sense, charming smile
and youthful looks, did manage to bring everyone on board.
His elevation to the ultimate seat of power—as a Guide—
was hence akin to a walk in the park.

During the meeting, Rajaji had come armed with diagrams, pie charts and statistics. Modern tools that allowed him to make the case in front of the other Guides that in order to develop Old City, some decrepit buildings have to be demolished. And in their place should arise newer ones, draped in their curtains of glass and concrete. New buildings that would be tall, reach the skies and scream out to the world about the potential that Old City concealed within it. Of course, the people living in these decrepit buildings would have to be relocated to someplace else. Where to, that could be thought of later. It wasn't a priority at the moment. Besides, the transition of Old City into a new entity, it's entry into the ballrooms of the modern world, one where it regained the glory that it once possessed, needed money. And that's where Inspire Corporation came in. The representatives from Millennium City explained their investment provisions. They would provide loans at a minimal interest for at least a decade. Jaideep, who was invited to participate in the proceedings was needed specifically because a project of this magnitude needed proper policing. It was up to him to ensure the people did not protest. That construction, once it started, would proceed without any hiccups. Shri Balaji Vishwanath, the oldest and highest-ranking Guide, didn't utter a word through the entire proceedings. Sitting just a few paces away, Jaideep knew that, while the old man might have appeared disinterested, not a word had escaped his attention. When the meeting was over, Shri Vishwanath swivelled in his leather chair, turned to look at Rajaji Prasad and gestured him to sit down. Dressed in an immaculate white kurta and dhoti, he slowly moved his hands from the armrest of his chair and put them on the conference table.

His fingers, bejewelled with eight gemstone rings containing astrological symbolism, clashed with each other. Jaideep, whose eyes escaped nothing, knew there was something on the old man's mind.

'Prasad, I am a man of few words. I speak what I want to speak,' he said. His voice, husky. His words, deliberate and measured. Rajaji Prasad nodded in agreement.

'The diagrams and plans you have are all fine,' he continued, 'but Old City has been around for a long time. And it will be around for years to come. Do we really require these changes?'

'But, Master ji, like I said during the presentation, our buildings are all in ruins. Our roads are in poor condition. We need to start rebuilding,' Prasad said.

'I trust your judgement. You have been a loyal servant of the Citadel. But why now? Can't it wait?'

'I am sorry to disagree with you, Master ji. But no, it can't. Look at the place where these gentlemen come from. Don't we want to regain our lost status? Become rich and powerful like Millennium City?'

'Are we less powerful?' Shri Vishwanath drawled. His eyebrows arched. His eyes were on Prasad. Almost piercing him like needles. One of the members from Inspire Corporation chimed in.

'Sorry to interrupt, Mr Vishwanath. But we, at Inspire, believe our future lies in sustainability. And Old City, with its present infrastructure, isn't sustainable. Besides, there's something for everyone. And Millennium City is your friend, sir,' he said.

'Master ji, we have to start thinking about the future. About tomorrow. About our children and their children.

The world isn't the same any more,' Prasad said. His voice
was shaky.

Jaideep discerned a sense of desperation. Prasad was
articulate, yes, but he panicked easily. Maybe this urgency
was what got him so far. Enabled his steep climb on the
ladders of political power. But Prasad, in his zeal to rebuild
the future, failed to understand the time-worn cogwheels of
the Citadel. Those wheels moved slowly. Shri Vishwanath
did not say anything. His face had become grave. He gave
the appearance that he was mulling over something. After a
brief pause, he gestured to the representatives from Inspire
Corporation to leave and go back to their guest house. He
did not fail to say that he thought they must have been tired.
When they left, Balaji Vishwanath turned towards Prasad.
His piercing gaze had returned.

'You used a curious phrase, Prasad. In your presentation.
I was listening. I wish for you to explain it to me. I am an
old man, after all,' he said. His voice, calm. Disciplined. But
everyone present in the conference room could recognize the
force beneath.

'Huh? What phrase, Master ji?'

'When you say that "these new skyscrapers will be the
temples of Old City", what do you mean by "temples", Prasad?'

As soon as the weight of these words fell on Prasad, he
visibly blushed. He rose to say something. To explain his
statement. But Balaji Vishwanath cut him off with a wave of
his hands.

'I don't mind these new developments that you've
planned. I don't even mind those black-suited men being
involved and paying for it. But remember, our future can't be
complete without our traditions. Don't forget that.'

Prasad nodded in agreement. He kept his eyes on the conference table. Ensconced comfortably in his chair, Jaideep smiled. Seeing Prasad discomfited, Balaji Vishwanath pushed his leather chair back and got up. He walked around the conference table towards where Prasad was sitting, halfway across him. Although he was nearing eighty, Balaji Vishwanath was agile. He walked with a certain gravitas, like that of a man with full knowledge of the fact that he exuded power and control. He placed his right hand on Prasad's left shoulder.

'You're a good man. A loyal servant,' he whispered.

'I . . . I am sorry, Master ji. If you want, I'll cancel the deal,' Prasad said.

'No. The deal is done. Tell that to those men tomorrow.'

Prasad looked back at Vishwanath. A familiar concoction of confusion and relief was plastered all over his face. Balaji Vishwanath removed his hand from his shoulder, wrapped them behind his back and walked over to the large whiteboard replete with pie charts. He turned around to face everyone in the room.

'I think it's time we start thinking about the plan I had floated to you men last year,' he said.

Jaideep's smile disappeared. He anticipated trouble.

'This plan of building the skyscrapers—how many people do you think will be displaced?' Vishwanath asked, looking straight at Rajaji Prasad.

'At least a few hundred initially. We plan to start slow. Take care first of the middle-class areas. Then we can scale up,' Prasad replied.

'There will be resentment. People will be angry,' Vishwanath said.

'My men are fully equipped to handle law and order, Master ji,' Jaideep said.

'Yes. And I don't doubt you or your men, Jaideep. But anger boils inside men's flesh. It makes them do strange things. Question order. Even our intentions. That can't be allowed. There has to be *anushasan*.'

'What do you have in mind, Master ji?' one of the middle-ranking Guides quipped.

No answer came.

Sharp breaths were heard in the room, as all eyes were glued to him now.

He continued as if nothing had happened. 'In the Muslim Quarters. It's long overdue. Besides, that land was ours. Our scriptures have pointed to that fact since time immemorial. Scriptures are our history,' Vishwanath said. Unlike Prasad, there was no urgency or desperation in Master ji's words. It was all matter-of-fact.

Jaideep's heart sunk. Not so much because he harboured any affection towards the Old Masjid, but because such an act would bring in trouble. Strife would break out. There would be blood. And yet, he could see the crystal clear reasoning behind Master ji's plan. Blood, like tears and laughter, was a human necessity. It had to flow if balance was to be regained. However, blood, unlike tears or laughter, bound people to a sense of tribal loyalty. There was only one other thing that worked in a similar way. And that was religion. When you combined these two elements, what you got was unfettered power to rule. Or, to use Master ji's language, anushasan. Many moons ago, when Jaideep was just a boy and was under the tutelage of Master ji, he had learnt that men in their very hearts were inclined towards that which

was familiar. What they feared most was the very idea of
change. Metamorphosis. Religion and ties of blood provided
that illusion of order. Of familiarity. It provided a picture of an
unchanging world. It cushioned their fears of change. Sitting
in the conference room, Jaideep couldn't help but marvel at
Master ji's wisdom. The only way to divert citizens' attention
from the chaos, which would ensue from the rapid changes
that Old City would soon start to undergo, was to draw them
back to the fountainhead of religion. And blood.

'There would be strife,' Jaideep uttered.

'It's necessary in the larger scheme of things. Besides,
mosques are demolished all the time. It's old. They can
worship someplace else. A temple, however, can't be built
just about everywhere. That land is sacred ground. It's time
we take it back.'

'It's time we assert ourselves.'

■ ■ ■

In Jaideep Singhla's cabin at the police headquarters, sunlight
filtered through the curtains, splintering and breaking into
a million triangular fragments. A dance of light and shadow
played on his face and desk. Yesterday's long meeting and
Master ji's words still rang in his ears. His unlit cigarette
dangled between his fingers and he gazed at the thick file
lying open in front of him. Although his eyes saw nothing. A
doubt—a residue from last night—bothered him. The next
morning, he found himself to be a troubled man. His elder
son, Hardik, had come into his bedroom in the morning,
expecting to see his father. Jaideep had come home late last
night, and instead of having dinner, had retired straight to

his room. Locking the door behind him. His wife had passed away long ago, soon after giving birth to their daughter, Ishita. This morning, he had brushed his son gently aside and had gotten ready to come to the office. He knew he had to go home early today. He would have to make it up to his angry son. Maybe he could pick up some mushrooms on his way back. Cook them into a curry. Just the way Hardik and Ishita loved. Lost in his thoughts, he hadn't realized that a junior officer was at the door. After his repeated knocks on the door went unanswered, the officer took a chance of opening the door to peep in and see if sahab was all right. That was when Jaideep caught his eye.

'Yes, Karandikar. Is everything fine?' Jaideep asked. The officer, sensing this to be his cue, walked inside and gave a light salute.

'Sahab, should I get today's roster of case files?' Karandikar asked.

'Yes, sure, get them. Also, Karandikar, anything happened yesterday? Fill me in.'

'Sahab, nothing extraordinary happened. We are still working on the old roster of cases. We also caught the water thief yesterday.'

'Achha? From where?'

'The Christian Quarters, sahab. He was hiding away in one of the shanties there. Drunk. It was only a matter of time before he was caught. Our investigation was on the right track.'

'That's great. Good job. Anything else?'

'Sahab, last night, our men were on a patrol in the Eastern Side . . .'

'The mines?'

'Yes, sahab . . . They found five trespassers there. Five children. Two of them were from the Muslim Quarters . . . Two girls also were there . . .'

'Oh . . . must be urchins. Were they clean? The Eastern Side is known for drug trafficking. Does it need any investigation?'

'Sahab . . . they were clean. But there is this thing . . .'

'What? What thing?'

'We found *the* Meta there, sahab . . .'

Jaideep's eyes widened. He sat up straight. His body taut. His mind raced back in time. Images that had long since settled down into the wasteland of his consciousness emerged. Easwaran. That man with a singular vision. Quiet. The man who spoke few words. The man who could have become something. And from there, to the days of the gangs. *Things were much simpler then*, Jaideep thought. The Citadel actively supported the gangs and encouraged participation. But the Guides soon realized that, left unchecked, these gangs could one day become a power unto themselves. And so, Master ji, devised the perfect plan. Yet again. The Citadel would follow the age-old practice of ambiguity. On the face of it, it would crack down upon the gangs. Imprison lower rung members. This way, it would enable Old City to put up a respected face when talking to Millennium City. But internally, the gang leaders who were loyal to the Citadel and who believed in the ideology the Citadel promoted, would be encouraged to continue with their shadow activities. As Master ji had taught, the real power lay not so much in *having* morals, but in *showing* that one was moral. The truth, of course, was open to interpretation. Over the years, from openly being a symbol of Old City's pride, the gangs went underground. And apart from dealing with water, also diversified into other areas—drugs and slaves.

Slouched back in his leather chair, Jaideep's mind took him to these large, soon-to-be-forgotten swathes of time. His rise in Old City's politics was largely due to his role in forming the gangs and recruiting its members. He was a young police officer then, but Master ji realized, if there was one thing Jaideep had a talent for, it wasn't so much in the actual mundane job of policing. But instead, in the subtle art of fixing things. And a fixer in law enforcement, and loyal to the Citadel, would always play into Master ji's hands. Jaideep realized this. If Jaideep's sense of right and wrong was fluid, Easwaran's was rock solid. In Easwaran, Jaideep saw a man of conflict. A man frequently torn between the necessity of being practical and yet unable to shy away from the idea of doing good. And that fascinated him. For a man, this conflict could be both a source of strength and weakness. And Easwaran was no exception. But Easwaran had, what Jaideep thought most—including his own self—lacked: a tremendous sense of will. And that will, if properly used and channelized, could be of immense use to the Citadel. It was this that drove Jaideep into Easwaran's house a long time ago, when he sat him down, looked him in the eye and made him realize the importance of what he was offering. Like a salesman. But then, plans don't always work according to your expectations. A man, caught in the throes of right and wrong, and perpetually so, had to choose one. Jaideep chose that Meta. He himself did not know whether it was the right choice or not, and he realized that Easwaran himself would have barely known that either. But it was a choice nevertheless.

Looking up, Jaideep saw Karandikar still standing. His eyes searching for an answer. Curiosity and concern woven together. Jaideep tossed his unlit cigarette away and got up.

'Take me to the Meta,' he said.

■ ■ ■

Hardik was sitting in his study, the window rolled up, when he saw his father's vehicle come up their driveway. He wasn't going to play ball, he decided. He wasn't going to give in. He would make sure his father saw that he was angry. Since the time he could remember, it was his father who had been around. His mother, on the other hand, was just a spectre. A fragment of a long forgotten dream. And in all these years, his father had been more than a friend to him. Hardik grew up as a lonely child. A far cry from the tough image of a police chief his father had of himself in the city. Hardik was studious. When he was five years old, his father had taken him to see the construction of Old City's water reservoir. That image of him in the dust bowl—concrete and ash flying all around him, and his eyes transfixed on the assemblages of steel and wood as they were woven by hundreds of workers—would remain with him forever. Since then, architecture and buildings fascinated him. He would pester his father with questions about buildings and tools and technology. Jaideep, unable to answer everything, managed to import texts from Millennium City for his boy. And Hardik would pore over them, day and night, fascinated and immersed in this new world.

Jaideep supported his boy in his endeavours and realized that with his love for architecture, he could easily secure a place for himself in the Citadel's technical department and maybe, just maybe, like Rajaji Prasad before him, rise through the ranks and become someone important himself. With Rajaji Prasad and a new crop of technicians, Citadel was on its way to revamp itself. It was paying far more attention to technical knowledge and sought out young people with an acute interest in it. Rajaji also, with his vast connections with Inspire Corporation, had managed to bring in experts from Millennium City to help train the technicians here. And of late, Old City's engineering college, housed in a rickety building in the Hindu Quarters, had begun to see a new activity thrive on its grounds.

But at the same time, whenever Jaideep looked at his son, he saw his increasing loneliness. Not that Hardik did not mingle with boys of his age. But Hardik sought to stay inside more. He preferred the quietude of his house to a life outside. Jaideep saw this as a sign of weakness. If Hardik was unable to spend time out, play and mingle with other boys, would he ever be able to rise up in the Citadel? His love of architecture notwithstanding, if there was ever one culture the Citadel sought to instil amongst its members, it was that of physical strength. One of the core properties the Citadel owned was a large open ground, attached to the back of its main building. Every morning here, scores of young boys were trained in physical exercises. The Citadel controlled four school across Old City, and each of these schools received funding to inculcate physical training amongst the boys who studied there.

Hardik went to one such school. And although it was compulsory for him to undergo physical training, he hated it. More often than not, he would feign sickness in order to get away from it. Jaideep would see through this. But the father that he was, without his beloved wife by his side, he would say nothing but just look on with dismay. These would be the times he'd miss his wife more. Maybe she would have been able to see through Hardik, talk sense to him in a way only a mother could. The times he'd attempted to speak to Hardik about the importance of physical education and exercise . . . The talk, would although begin in earnest with his tone balanced perfectly between concern, reprimand and friendly informality, it would eventually devolve into a fight between the two. Hardik would then pretend to stop talking to his father, and the latter would be driven by pangs of guilt. It was a quality Hardik's mother possessed—to bend Jaideep to her will by making him feel guilty, even on those occasions when he knew he was correct and his wife wrong.

Hardik's sister, Ishita, on the other hand, was more like Jaideep. From an early age, she exhibited signs of meticulousness and practicality. She was far more able to fit herself into the social structure of Old City by realizing the importance of womanly grace, making Jaideep worry least about her. He knew, somehow, Ishita would make do. It was Hardik who ate away at his sleep.

As the wheels of the vehicle crushed the gravel outside their house and came to a standstill, Hardik saw that Jaideep wasn't alone. At first, he thought his eyes were deceiving him. But no, there was no illusion here. His father was accompanied by the Meta and the girl he was known to play with. He stood still, near his open window, as the trio made their way to their front door.

■ ■ ■

Rajaji Prasad was in Master ji's room in the Citadel when he heard the news that his daughter had been picked up by the police from the old mines. He had reached home the day before, later than usual, his mind heavy with Master ji's words from the meeting. No sooner did he enter the house than he saw his wife and elder sister greet him with tears and worry plastered on their faces. His body was heavy with fatigue and his mind blank, the meeting and the heavy work he had put into that presentation having sapped his energies. Besides, Master ji always had his own way of making his presence felt. For a few minutes, when he had walked over to him in the conference room, after bidding the guests from Millennium City goodbye, Rajaji could have sworn Master ji would sabotage the deal. And worse, throw him out perhaps. When Master ji elucidated his grand plans for Old City, he couldn't help but marvel. Maybe that was why he was the undoubted master, the most revered man in Old City. He realized it would take him years to reach that position.

At the same time, his other suspicion that somehow the Citadel and other Guides were coming around to see his point of view was correct. When he joined as the newest Guide in the Citadel, he would have trouble explaining his radical ideas to the other members, what with them being entrenched in their chosen comfort zone. But he persisted. If there was one thing he knew he could do, and do well, it was talk. And so, he used his gift of negotiation on the other Guides. There was friction at first, and there were even times when he was on the verge of giving up, but he persisted. And now, he was able to see the fruits of his persistence. The skyscraper project was an idea he had harboured since long. And now he was close, frighteningly close, to seeing it materialize before his eyes.

'Ruby isn't in her room,' Aditi, his wife, said. Her voice precariously perched between her normal tone and a silent scream, as if deep inside her, she was still unable to process the fact that her daughter wasn't in the house.

'Huh? What do you mean?' he said, perplexed.

'Didn't you hear? Your daughter isn't in her room. And I don't know how long she hasn't been around,' Aditi said. Her voice was wavering now. Rajaji could see she would break down into sobs any moment now.

'Didn't you see her today? Have you spoken to the neighbours?'

'No, I didn't . . . I mean, I thought I did . . . I don't know.'

'What do you mean? You're not talking sense. If you were home the whole day, you would have seen her, Aditi.'

'I wasn't home the whole day. We had all gone to the temple. To visit Guru Maharaj. Listen, she's always home. She has *always* been home. I don't know what to do now. It's all my fault,' Aditi said, her sobs perforating through her otherwise calm exterior.

'Calm down, calm down,' Rajaji said, his hands trying to grab hold of his wife's arms. There were times when he wanted to be anywhere else in the world but here, in his home and involved in its myriad domestic problems. And especially now, when all he wanted was a cold bath, wash off the day's tiredness from his body and sleep. He could feel a headache coming on.

'Listen, listen . . . Shhh . . . Aditi . . . Did you talk to the neighbours?' Turning to his elder sister, he said, 'Didi, did you?'

'Yes, we sent the servants everywhere . . . everywhere . . . No one saw anything,' his elder sister answered.

Rajaji Prasad had spent that whole night going to the neighbours again, asking everyone about his daughter's whereabouts. He had come home defeated, angry and tired. While his wife let her sobs lull her to sleep, Rajaji Prasad resolved to see this matter through with Master ji in the morning. Knowing full well that Master ji would leave no stone unturned to find his daughter for him, Rajaji Prasad finally fell asleep, against his own wishes. Allowing the weight of the day's events to conquer him.

Now as he stood in Master ji's presence with the redness of his eyes indicating the turmoil in his heart, Karandikar hurriedly came in, bearing the news that his daughter was safe and in the custody of the Citadel Police. Karandikar waited for an order. Feeling a huge sense of relief, Rajaji Prasad was about to take leave of Master ji when he stopped him short with the familiar gesture of his hands. He motioned Karandikar to leave and asked Rajaji to take a seat.

'Your daughter was found in the mines, with boys from the Muslim Quarters. Is everything all right in your house, child?' Master ji asked, offering Rajaji Prasad a glass of lemon water.

'I am sure there must have been some misunderstanding, Master ji,' Rajaji Prasad said, fumbling with words.

'Maybe. Maybe not, child. How can you be so sure?'

'Wha . . . What do you mean, Master ji?'

'Well, I could be wrong. But you see this hair, crisp white, it hasn't happened in vain. I know something about the world.'

'Of course you do, Master ji. That's why you have been continuing to guide us through all these years.'

'Ruby is your daughter's name, is it?'

'Yes, Master ji. And she has always been an obedient child. Always. Never did anything to hurt us.'

'Children never do, child. But they don't remain children for long. Time, you see, child, is uncaring. It removes and uproots children from their parents.'

'I understand, Master ji. But we've inculcated a sense of proper and correct culture in Ruby. Both Aditi and I.'

'And I believe you. I tell everyone how perfect your family is. How cultured. Seeped in our age-old traditions.'

'I . . . I am sure there's been a misunderstanding. I'll talk to Ruby. Punish her if need be, Master ji. This is surely unacceptable.'

'How much will you reprimand, child? She's a woman. Not everyone can be Sita. You require good karma to be born as one in today's bad world.'

'But she is a good child, a good daughter.'

Master ji got up from his chair and began to pace around, making Rajaji Prasad turn around.

'No . . . Keep sitting, dear child. You have had a rough day. I can see it in your eyes,' Master ji said.

'What is happening, Master ji? My daughter being found in the mines. It has never ever happened in our family.'

'I am sure it's a misunderstanding, child. Nothing more.'

'But why would the policeman talk about *those* boys?'

Master ji walked slowly near Rajaji Prasad and sat down on the edge of the large table that adorned his room. His eyes were now on Rajaji. His fingers were fidgeting, playing with the rings on his fingers.

'That, child,' he said after a brief pause, 'should be a cause for concern, don't you think? Of course, you're her father and you would *know* better.'

'Master ji, you know everything. Please guide me, as you have guided all of us through the years. My heart sinks every time I try and think of that policeman's words about my daughter in the mines . . . with those Muslims. Hey Ram!' Rajaji's words had come loose now and were on the verge of being tied up together with his oncoming tears.

# 10

*How long does it take for change to occur? A year, a lifetime or just a minute?*

Long after it was all over, Haksh would return to this question. When exactly did things change? At what precise moment? Was it when he decided to give in to Chhaya's desire to go search for the Mad Baba, deep into those damned ancient mines? Was it when they were caught by the police? Or was it when the chief of police, Jaideep Singhla took them to his house? Or was it when they were finally returned? Did that one night in prison change it all? Did change implant its authority in the form of minor bruises on Chhaya's legs— the origin of which she never spoke of, despite his incessant requests to her to tell him what transpired in the prison? Did she know what had happened to Latif and Abdul? Did anyone know? Or could it be said that change made itself felt in the dead and dying Old City years ago when Easwaran, despite facing opposition, decided to pick Haksh up and bring him here? Much like all questions that plagued him, Haksh knew that he might never receive answers to these.

And he also knew things would never be the same again.

He had *felt* it in his bones back in the mines. He saw it written in the embers as it flew out into the darkening sky.

Or maybe he saw change writ large on their collective lives when, long after they had been returned, he had sneaked into the house like he always did, without making his presence felt, and was greeted by Dayani's silence.

Everything was the same.

Everything in the house was there in its place. The same smell of death and decay filled the air. As it always did. He had sneaked in, trying to catch Chhaya's eye to entice her to go outside. Or to sit close to her, as she would put an earphone in his ear and the other in hers, with music reverberating everywhere. But there was something that wasn't the same. Chhaya stood with her back against Dayani, who was holding a comb. There were no earphones, no music. As Dayani combed her hair straight back, applied oil and pulled her hair into a ponytail, Chhaya did not resist. She had a vacant look that suggested that she was far away—a place Haksh couldn't reach. He kept looking at her. She straightened her white pinafore dress. And when the ritual was over, her hands did not move back to untie the ponytail. She slipped her feet into a new pair of shoes Dayani had bought for her and walked out. It was evening. The sunlight had receded. Haksh saw the darkness descending upon them, as it did every evening. But this time, there was no breeze. The ash particles lay suspended in the thin evening air. Her eyes did not meet his.

■ ■ ■

The third floor of the Citadel contained a large hall called the House of Justice. Men and women filed in, one after the other. The news had spread thick and fast through the shanties and rickety streets of Old City. Through their official channels, the media division of the Citadel was quick enough to broadcast news about a public hearing, requesting everyone to tune in to their channels on the said date and not failing to mention that they were welcome to attend the proceedings.

That same day, Haksh had walked upstairs towards Easwaran's room. The man looked older, bent. As if time had managed to incarcerate him within its walls. Since they had returned, the Old City and everything in it appeared distant to Haksh.

He had walked to the Muslim Quarters, trying to find Latif and Abdul. But the Old Masjid only wore a deserted look. If only Latif was around. He had never felt at home in Old City, and that was a fact. But earlier, there were at least people who made him feel wanted. Who walked alongside him and took his side. And now, finding no one, he felt like running away. To what he did not know. A future he did not recognize. The present was too much for him. Although he had never felt rooted and attached to this place, Chhaya and his friends still provided an anchor, which made him feel some sort of an inexpressible allegiance. But now, he barely met Chhaya. On the days that he did, they spoke cordially—each keeping the pretension alive that things were still the same. But Haksh realized, cordiality was akin to a death knell to whatever they had and felt between them earlier. It reached a point where he was unable to comprehend the images from the past that floated as clear as water in his mind, and he felt unsure about even trusting those memories. Maybe they were false memories implanted by an overseeing lord to illustrate a cruel jest. But at the same time, he knew and was willing to even swear that things were fine, that all this was nothing but a hiccup, and things would return to the way they were.

As he walked up to Easwaran, these myriad thoughts played over and over in his head. *This too shall pass*, he kept telling himself. Easwaran was on his bed. The window was ajar and a warm breeze was in the offing. He was holding what looked like an old book, its pages bunched up by a knot that ran through its spine.

'Are you feeling fine, Easwaran?' Haksh asked. Of late, Easwaran's health had begun to deteriorate and the cough had become chronic. On a few occasions, he'd even spat blood. Easwaran nodded in answer. Haksh walked up to the edge of the bed and sat down.

'Are you still trying to read this book? You've been at it for so long now,' he said.

Easwaran answered again with a nod, this time half-heartedly. Silence ensued for a while. Haksh sat, his feet dangling down, and scanned the room. Books, reams of paper and fragments of dead leaves were strewn everywhere, giving the room a musty smell. Near the bed, lay a half-broken wooden chair, leaning over a dusty table. A lamp stood guard near its edge.

'Easwaran, do you think I belong *here*? Do you think I will *ever* belong here?' Haksh asked. The calm in his voice did nothing to hide the turbulence raging within. Easwaran looked up from his book.

'What do you mean?'

'You know what I mean. You know what has been happening and what has happened.'

'There are things you just can't control, Haksh. You should learn that,' Easwaran said.

'But how can I let go when it troubles me so? If only, Easwaran, if only you knew the place I am in. And what I am going through.'

Easwaran got up from the bed and walked closer to Haksh. He put his hands on Haksh's forehead and exclaimed, half in jest and half seriously, 'Phew . . . your head seems hot. That's why I say, don't overthink. The lid will blow off like a pressure cooker.' Haksh brushed Easwaran's hand away and shifted in his spot.

'You can joke all you want, but you know, and I know you know, that what I'm saying makes sense,' he said. Without uttering a word, Easwaran walked away towards his stack of books. There was silence again.

'You'll do good. I know you will. You just need to hang in there. And you will figure something out,' he managed to say.

'Figure something out? I was put in a prison, Easwaran. And not *once* did you or anyone here ever reach out to me and ask me what I must have gone through. There are days when I can't sleep. All I imagine are dark cells closing in on me, and I can do nothing but scream.'

'A boy has to become a man someday.'

Exasperated, Haksh got up. He shouldn't have come up here. He had no idea what made Easwaran so bottled up. Maybe he was right in not confiding in him earlier. Maybe it were his deep instincts that rightfully made him steer clear from everyone in the house. The only person who ever saw him for what he was, was Chhaya. And now even that possibility seemed distant. Earlier, on bad days, he would walk out and stand under the dead tree outside their house. And Chhaya would walk up to him. Somehow she just knew. And he wished, against all odds, that people like Easwaran would just *get* things. Get him. Haksh wasn't the sort of person who'd express himself openly, and yet, in this moment, he felt this tremendous rising urge to shout and to scream. To yell out to the world how he felt. Maybe only then would they understand. Pay heed to him.

Easwaran had gone back to his book, nodding to himself as he read. On any other day, Haksh would sneak up and read along with him. But now, all these objects, antiques and remnants from a time he did not know, seemed all the more debilitating. What was the use anyway, if they did not speak to him, if they did not comfort him? Then, as he looked on at the shadowy figure of Easwaran—his white hair with a bald spot in the middle of his head, his black trousers dirty with the soot from his cigarettes and the ash from outside, bent over his book—a sudden revelation dawned on Haksh: there was no way he could keep living here. If he did, he would go mad. And like Easwaran had jokingly mentioned, these overcrowding thoughts would blow his head up into smithereens. Or maybe he would become something he wasn't before. And gradually metamorphose.

What was that story again, the one that Easwaran had recounted to him many days ago? The story of a man who woke up to find he had turned into a large insect, while his family members and everyone around failed to recognize him. That story had stayed with Haksh, and on countless nights when sleep eluded him, he would lie wide awake thinking of it. His daydreams crashing against each other to a point where he would imagine he had become this huge insect, drifting away from everyone, into the vast emptiness of outer space and falling freely into nothingness. Haksh walked towards the door. His feet suddenly felt heavy. As if somehow his chaotic thoughts swirling around inside his head had made their way to his limbs. Making them go numb. Before closing the door behind him, he looked at Easwaran. That man kept nodding to himself.

Outside, standing on the ash-drenched sunlit porch as the warm breeze blew against his face, Haksh lit up his cigarette. Consumed by his thoughts, he opened the main gate to make way to the familiar spot of the large dead tree. As he stepped outside, he saw nailed to the front walls of his house, a poster. The edges were serrated. On its upper left corner was an image of a castle. The emblem of the Citadel. Daubed in jet-black ink, the poster announced the date of the public hearing in the Citadel's House of Justice.

■ ■ ■

The House of Justice buzzed with activity. The number of guards at each of the four entry gates had been doubled. Hordes of people were sauntering in, some with curiosity, some because they had nothing else to do and some because they had been paid by the Citadel to come and be a part of the proceedings.

Jaideep Singhla felt jittery. He had deployed police personnel in plain clothes across the Citadel and beyond. He anticipated problems. But then, being a policeman, it was his job to anticipate and to sniff out bad news, irrespective of whether it turned out to be true or not. His children, Hardik and Ishita, were sitting in the front row, and every few minutes, his eyes turned towards them. He did not want to bring them here, but he knew Master ji would ask him the reason for this and then he wouldn't know what to say. Better to avoid trouble. He wasn't too worried about Ishita. She seemed at ease, sitting, dressed in a frock patterned all over with yellow flowers. What worried him was Hardik. He was sensitive, and Jaideep could see how awkward he was. To help matters, Jaideep had even devised a plan. He brought Chhaya and the Meta to his home and introduced them to Hardik with the hope that it would enable Hardik to come out of his cocoon. And part of that plan did succeed. Hardik took to Chhaya, and he could see their friendship blossom. But he worried about the Meta. Even at their house, it hadn't spoken much. Maybe it was the effect of the prison. After all, it isn't the place for children to be in. Even if it was a Meta. But Old City itself wasn't the place for it to be living in. Easwaran should have realized it when he'd made that drastic decision. It's a miracle the Meta lived in the city for so long. But everything comes with an expiry date. Who knows when such a date would arrive?

The hall was chock-full of people. Master ji, like an ace magician, knew how to conjure up crowds out of thin air. A tactic he felt was the very source of his power. That Master ji was able to validate his immense power by creating the illusion in front of people that he was their representative, that it was them who created him and it will be them who can remove him. No one else. As the sun rose overhead and streamed its light through the translucent curtains, the hall appeared to be bathed in a yellow glow. The crowd soon began to appear restless. Sounds of chattering filled the place. Before Jaideep realized, he saw the crowd rise in unison. He looked at the polished wooden stage at the furthest end of the hall. Master ji was walking in, followed by all the other Guides. Rajaji Prasad entered last. Each took their positions on the stage, and Master ji walked up to the podium on the right to address the crowd. No sooner did he stand, the crowd buzzed. It seemed like currents of electricity were passing through them. Master ji raised his right hand, trying to quieten them. The rings on his fingers glistened in the sunlight.

'Do sit, my brothers and sisters. Do sit,' Master ji began. His voice was gentle and strangely warm.

'Do sit, my dear people, please do sit.' When the crowd quietened, Master ji looked hard at the crowd through his large black spectacles and continued. 'A time comes less often in the life of a nation when we gather together, each one of us, as brothers and sisters, to take stock of the present. To assess our strengths and our shortcomings.' There was a hypnotic quality to his words, which seemed to be binding the people together in a singular rhythm. 'I know each one of you assembled here has left behind your work, your lives. And I assure you, I will not take long. First of all, let me thank my fellow brothers, with whom I have shared the better part of my life. It is their undying devotion to the betterment of Old City, the example they have set for the public, which gives me strength each day. And, of course, my dear brothers and sisters, no example can be greater than you. Your joys and sorrows have become a part of mine. I stand in front of you, reeling with gratitude.' The crowd cheered. He turned around and looking at the other Guides, made a slight gesture of obeisance.

'Why we have assembled here, you all might be wondering. On a beautiful day such as this one that Hari has blessed us with. Can anyone tell me?'

The crowd cheered again. A few voices shouted 'yes', while a few shouted 'no'. Master ji smiled.

'What do we know of purity, my brethren? Can anyone tell me?'

'Purity is godliness,' someone from the crowd shouted. 'Purity is the incarnation of Hari,' someone else clarified. Master ji's smile widened.

'You're right, brothers and sisters. You're absolutely right. Purity is the very essence of our civilization. It is the very soul of Old City and everything beyond. What do you see when you look outside, towards our neighbouring region? Do you see purity? Do you? Brothers and sisters, tell me!' Upon hearing the reference to Millennium City, the crowd jeered. 'Do you want to become like our neighbour? Where the distinction between people is not held, where *anything* is permissible?'

The crowd roared a resounding 'NO!'

'Do you prefer to live like dogs?? Just the other day I heard, from someone who had just visited our brotherly neighbour, about the deplorable life there. People live like animals, they eat whatever they want to eat and they dress however they want to dress. Their tongue is a mixture of many languages. Is that how a nation should be, brothers and sisters?'

The crowd, now bursting through the seams of the hall, shouted its disapproval in one electrified response.

'What do you do when rules are breached?'

'Punish, punish, PUNISH!' the crowd blared.

Master ji paused. He took a sip of water from the glass placed next to his hand. The smile had grown thin. Furrows appeared between his brows. Deep, like trench warfare.

'A few days ago, an incident transpired in the very soul of Old City,' he said. 'An incident that should scare every family here. An incident that cannot be tolerated. When the rules about dividing up the town into quarters were laid down by our forefathers, it was done with wisdom. They only sought to protect the purity of each community. While the vile propaganda from some people here will say that barriers should be broken, that these rules make no sense,' Master ji's voice had grown louder and deeper. 'I tell you all, our ancestors made these rules not for one community, but for all. They believed that the only way to protect communities from destroying themselves was to insulate them from each other. In other words, purity. To ensure we are pure. Wealth, my dear brethren, comes and goes. But our culture, which makes us what we are, is sacrosanct. Right or wrong, brothers and sisters?'

'Right!' the crowd intoned in unison.

'Sometime back, our very own Guide, Shri Rajaji Prasad,' Master ji said, turning and pointing at him, 'came frantically to my room in the Citadel. He is a Guide, yes. Dedicated to the life of Old City, yes. But he, like you all, is also a family man. He was upset, on the verge of tears. When I asked him what the matter was, he told me his daughter, Ruby, was missing. They had searched everywhere and she was nowhere to be found. Imagine the anguish of a father, my brethren. Imagine what must have gone through his mind. I immediately organized a search party. And very soon, with praise to Hari, she was found. Safe and sound. But do you know where she was, my brethren?' He paused again.

The crowd said nothing. It seemed to be steeped in a captivating silence.

'Two miscreants had somehow sneaked into Rajaji Prasad's house, when he was busy with the affairs of the state, and his wife was in the holy temple, offering prayers. These miscreants stole her away. They were about to cross the border, when our police, our able-bodied men, found them. Do you know how these miscreants look, my brethren?' A long pause, again.

'Behold.'

He turned around and stretched out his hands towards the side of the stage. The door opened and five policemen emerged. They were tightly escorting two young boys. Their hands and limbs bound by chains. Their torsos bare. Their faces were coated in what looked like dried blood. The younger boy had a heavy face. Puffy. His right eye sewn shut. Thin scratches criss-crossed across the contours of the elder one's bare chest. His face bore signs of trauma. He scanned the blank faces of the men and women in the crowd. Searching for something. Someone. When he saw nothing, he shifted his gaze and stared at his feet.

The crowd had gathered momentum. Some gasped. Some screamed. Abuses were hurled. Jaideep, alert, motioned the guards to enter. And just when he did, his eyes caught someone familiar. The Meta. Standing near the door, he seemed one amongst many. But unlike others, he was quiet. Deathly quiet. His eyes hovered over the faces of the two Muslim boys standing near the pulpit, then to the front row of the hall, where his son Hardik stood. Ishita sat next to him. To his other side was a face the Meta would also be familiar with. It was Easwaran's daughter, Chhaya.

'Shanti, shanti,' Master ji chanted, trying to soothe the crowd's jittery nerves. 'Be still, my brothers and sisters.

I understand what you must feel. I understand. But you must
be still,' he said. When the crowd finally regained composure,
he turned towards Rajaji Prasad and motioned. Rajaji got up
immediately after and walked back behind the stage.

'The faces of these criminals, my dear brothers and
sisters,' Master ji intoned. 'Don't be fooled by their youth, the
innocence in their eyes. For hidden behind that innocence is
devious machinery. Machinery to abduct our daughters, our
goddesses. To defile them,' his voice rose again. 'And because
we are an ancient civilization, with proper rules of conduct,
law is everything.'

As he said this, he pointed to the door at the other side
of the pulpit. The door opened and Rajaji Prasad stepped
forth. Beside him walked Ruby. Her eyes were red. It either
meant she hadn't slept or that she was crying. The truth, of
course, was lost. Rajaji Prasad clasped her palms. Tight. He
brought her in front of the stage, to face Master ji and other
Guides. He bent down, gently caressed his daughter's head
and whispered something in her ears. Master ji's eyes did not
leave them all throughout. He smiled again. He stretched out
his hand and invited Ruby up onstage. She hesitated. And
the more she did, the tighter Rajaji Prasad's hands clutched
around hers. He gave her a slight nudge on her back, egging
her forward. Taking nimble steps, she climbed the stairs
of the stage and walked towards Master ji. As soon as she
reached near him, Master ji extended his hands and took hers
in them. He then gently placed his hands on her shoulders,
brought her forward and turned her so she could face the two
Muslim boys. The older boy looked up to face her. Their eyes
met for a few seconds. Ruby hesitated again. But this time,
Master ji ran his hands through her hair.

'Don't be afraid, child. Don't be afraid. Tell us, are these the two criminals who abducted you?' he asked. His voice was matter of fact. Ruby looked at him and then at the boys. A hint of tears formed in the inner corners of her eyes. She turned around to face the crowd and nodded.

'Are these the criminals who tried to defile you, child? My child?' Master ji pressed further, now addressing the crowd. Ruby did not answer immediately. Silence ensued again.

'Yes.'

# 11

L ouie sat on a bar stool, in front of the counter, elbows resting on the counter desk and his head in his hands. The evening had come down thick and fast. And now night was approaching. Coupled with smoke, dust and fragments of ash, neon lights drenched the pub in its usual velvety sheen. It had been a long day. All Louie ever wanted was to have a normal day, a day that did not stand out in any which way from the other days that he'd survived. Heck, wasn't that the reason he'd opened the pub in the first place? But then Old City had its ways of surprising you, make you jump out of your own skin. The pub he'd started—Louie's Brewery & Inn—did well in the initial few years. Allowed him to make money. He bought a house in the Christian Quarters. Went down on his knees and asked his then girlfriend Malini to marry him. Just the way it should be. It was a normal wedding. They had a normal life. Had bacon and eggs for breakfast every morning. Normal. The normalcy allowed him to imagine a life that could be designated with this clichéd euphemism years later—'a life well lived'. *Cliché!* What was that his schoolteacher told him, many eons ago, about that word? 'Cliché is a truth that is tired of repeating itself.' Which in other words, he thought, meant normal.

But things hadn't been on an even keel lately. The pub was losing business. And that wasn't normal. No sir, not at any cost. When he'd opened it, it was one of the relatively few pubs in Old City. And while the Citadel allowed drinking in the Christian Quarters and prohibited it in the rest, it allowed Louie a splendid monopoly. But that was almost ten years ago. Things were simpler then. Now, pubs sprang up even in the Hindu Quarters and competed with pubs elsewhere in the city. Newer pubs. With alcohol imported from Millennium City and elsewhere. Posh. Some were even adorned with fairy lights. Who the hell puts up fairy lights in a goddamn pub of all places! Come, drink, talk, flirt with the waitresses, have a good time, thank you, buh-bye. End of story. Normal day well spent.

He had started the day with a fight with Malini. Like every woman out there, she could just be exasperating, he deduced. And didn't he just last week give money to her for groceries and stuff? How could she ask for more money in less than a week? Does she think that money grows on trees? The moment he skipped breakfast and left his house this morning, he realized that it was going to be a long day. And boy, was he right about that!

As evening dawned in Old City, men had started filing in. Well yes, not as many as what used to be earlier, when there would be no room to sit inside, but today wasn't a total disappointment either. And that's when it all began. He should have noticed the man in a black coat. A cigarette dangling from his lips. As the evening faded away, so did the people. And Louie knew, for a bar owner, this was the most sensitive time. The light drinkers and merrymakers would leave, and those that remained were either those who drank for the love of drinking and ending up with a massive headache the next day, or the lonely kinds, who came to drink because they could be nowhere else at this late hour. Such pity he felt for them. But a bar owner ought to mind his own business and just fill the jug when it is empty. The man had set foot inside quite late. His knee-length boots were caked with mud. His long wavy hair, awry. His jawline, chiselled. Not bad looking at all. From the outset, he had an air of loneliness. He had stepped in and taken an empty corner table. The cigarette never left his lips. When Josy brought his beer, the man did not raise his eyes to look at her. He just drank quietly. As quiet as he had walked in. It wasn't the air of loneliness that troubled Louie. It was just the oddity of the man. He couldn't quite put his finger on it. It would then dawn upon him—when he would go back to his house, lie down on his bed, allow the proceedings of the day to wash over him, lulling him to sleep—that it was his instinct. Yea, he just *felt* weird.

The man kept drinking, and yet showed no signs of being intoxicated. He looked balanced. Just then, two men walked in. They didn't look like they were from this quarter. Hindu Quarters, maybe. But why would men from the Hindu Quarters walk into a shady bar like Louie's Brewery? Didn't they have better places to go to? One of them was undoubtedly rich. Moneyed. He was wearing a long coat, with his hoodie covering his head. He was treading on thin ice because his choice of attire, slightly suspicious as it seemed, would make anyone do a double take. Louie was a bar owner, who'd flunked mathematics in school and whose teacher had thought he'd die in the homeless shelter, for that's where all the dumb kids ended up. But good ol' Louie was sure as hell not stupid. It was a hot day with absolutely no breeze.

And here was this gentleman wearing a hooded coat. Either he felt cold or he didn't want anyone to recognize him. And Louie knew *no one* felt cold. That was just bizarre!

The two men had walked in, and without looking anywhere, pulled up two chairs and sat beside the lonely man. He looked up and nodded. The three sat there for some time, talking in hushed tones. When Josy went to their table to ask for their order, the hooded man waved his hand, motioning her to leave. Again, this did not seem normal. You can't just come into Louie's Brewery & Inn and not be enamoured of the waitress and not order. After conversing for some time, the two men got up. The hooded man shook hands with the lonely man and left with his ally. No questions asked. As if Louie had dreamt the whole thing.

Just when Louie returned his focus to the ledger in front of him, the lonely man walked up to him. Louie looked up. Yep. The man was good-looking, all right. In his deep voice, he asked for a room. Louie should have said no. That man could be trouble. Maybe he was. But then maybe he wasn't. The man took a thick pile of notes out of his pocket and placed it on the counter. Money, of course, speaks louder than anything else. Louie nodded approvingly. When the man took his keys and walked upstairs, Louie noticed a tattoo on his neck. Five evenly placed dots. And that's when Louie knew, something was brewing in Old City.

There was something in the air.

■ ■ ■

Phantoms. Ghost bodies. Shapes that changed. Whooshing in and out. Along with a fugitive, running away from his own self.

And after all this, his paths would bring him back to the one place he swore never to return to. Old City. Teeming with decrepitude and the change of time. Haksh lay on his bed, staring at the ceiling. The walls of the inn were colourless. The paint had come off in some spots, revealing the dirty concrete underneath. *Dirt and Old City were soulmates,* he thought. Would it matter, after all these years, to face that part of his life again? To conjure up images from his past he had long suppressed. But he also knew he hadn't suppressed anything. The past stayed with him. His constant companion. Nudging him. Thickening the walls of his heart. Wrapping its dense claws around his soul to the point where the only thing he desired was comeuppance. He closed his eyes. Phantom bodies sprang up from the deep tunnel through which his consciousness flowed. Bare torsos. Dried blood caked on their faces. And the moment he stretched out his hands to touch those faces, it all turned to smoke and dissolved in the darkness of the night. And then there was another face. Of a girl, her hair awry. Barefoot. The girl who dreamt of music. The moment her face appeared, a gush of anger surged through him again. The past spoke in many tongues. And to him, it spoke of retribution.

■ ■ ■

The boy ran about the courtyard. Dayani ran behind him. Harish stood in a corner, looking at the two. A smile danced across his face. Yea, the boy had the same green eyes of his mother. The same fair skin. And yet, he was too impetuous. Hated his meals. Hated being dressed. If left alone, he'd go back to playing in the mud. But somewhere behind

Harish's smile, lurked a sense of loss. If only his wife had been around to see the boy grow. Dayani was getting old. Things weren't the same as before. Easwaran had left the house in dire financial stress. All the money saved up from his days in the gang had been depleted. If only his father had realized this, instead of prioritizing other concerns, before passing away. If only he'd prioritized his family over his other stupid concerns.

As soon as the funeral rites had gotten over, Harish had walked up to his father's room upstairs and searched every nook and cranny. For long, Dayani had believed that Easwaran had hidden his money and kept it under lock and key somewhere in his room, while he wasted himself on books and papers that made no sense. Harish had found nothing. The books he had left behind were of no use. And so, Harish sold them to the scrap dealer. As time passed, Harish was able to believe that a better future lay ahead. He had met his wife, fallen in love, gotten married and fathered a beautiful son. He had begun working as a clerk, in a permanent position, in the Citadel. He had gotten his sister, Chhaya, married to his father's old friend Jaideep Singhla's son, who ran a highly profitable construction business.

Old City was going through a construction boom. Since Master ji passed on, and the mantle of the Chief Guide was taken over by Rajaji Prasad, things in Old City had begun to change. The cogwheels in the Citadel that otherwise ran slow had picked up speed. Harish had heard veteran clerks speak of how work was done during Master ji's time—how the day would begin slowly, numerous breaks would be taken and it would take ages for files to be passed from one department to the next. But Rajaji Prasad was relatively young.

He brought with him energy and a new way of doing things. Of course, the office grapevine suggested that he enjoyed a cosy relationship with his peers in Millennium City. While Master ji was known for his sartorial sense, Rajaji Prasad had decadent tastes. He loved his cigarettes, his finely woven clothes and his imported alcohols from Millennium City. Of course, Harish did not know how true all this was. But he tended to believe in the eternal wisdom of gossip.

The money that Harish earned was good. Enough to live a comfortable life and to ensure he was able to at least fulfil his son's dreams. The very thing his own father did not. He had begun saving. But, of course, he could have done with a little support from his brother-in-law. Although none came, he still held out hope. He had asked his brother-in-law on more than one occasion to help him buy a plot in one of the posh areas of the Hindu Quarters. Hardik had promised he'd look into it. Harish wasn't a man to easily lose hope. But then things changed. The same chronic cough that took away his father's life returned to take away his wife from him. And that's when he had started to despair. A comfortable amount of time had passed since his wife's demise, but grief is a strange thing. It persists, even when you know it isn't around. And the only way to keep it locked out was to lose one's sense of the present. So Harish took to alcohol. There have been times when Dayani, unable to see her beloved son deteriorate, had implored him to remarry, to restart his life. He wasn't old. He still had his youthful looks. And it is never too late to start all over again. Harish had promised he would. He had sworn he would not waste away, become the phantom that his father had become. And that his son meant the world to him. But then grief had pulled the strings, and Harish, like a puppet in thrall, had obeyed its call.

That was where things stood, this morning. Harish had woken up in a good mood, which was so rare these days. His son was happy too and had been taking his meals on time these days. As he stood looking at the boy playing with his grandmother, the smile, unbeknownst to him, had come on its own volition.

'He is going to look like you when he grows up,' Dayani said. Holding the boy close, she picked him up in her arms.

'No. He's going to look like his mother when he grows up,' Harish said. As soon as he said this, his smile disappeared. Dayani opened her mouth to say something, but closed it soon after, swallowing her unsaid words.

'Mala wanted him to grow up and work in the media or something. She said, his green eyes meant he'd have looks to die for when he grows up,' Harish said.

'There's a long time to go before that. But in order for you to help fulfil what Mala had dreamt of, you have to get your act together. Did you go to work yesterday, Harish?'

Harish did not immediately answer. His smile had returned, but Dayani knew his mind was somewhere else.

'I am asking you something, Harish. Did you go to work yesterday?'

'Yes, I did. God, why do you have to be after me all the time? I am not a kid any more, Ma.'

Dayani put the boy down, who started running as soon as his feet touched the ground. She walked up close to Harish and stared deeply in his eyes. Harish did not look at her. Instead, he kept his gaze fixed on his son. Dayani knew he was lying. A heavy odour of liquor emanated from his breath and clothes. But she did not prod. She knew it would just make Harish angry. No matter how much Harish protested to the contrary, he could not change his genes. Harish was different from his father. Chhaya took after him. But there were also elements, thought Dayani, when Harish resembled his father much more than Chhaya did. As her children grew up, these hidden specificities manifested more clearly. Chhaya had grown comfortable in her new life. Harish, on the other hand, was in danger of dwindling away.

Just then, Harish began running around the courtyard, pretending to chase his son. Dayani shifted to where her son had been standing, lost in her own thoughts, when she heard footsteps, dark and heavy, squishing the dusty gravel outside their house. As she turned around, a man materialized out of thin air. Tall and thin. His skin, a shade darker. Long, wavy hair. Chiselled face. At first she did not recognize him. Took him to be a stranger who had lost his way. Age had rendered her eyesight weak, and so, she took recourse to her spectacles and adjusted them on her nose. The man walked up to her. As she was about to open her mouth to ask who he was, she saw the man's eyes and a tattoo. Dayani knew who he was.

'Haksh. What are you doing here?' Harish, who was a short distance away, rubbing the mud off his son's clothes, looked up.

'Biding my time, Dayani. Revisiting some old and fond memories of a boy who once lived here,' Haksh answered. His voice was deep and calm.

Dayani did not utter a word. Although her words and her voice gave nothing away, there was a fear that was so familiar to her that had made its return. Harish walked up beside her. Dayani instinctively drew her hands towards Harish's son and clutched him.

'How are you, Harish?' Haksh said. Harish was still in shock. It was written on his face.

'Why are you *really* here?' Dayani asked again. Haksh did not reply. He took the liberty of opening the front gate and walked inside. Dayani did not resist and nor did Harish. Their eyes followed every inch of Haksh, his every movement.

'Where's Easwaran?' Haksh asked. He looked up to scan the house. The house looked the same more or less, only older. Time had finally caught up with it. The dead tree was where it always stood. Aloof, distant, away from the house and yet never outside of it. An oddity. Haksh lit a cigarette.

'Don't. Don't light that. Can't you see the child?' Dayani snapped. She could sense anger rising inside her. The same old familiar feeling. Haksh put the cigarette to his lips, as if Dayani's words hadn't reached his ears. When she had found out that Haksh had left, disappeared, she did not raise a hue and cry. In fact, she had felt relief. Easwaran, on the other hand, was distraught. He remained stoic and never showed his feelings, but Dayani knew. And she hated Haksh all the more for it. She also knew Haksh's departure could have hastened his eventual death. There was a time, just a few days after Haksh had disappeared, when Easwaran had come out of the cocoon of books he had built to shield himself from facing the reality of their empty lives, and he had implored her to approach Jaideep to search for the missing Meta. Dayani knew the things that man was capable of . . . The extent to which he could manipulate. And yet, she had refused to budge. She had given in earlier and suffered for it. She would do no such thing again.

And Easwaran had stopped talking altogether, retreating to the safety of his make-believe world. As Haksh, no longer a boy but a full-blooded man, stood in their midst, still encased inside that same darkness she felt in him when she saw him as an infant, all these ancient memories came flooding back to her.

'Where's Easwaran? Is he back up there?' Haksh asked again.

'He's dead,' Harish said. Haksh's eyes met his. Haksh walked up to Harish, and on noticing the young boy standing in front of him, knelt down.

'What is your name?' he asked the boy, who moved his eyes from Haksh to his father. Haksh gently caressed the boy's hair. Dayani took the boy's hand and drew him towards her.

'Not your business any more, Haksh. Not your business. If you're done with whatever you've come here for, I suggest you leave,' she said.

'I have not even started, Dayani,' Haksh said.

■ ■ ■

Hardik hadn't been sleeping easy.

There was a niggling thought bothering him. And as was his wont, he tried to dissect it, reach its core and see what he could do about it, but he was left fumbling in the darkness. He wasn't even able to fully comprehend what it was that he was feeling, but nevertheless, he knew that it was there; it was real. Lurking in the back of his mind all the time. And he also knew it was about his wife. When he'd married Chhaya, things were as they were supposed to be. They led happy lives—at least that's what he thought. He believed the love he had for her was reciprocated in kind. Yet, ever since he had been friends with her, going back to the time when they were still children, he always found something amiss with her. It's like on some occasions, she just stopped existing. As if somewhere she was plagued by a sense of melancholy that even she herself could not have explained.

In their growing years, this sense of being off, of completely removing oneself from the world around you and returning back to it as if you'd never gone, which Chhaya could do so well, never bothered Hardik. He had looked at it as a quirk and everyone was entitled to their quirks. Heck, if Hardik were to list out his, he'd never stop. Maybe it had something to do with that Meta whom Chhaya grew up with. But then she had mentioned him offhandedly only on a few occasions, never really spoke about him. Besides, Hardik had come to believe that they weren't that close anyway. After they got married, Chhaya's disconnect with the world only grew. He had tried to ask her, talk to her about it, but each time he wouldn't let the words come out of his mouth, distrusting his own powers of observation. Maybe he was wrong after all. Maybe she *was* like that. Otherwise, in all their other aspects of domestic life, he found nothing amiss. On social occasions, they conducted themselves as a young married couple who were still very much in love. And they indeed were, at least Hardik wanted to think so. But then, this niggling feeling would gnaw at him on many of those nights, with his wife sleeping next to him, and he would lie wide awake, wondering, *were they really in love?* If it was love, should he even question its presence? And because he was questioning its presence in their lives, did it mean that if it really existed for him as well, he never have would brought himself to question it? Labyrinthine thoughts like these had begun to trouble him of late. And it was what had kept him awake.

Hardik was in his study, his files open in front of him. The sunlight streamed through the yellow curtains. He was half groggy with sleep and was unable to focus his attention on the plethora of blueprints of buildings that were sandwiched between those thick files. He had followed his childhood passion of building things and eventually moulded it by forming a construction company. When he'd started out, things hadn't been easy. Labour in Old City was cheap, but that only meant they were prone to frequent strikes. Rajaji Prasad, as the new Chief Guide, had introduced a series of legislations to tackle this issue, and Hardik could see they were bearing fruit. These laws sought to make business and entrepreneurship easy in Old City, something that was not so during Balaji Vishwanath's time. And this definitely helped a nascent company like his. As other companies, like Hardik's, sprung up, competition grew. Just last year, Hardik's company saw a huge profit with all the projects on track. *Like a well-oiled machine*, thought Hardik. This money was used in renovating his old house.

On many occasions, Chhaya had insisted they sell this property and build a better house somewhere. But ever since his father, Jaideep Singhla, had passed on, leaving a gaping hole inside him, he wasn't able to bring himself to sell this house. It was all that remained from his childhood years. Besides, it was the same place where he had met Chhaya, many moons ago, in the same study, looking out the same window. It was true that as things change, one has to move on and adapt, but then, did it mean one had to abandon certain elements that still tied them to their past? Can the past ever be buried?

The servants entered one by one. He noticed their movements from the corner of his eye, visibly distracted. The house was being decorated today. His company had signed a memorandum of understanding with a subsidiary of Inspire Corporation, which would allow the sale of cement and other building supplements at a reduced price to Hardik's company. This, in turn, Hardik realized, would bring down his company's cost of production, making it more profitable in the coming years. This will provide a huge shot in the arm, and so, it called for a celebration. Ever since he was a child, Hardik hadn't easily taken to the idea of socializing. But as he grew up and went on to assemble his company from scratch, he had grown to realize the importance of talking to people. It was all about the dharma of negotiation, as Rajaji Prasad had spoken of in many of his public self-help lectures, which had helped Hardik overcome his social awkwardness and assert himself. The small party he was throwing today was just an effort in that direction. Invite people, mingle, negotiate and build one's contact network. Who knows who might be of help in the near future? When his sister, Ishita, found out about Hardik's party, she had thrown up her arms in mock desperation, proclaiming how boring he and Chhaya were. She insisted on spicing up the event, to make the Singhlas stand out from the rest of Old City. Her suggestion: theme party. Hardik straightaway objected to that, which led to a lot of back and forth, but eventually they decided to have a masquerade party.

As he was poring over his file, he saw a maid come into the study to dust off the ash that had streamed in along with the sunlight.

'Has Chhaya woken up?' Hardik asked.

'Yes, sahab, Chhaya ma'am has just woken up,' the maid replied.

'Did she ask about me? Call for me?'

'No, I don't think so. She hasn't said anything. Do you want me to tell her that you're calling for her?'

Hardik mulled over this suggestion. The same shroud of doubt, which had plagued him last night and on several nights before this, returned.

'No. Don't. I'll be there shortly,' he said.

Just then, the doorbell rang. One of the servants rushed to open the door. Hardik then saw Umesh Kumar, his associate in the firm, walk up towards him in the study.

'*Arey*, you're here early. Did you manage to finish reading the file?' Hardik asked. He did not get up from his seat to welcome him.

'Not only did I finish reading the file, but I also started working on the presentation. Ha! Damn. After that bit of a dry run, I think I am going back to being productive all over again. How are you this morning? I see you're still going through the file,' Umesh said, taking a seat across the table from Hardik.

'That's good, that's good,' Hardik said absent-mindedly.

'Whoa . . . someone got up on the wrong side of the bed. Is everything all right?'

'Yes, yes. Things are fine. I am just tensed up about this tender. When do you think the Citadel will decide? Any players we need to be wary of?'

'Not that I know of. We're still the number one contender. Although—'

'Our profits are up, we have the MoU; nothing should go wrong, right? This Citadel tender is big money,' Hardik said in one breath. On being cut off mid-sentence, Umesh flinched. Hardik then asked, 'What was that you were saying?'

'Just that we might be number one in the region, but things are not like they were before. New companies have come up. I know one, particularly, that has a direct line of contact with Inspire.'

'Which company is this?'

'I don't know. Some company that goes by the name of . . . umm . . . Latif Associates.'

'Never heard of it. That's strange. When did this company register itself?'

'No clue. But rumour has it that this company is hot.'

'Then get a clue, Umesh. I have not hired you to just sit around and flirt with waitresses in the bars you frequent. C'mon yaar, at least give me something here,' Hardik said.

'Umm . . . Don't worry. I'll get our men working on this,' Umesh managed to utter. He did not conceal his displeasure with Hardik's commanding tone, but that little detail was lost on Hardik, who quickly returned to his file. Umesh sat there, looking at Hardik intently and realized something wasn't quite right with him. And it wasn't just the tender from Citadel that was bothering him. There was something else. But then, he was just his associate, his business partner. And Hardik, no matter how great he was in forging partnerships in his professional environment, knew next to nothing about friendship. And so, Umesh did not persist.

'Do one thing, Umesh, extend an invitation to the owner of this Latif Associates. Find out who he is, and tell him I would love to meet him. In fact, call him to the party tonight.'

'Huh? Are you sure, boss? We hardly know him.'

'Well, we don't know a lot of the other invitees as well, or even if we do, just barely. My father used to say, if you find someone who seems to be your competitor, keep them close *and* at arm's length. Let's see what he's like.'

Umesh slowly nodded. When he realized there was nothing for him to do here, he excused himself, got up and left as abruptly as he had come.

Hardik thumped the file on his desk. No, enough was enough. The elephant in the room had to be addressed. He had to have a conversation with his wife, about what he had been feeling and noticing. He had to apprise her of the gravity of the situation. The despondency in his house was eating its way into his work, and he realized that was the cause behind the glaring mistakes in his work. Sure, it was Umesh's job to go out and gather intelligence about the other players in the market, which at least would have given their own firm an advantage when it came to quoting a price for the tender. But if Hardik himself would have been in his element, problems like these would have never arisen. After all, to what extent can you depend on your associates and business partners?

Hardik walked into the bedroom. Chhaya was sitting at the dressing table, straightening her hair. The first thing Hardik saw was Chhaya's reflection in the large rectangular mirror, and at that very moment, the resolve that he had built up just a moment ago, died down. She smiled as she saw him walk towards her.

'I thought you weren't well,' Hardik said. He came behind her and kissed the top of her head.

'No, I have been feeling much better. The cough has not been that bad lately. The medicines are working,' she said.

'The servants have been running here and there since morning. Cleaning the house, decorating. Are you sure you'll be well for the party tonight?'

'Don't worry about me. I'll be more than well. See, I'm absolutely fine!'

'Ha! Hardly! Why do you have to straighten your hair all the time? Just keep them curly, no?'

Chhaya did not respond. A moment later, she answered, 'No.' Such moments bothered Hardik. It was as if there were secrets that Chhaya had bottled up inside of her, secrets that Hardik was not privy to. And the more he thought of this, the more he wanted to peer inside her heart. But the more he tried to do so, the more distant Chhaya would become.

'It was just a simple suggestion, you know,' Hardik said.

'Mhmm . . . yes,' Chhaya mumbled. Looking into the mirror, Hardik could see that Chhaya's eyes were still on him, yet he couldn't help but feel as if she was looking at someone else, with her thoughts someplace else.

'How many guests are coming?' Chhaya asked.

Somehow that question irked him. These weren't things he was supposed to know. If only, for once, Chhaya would do what she was *supposed* to do. Take charge of the household. Maybe by doing that, she could become more accustomed to the house, and by extension, to him. And this distance that Chhaya maintained from everything around her and the duties of domestic life, was just another manifestation of the malaise Hardik thought was plaguing his married life. He had seen his married friends and colleagues and their lives. It wasn't this dull. And no, it wasn't monotony that bothered him. In fact, as a man, he even welcomed it. Craved those mundane activities of domestic life, which he had witnessed in the company of other couples. What bothered him was one, his complete inability to fathom just what exactly his wife wanted out of their marriage and out of life in general, and two, her near total desire to keep him out of her life. She was staying with him, and they were doing everything a married couple does, but at times, he felt as if she was some sort of ghost who, at his mere touch, would disintegrate into smoke and fade away.

'Not many. But I have called Rajaji Prasad and a few important ones. Did I not mention this to you, Chhaya?'

'Mhmm . . . yes you did. I guess,' she answered, as she continued straightening her wild, wavy hair.

■ ■ ■

Haksh walked through the alleyways of the Muslim Quarters. Every lane bifurcated into multiple lanes, each smaller and thinner than the one before it. The area had changed so much since he was a child. The masjid was no longer there. What remained in its stead was rubble. Some houses had grown in size, while some had shrunk. There were new faces. And yet, there was an odd familiarity to the place. It didn't feel like Haksh had come here after several years.

As he walked, he felt like there was someone behind him, following his every move. He looked behind him and saw no one. Just a large mass of people going about their daily lives. A vegetable seller called out seeking customers, while shopkeepers tended to their daily affairs. Just then, someone came up behind Haksh and tapped him lightly on his shoulders. He turned around. He saw a young man, who must have been around the age of eighteen. The man gave a smile and nodded. Haksh nodded in acquiescence. Suddenly, two more men surfaced and surrounded Haksh on all sides.

'Where are we going?' Haksh asked.

'You'll see. It's just round the corner,' the eighteen-year-old man said.

They then turned towards the right to a narrow lane. Haksh saw that the path came to a dead end. But at the end of the lane was a black iron gate. One of the men opened the gate and ushered Haksh in.

It was a double-storeyed house. But because the area was quite old, houses like these had stood cheek by jowl with each other for ages past, to the point that every such lane inevitably led to old houses like the one Haksh was in at present. A long, narrow flight of steps led them to a wooden door with carvings on it. Haksh was escorted to a large room, the floor of which had chessboard patterns. The light was low here and a feeble bulb buzzed. A decrepit ceiling fan whirled away. Green curtains adorned the window, although there was no need for a curtain anyway, for the sun rays were mostly blocked by the buildings glued to this one. A bed stood on the furthest end of the room, draped with a mosquito net. Haksh walked towards it. An old man lay on it. As soon as he heard footsteps, he sat up in bed and removed the net to see his visitor.

'When did you come?' the man asked. His voice was gruff. Haksh could see that he was tall, tall enough for the bed he was sitting on.

'Just now,' Haksh answered.

'No. When did you arrive here, in Old City?'

'About a month ago. I was lying low. Biding my time.'

'Hmm . . . Did you meet everyone?'

'Just the woman Easwaran was married to. And his son. And a few others.'

'Old City has changed, hasn't it? Some say for the better, while some say for the worse. This new Guide seems to know his job well.'

'So do I,' Haksh said coldly. He could see the man was surprised on hearing this. He got up from the bed and walked towards Haksh.

'Did Aakash tell you I knew Easwaran? Very well. We were in the same gang. I was there when he brought you here into this world, into Old City,' the man said.

'Yes, he did.'

'I can sense something inside you. Something I thought wasn't there.'

'There's nothing inside of me.'

'Hmm . . . Easwaran would have been disappointed to know that. God bless that man.'

'Maybe.'

'When you ran away and were in hiding, Easwaran came to me. He knew what was going on; he might have been senile during his later years, but he wasn't stupid.'

'And I thank you for that, Eaklavya, thank you for not keeping me here. Thank you for smuggling me into Millennium City and keeping me safe there. But I believe I asked you for nothing. I would have survived even if you hadn't helped me. Even without Easwaran. Without

anyone,' Haksh said, his voice rising. Over the years, he
had realized that the anger that festered in him, the same
anger that drove him away from Old City and brought him
back here, was what he had to embrace about himself if he
wanted to survive. For it was only anger that made him
see reason. Not love or whatever it was that he felt during
those hazy childhood days, running after Chhaya, believing
in the world of books and stories and pictures from faraway
lands. The truth was that nothing mattered. Something had
collapsed within him that day, in the Hall of Justice. No,
that's not quite right. The Hall of Justice had delivered its
verdict against two boys he once knew. But it also made him
grow up.

Eaklavya said nothing for a while. He then went back
to the bed and sat down again. He motioned to Haksh to
walk towards him. Haksh hesitated. One of the men standing
behind him stepped forward and poked his back. Upon
reaching the edge of the bed, Eaklavya asked him to kneel
down in front of him. Taking Haksh's face in his hands, he
scanned that chiselled face for some time in utter silence.

'You've grown up fine. And yet, I see that you are troubled.
I don't have a remedy for that, of course. Anyway, Bashir there
will give you the number of the locker where the rest of the
money is deposited. Easwaran's hard-earned savings from our
days in the wild together. Do what you want to do with it. But
remember your father. Always remember him.'

'He's not my father,' Haksh replied. He removed the old
man's hands from his face, got up and walked towards the
door. As he was about to go out, Eaklavya called out.

'Do you know why Easwaran picked you up? Do you
know why he even let you go away? All these years?'

Haksh turned back.

'A father's love. That's what it was,' Eaklavya added after a moment's pause. 'But I won't stop you. I am no one to stop you. Easwaran wouldn't have either. But know this, before you proceed with your plan, know that the greatest truth—something I myself have learnt the hard way—is that love transcends.'

■ ■ ■

As the evening came over Old City, businessmen, dignitaries and powerful bigwigs dressed in their finest attires, made their way to Hardik's bungalow. The house was decked in fairy lights. Hardik and Ishita stood at the door to greet the guests. Entertaining the guests inside was Chhaya, dressed in a red sari. Her straight hair flowed down to her hips. A bright smile on her face. While Hardik welcomed the guests, he saw Chhaya from the corner of his eye. While on other days, her smile would fill him with love for her, today it just made him angry. He found it fake and would even have preferred her distant, aloof self to this show of joviality that she had put on. He knew very well that she wasn't happy. So why pretend? Why show that she loved him, when she didn't even accord him the respect of responding to him or taking an interest in his affairs. And the more he allowed the anger to grow inside him, the steelier his resolve became. He would have to have a talk with her, even if that contained the danger of things getting out of hand. He just had to.

When most of the guests had come and the house was almost filled, Hardik and Ishita went inside. Ishita went up to the front, where the food was laid out on a table, so she could see the entire room and motioned everyone to pay attention. All faces turned towards her.

'Ladies and gentlemen, dear friends of my brother and his lovely wife, as you all know, we don't really need a reason to give a party, now do we? But it is also a fact that this party is happening for a reason. It is to celebrate his success and the remarkable part each one of you has played in it. And it is an attempt from him to showcase how indebted he is to all of you. Now please do enjoy yourself, don't hesitate, and please, please, put on your masks!'

The party went on at its own pace. Men and women chatted through their masks. Laughter was heard. Glasses were clinked. Chhaya moved from one group of guests to the other. She still hadn't put on her mask. Hardik walked up from behind, holding her by the waist and led her to a corner.

'What's wrong, Chhaya?' he whispered.

'Nothing, what's wrong?' Chhaya answered, surprised.

'Why haven't you put your mask on?'

'Oh c'mon, do I have to?'

'*Yes*, you have to. You very well have to. C'mon yaar, don't spoil the fun. Ishita has done so much to put this party together. Put on the mask, please,' he said. Chhaya removed his hands from hers and walked away. He saw her go upstairs. Resting his head against the wall, Hardik cursed under his breath, 'Shit.'

Just then someone patted him on the back. Hardik turned. For a moment, he did not recognize who it was, but as soon as he opened his mouth, Hardik realized it was Umesh.

'Ha! What do you think, boss? This mask works?' he said excitedly.

'Clearly,' Hardik replied in candid jest and also with relief.

'Oh, by the way. There, standing beside Rajaji Prasad is the owner of Latif Associates,' Umesh said. Hardik looked at the man in question. He was tall, had long hair. From this angle, the man seemed to have a well-proportioned and chiselled jawline. *Attractive*, thought Hardik. No wonder all women seemed to gather around him. He was dressed in a black tuxedo and a crisp white shirt. His face was covered with a black mask.

'Why is he talking to Rajaji Prasad?' Hardik asked. His eyes still on the stranger.

'Oh c'mon. He is at your party, he is going to talk to the primary guest you've invited. But the difference, boss, is that Rajaji Prasad has come to *your* party. Not his. Let the new bees taste the honey. Only we control the source.'

Hardik laughed. Just then, the stranger turned around and glanced at him. Their eyes met. There was something in those eyes, black as coal, which seemed vaguely familiar to Hardik. But then he turned around to see Chhaya walking down the stairs. Her face was covered with a black mask.

When she walked towards him, Hardik pulled her aside again and attempted to kiss her lips. She resisted and the kiss landed on her cheeks instead. If Hardik had paid attention, he would have seen that the stranger's eyes were fixated on his wife. That nothing escaped his eyes. They had seen every little detail unfold—Hardik pulling his wife to a corner, their little tiff, her aloofness and now her mask.

The stranger put his glass on the drinks tray a servant was carrying and picked up another. He then walked towards his host and hostesses. Umesh, who saw him coming, nudged his boss gently. Hardik turned.

'Oh, welcome, welcome, Mr Chawla. Boss, meet the proprietor of Latif Associates.'

When the man approached, Hardik extended his hands and received a firm handshake in response. The man nodded towards Umesh, acknowledging him, and smiled. While his eyes stayed on both the men, what he actually focused on was the hostess of the evening, dressed in a red sari, the mask covering her face. Those eyes also saw that the hostess hadn't moved her eyes from him either. She had the same smile on her face that used to irritate Hardik earlier. She responded to every nudge, every little joke her husband and his associate cracked. Laughed when she had to laugh. But Haksh's eyes also saw that beneath this composure and grace, she was battling a raging storm inside her. There was no need for introductions between them. She knew and saw who he was. The mask was unnecessary.

# 12

Sitting behind the reception of his inn after dinner, Louie was staring intently at the ledger, but his eyes saw nothing. He knew, at a time like this, he should have been preoccupied with finances or with his wife, but the new tenant in his inn seemed to have drawn all of Louie's energies towards him. *I should have said no. I am too old to have new drama in my life. Was it because I was intrigued by this man's aura of mystery or was this a premonition?* These thoughts refused to leave Louie's mind.

While these thoughts flitted through his head, Louie heard footsteps outside, which only grew louder and louder, until the figure of the man, who had been the subject of Louie's recent concerns, came into view. Louie noticed how he was impeccably dressed, which just ignited his curiosity even more. Haksh slowly walked inside. He rested his palms casually on the reception desk and peered intently into Louie's eyes. He looked into Haksh's coal-black eyes but quickly looked down and placed a key on the desk, next to Haksh's hands. Louie would have wanted to engage his tenant in a conversation, speak about the weather maybe, about his day even, but no sooner did these ideas come to him than he realized the man wasn't standing there any more. It was as if he was never there and Louie had been dreaming all this while.

*No*, Louie thought. Enough is enough. He should stop thinking about him. The man was only a tenant and would soon leave. And Louie was overworked. He needed a vacation, some time off. Maybe Louie would talk to his wife tonight, about going to Millennium City for a few days. Soak in its sights and sounds. She had been suggesting this for a long time, and he even had some money saved up—which he thought he could use in renovating two old rooms at the inn—but all that would need to wait. Right now, more than anything else, it was time to close for the day. Time for him to go to his room, snuggle next to his wife and sleep.

But it seemed that there was more in store for Louie. For as soon as he closed his ledger and turned to turn off the lights, the main door of the inn opened and there stood a well-dressed woman.

■ ■ ■

Dressed in a long black skirt and a T-shirt, Chhaya stood outside Haksh's door. Earlier that evening, the moment she'd looked into those dark coal-black eyes, she knew who it was. One may meet uncountable people throughout the course of their life and not remember who they once were. But Chhaya could never forget those eyes that peered straight into her soul. She felt like her own shadow had disassociated itself from her body and leapt into nothingness, only to return years later. And now, in this decrepit hotel and its clammy crumbling walls, Chhaya stood, feeling decrepit. Her long, curly black hair cascaded down her back. The light mascara that she had worn for the party on Hardik's insistence was smudged. And here she stood at Haksh's door, breathing heavily, wanting to knock at the door of his heart, to scream. But something inexplicable stopped her. Was it right, after all these years, to embrace the past that had come rushing back to her as easily as it had abandoned her? What should she do? Her mind veered back to the wee hours of those foregone nights, when soon after Haksh had left. She tried to recollect their childhood years, when Haksh was around . . . But she was only able to remember fragments of memories, never in their entirety, as if she'd just woken up from a deep slumber. Somehow, she remembered every little thing about Haksh. How he smelt, how he walked, his voice. During the years in which he was not around, at times she'd even suspected she could hear his thoughts, whichever corner of the world they were travelling from. But then, when morning came, she would know it was only her imagination. What kind of a strange conundrum was this, where you barely remembered the time spent with someone but seemed to know almost everything about them?

She heard footsteps behind the closed door. Her heart leapt. They grew louder and Haksh opened the door.

She saw his chiselled face, his long hair and those eyes . . . That unwavering gaze. Not a word passed between them. But words had never been necessary between them. She walked inside and heard the door close behind her.

'Why are you back?' she managed to ask.

Haksh did not reply.

The bed was neatly made. Everything in the room—spare and ornamental—was in its place. A desk near the bed. A flower vase sat atop the desk. A painting of a ship anchored in a harbour hung on a wall. A water bottle. Two bags placed near the bed, both neatly closed and zipped.

'Why are you staying here?' she asked again. Strangely, her voice did not quiver nor did it quake. 'Where were you all these years?'

'I followed you, you know? And God, it's been so many years, but you still take such long walks.'

No answer emerged.

'I got married. As you've noticed. And I'm happy,' she said. Haksh, who had been standing near the door all this while, moved towards her.

'Why are you back? What do you want after all this time?'

'Answers,' Haksh finally answered. His voice had grown deeper.

Chhaya smiled. 'You know, I somehow thought your voice would be the same as it was years ago. Do Metas grow up like that? Like *us*?'

He flinched.

She continued, 'I guess I just imagined all of it. There are times when I wake up in the morning with this feeling that everything that happened then was maybe part of my imagination. That you never even existed, that maybe I had dreamt about you or something.'

'You're not happy,' Haksh said.

'To see you? Of course, I am not. What did you think? You'll come back years later and find me leaping with joy?'

'You've not been happy.'

Before she could answer, a bout of ragged cough deep within her body rose in her throat.

When she recovered, she said hoarsely, 'Why are you here? What do you want? What are you looking for?'

'Answers. From you, from everyone.'

'As if answers were that easy to come by.' She moved towards him to study those coal-black eyes as she couldn't endure this any longer. 'I see only hatred. You're here to destroy everything,' she said quietly.

'If that's what my search leads to, then perhaps yes.'

'Don't do this. Whatever you're here for. This terrible path you've chosen. I don't know where you were or what kind of life you led, but we've made peace with everything, with our lives—even if you see no happiness, there's *at least* peace. Don't disrupt that. *Don't,*' she whispered, pleading with him.

'What happiness? What peace? I came back to take everything that was *mine.* All my life, I was made to live with the fact that I did not belong here. I tried to find my way, but you and everything that is here, stopped me at every step of the way. I will not rest till I incinerate everything.' Haksh's voice had risen, his pupils dilated. Looking into those eyes, Chhaya recoiled.

'You're not human. You can never be human. Never.'

'I know. And now I intend to show it.'

# 13

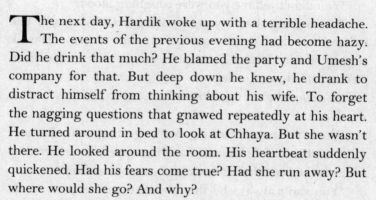

The next day, Hardik woke up with a terrible headache. The events of the previous evening had become hazy. Did he drink that much? He blamed the party and Umesh's company for that. But deep down he knew, he drank to distract himself from thinking about his wife. To forget the nagging questions that gnawed repeatedly at his heart. He turned around in bed to look at Chhaya. But she wasn't there. He looked around the room. His heartbeat suddenly quickened. Had his fears come true? Had she run away? But where would she go? And why?

But the cacophony in his mind subsided when he heard the muffled noise of someone coughing in the washroom.

Hardik knocked on the door. It was answered with more coughing. He began to bang on the door. When he didn't get a reaction, he began preparing himself to break it open. But just then, he heard the latch click open. He opened the door and saw Chhaya stooped over the washbasin. Her hair strewn about her face. A crumpled towel thrown on the floor. He picked it up. Its soft fabric was marked with tiny bloodstains. Hardik walked towards Chhaya and touched her shoulders. She turned. Her face, dripping with water, seemed pale. Drained.

'I am all right. I just coughed a little bit more today, that's all,' she said weakly.

'Are you out of your mind? You were coughing blood. This towel, the washbasin. Those are bloodstains.'

'No . . . no . . . It's normal. It has happened before too.'

'What? Happened before as in?'

'Nothing . . . nothing.'

'You didn't tell me you were coughing blood?'

'It's nothing. I told you it's *nothing*,' Chhaya said. The irritation in her voice was evident and it made Hardik slightly flinch. However, it wasn't enough to deter him from pushing this topic further.

'We should get you a doctor.'

'No.'

'Your "no" means nothing. We're getting you a doctor.'

'NO, Hardik!' Chhaya said as she stepped out and walked towards the bed. She sat down and caught her breath.

'You can't always be this obstinate and expect me or everyone to kowtow to your wishes, no matter how mad they are.'

'What wish of mine did I ever tell you?'

'That's the problem. You *never* tell me anything. It's like I am not even here.'

'Yes, you're not. You're not around. I don't see you. Now leave me alone,' she said quietly.

Hardik couldn't understand what pricked him the most. Chhaya's words or the way these words came out. Had she been angry, yelled at him, he wouldn't have cared. In fact, it would have made him happy. But Chhaya did nothing of that sort. Her voice was low. Nonchalant. If it was hatred, Hardik would have understood. But what he was unable to precisely understand—and even accept—was this indifference. It was exactly as she said. It was like she never did see him.

■ ■ ■

'You know, you might think you know the Muslim Quarters, but you actually don't,' Bashir said, 'which is why you need a guy like me to show you around.'

Haksh didn't say anything.

The two walked through the busy narrow streets, and every few minutes, there would be a sharp bend leading them into yet another narrow lane.

'We'll be there soon. Don't you worry. I have been entrusted to take you safely to your destination. And safely I will. By the way, you're from MC, aren't you?'

'MC?' Haksh asked.

'Millennium City . . . MC. It's not always possible to say the full name. So I shorten them. Not always. But just to save time.'

Silence.

'I sometimes wonder why would someone come to OC from MC anyway. You do seem like a person who's come to OC before. But that still doesn't explain things. What brings you here, to this quarter? I mean, I don't see many people from your part of town come here. Not that I am judging you or anything. I mean, who am I to judge? I was just asked to take you to Khan's, and get you out.'

'Yes.'

'You know, one day, I would go to MC too. I guess I am old enough now.'

'How old are you?'

'Seventeen. That's almost adult, you know.'

'Almost.'

'Well, if you ever think I am talking too much or asking too many questions, you can always stop me. I mean, it's okay. Chill, as they say in those richer quarters. But you can also talk to me about anything. Love problems, family problems, health problems, anything. Everyone comes to me to seek advice. Maybe I should start a business or something.'

Silence.

'Do you think I can go to MC and start a business and come back rich and all? I think if you have money, you can be anything. Anyone. I mean, I am not saying I want to be anyone else. I am happy the way I am. *Bindaas.* But sometimes, just sometimes, I wonder what it's like to live over there, you know.' Bashir stopped walking, removed his breathing mask, turned to face Haksh and winked with a smile on his face.

'Oh, and here we are,' Bashir added.

They were standing in front of a double-storeyed house with green walls. Bashir thumped the door thrice. The door opened and an old man, albeit fit, stood on the threshold. He had a long, flowing beard.

The man led the duo into a narrow passageway, which in turn opened into large veranda inside the house. Haksh could see three rooms lining the veranda, giving it the semblance of an amphitheatre, with each door separated by a large pillar.

'Arey, Khan Sahab, I was told to bring him here. I guess he has come to take the money.'

'I know who you are,' Khan said, addressing Haksh. 'I received the message last night.'

Haksh nodded.

'Wait here. I'll get you what you came all the way here for.'

Khan disappeared into one of the rooms and emerged soon, carrying a large black cloth bag.

'It's all there. Must be enough. Easwaran was a good man. He saved it all with me. If you ask me, he must have had a premonition. Strange are the works of God. Who knew, really?'

■ ■ ■

The signboard 'Latif Associates' glistened in the hazy sun. Standing near the balcony, Haksh was staring outside at the falling ash. An array of thoughts were criss-crossing his mind.

*Had she really come? Why did she look so frail? And that cough. That woman had the gall to talk to me like that. But why was she so frail?*

Questions. He had come to Old City, after all these years, to resolve the questions that had plagued him every night. But all that he met with were more questions.

*Did she not see that I am doing everything for* her? And yet, she saw hatred. Was he really incapable of love, of showing love and of receiving it in return?

But the biggest question of all that haunted Haksh was this: was it really love? Long ago, in one of those smuggled books that Easwaran had brought from Millennium City and carried with him everywhere like a talisman, he had read this line: *if I cannot inspire love, I will cause fear.* But the character in that book who really did cause fear was a monster. Did it make him a monster too then? But the monster did what he did because he was rejected by his own creator. So who was a monster then? The one condemned, or the one who condemns? Easwaran had once told him that the line separating love from its opposite was thin, which meant it was easy to breach it. But once breached, the difference could never be restored. Did that mean that he'd finally breached that thin line?

There was a soft knock on the door, which broke his daytime reverie.

At the door stood the man good ol' Louie from the bar would have recognized as the hooded man. But in broad daylight, this was a different man. He was dressed formally in a cream-coloured shirt, grey trousers and black leather shoes.

'Didn't I tell you, boss, this place you've rented is one of the best office spaces in the Hindu Quarters?'

'Yes. I should thank you for that.'

'No, no. Please, you're embarrassing me. I think it's high time we start getting some people to work here. Or else it can raise suspicions amongst the old men in the Citadel. And raids on shell companies aren't rare.'

'The Citadel has to show who's in control. I know.'

'Exactly. Which is why you should hire employees, especially if you bid for that contract.'

'Yes. What news do you bring?'

'Oh, Hardik was just enamoured of you that day at the party. He kept asking me, "Umesh, tell me more about him, where does he live, where has he studied, blah, blah, blah". I told him your father worked for Inspire back in the day. That got him even more excited.'

Haksh did not react. But Umesh could see he had piqued his interest.

'Apparently, even his sister seems to have been a bit too taken with you. I did notice she was hanging on to your every word. That's a master stroke, if you ask me. A great way to get into their society.'

Haksh turned away from Umesh, moving towards the balcony. A smile played on his lips.

'How is Hardik as a person?'

'Not bad. Needs attention, because he doesn't get it from his wife. Though I must also add that she hasn't been doing well. Just yesterday, she collapsed or something. A doctor was brought in against her wishes, a whole lotta drama happened,' Umesh said, arching his eyebrows just a tad whilst maintaining a casual tone.

Haksh did not turn back. Nor did he say anything.

'So . . . Hardik . . . I don't think you ought to be much worried. It's the Citadel you should focus on, if you want your money to grow.'

'I'll handle the Citadel. I have a job for you, Umesh.'

'Why, of course, yes, undoubtedly. Tell me, boss.'

Haksh turned around and led Umesh towards his desk. He opened a large briefcase to show wads of Millennium City currency.

'Do the job, and this is your fee.'

'Oh, boss, you're so generous. Even if you'd ask me to bring you the moon, I would have tried to get it for you. And please, you're embarrassing me with the money. I'd do it for free if you like.'

Umesh knew he was doing a bad job of playing it cool. His glee could hardly be suppressed and Haksh was well aware of that.

'Get me Harish,' Haksh said.

# 14

The message had left Harish bewildered.

Things were never the same for him, especially since Easwaran died. For some time, things had started looking up. He'd secured a job at the Citadel, gotten married and had a son. But his happiness was short-lived. The point was, he could never fit into the dry bureaucratic rigours that a job at the Citadel entailed. The slow passage of files from one department to the next. The need to say 'yes' when asked and 'no' when demanded. But then life—which he had taken for granted—struck him hard. The plague of mosquitoes, so common in Old City, struck his wife. She came down with a fever that refused to leave her body, gradually eating away at her.

After her death, Harish descended into a state of complete depression. He was lucky that Dayani was still around to take care of the baby. He neglected his job, earned the ire of his peers and gravitated slowly towards the bottle. During long and lonely evenings, he would visit one of the shady bars in the Hindu Quarters and get inebriated to the point of senselessness. And during those odd days when he wouldn't drink, he would spend it in the company of friends from those bars, crouched inside a makeshift hut in a dingy lane, trying his luck at earning a quick buck through a game of cards.

But his luck always ran out, and he'd end up losing. The losses had accumulated to a point where Harish became desperate. He had considered mortgaging his house to one of his bosses in the Citadel, get the money and pay off his gambling debts. He would then later try to pay off the private loan. Though he had no idea how he'd do that. But that was for later. At least his boss won't kill and dump his body in a trash can. But Harish didn't know that the men he had befriended in those dingy bars most likely would, if Harish didn't pay up on time.

The message, therefore, couldn't have come at a more opportune time for Harish. Now, plopped on the edge of his bed, he could see the dying rays of the setting sun cast shadows on the wall in front of him. He focused on those shadows, the way they changed shapes every now and then. He looked back to the days gone by. When as a child, his father would pick him up and take him along on those numerous journeys to Millennium City. The rugged terrains of the Interstate. And the journey back.

Did everything change when his father picked up that Meta? Was it then when things began to go downhill? Was that fate? Or do we live our lives responding to the choices we have made, when there is no stopping the effect each choice would create in its wake, like a single falling domino? He had no idea. If Easwaran had been around now, maybe Harish would have gone and asked him. But thoughts like these would hit him with a wave of regret, and the pursuit of its denial, which would eventually lead him back to the bottle or those dreaded cards. And Harish could feel himself slipping. His throat began to dry up, his fingers twitched and he felt light-headed, although he hadn't touched the bottle all day. It was like being drawn towards an illusion of a better life, a dream that he wouldn't want to wake up from.

*No.* Suddenly something broke his reverie. The message. That message. That man. He seemed familiar. He had seen him around in the Citadel.

The guy who spoke to the men higher up on the Citadel ladder. A political fixer, maybe? But why come to me? And how would he know that I was someone in need? Harish tried to understand. But this train of thought, instead of making him feel at ease, grew into a disquietude. If Harish was the recipient of a message, which on the face of it was about help, then it could mean two things. One, that the news of his house being mortgaged must have been doing the rounds, in turn making him an object of ridicule. And two, why would a stranger come up and offer help, unless and until there was some profit to be made? Is this some elaborate game of chess, the moves of which were eluding Harish?

But Harish also knew that at this juncture, he had nothing to lose. Down and out, pushed against the wall, Harish had to see the message to its logical conclusion.

■ ■ ■

Dressed in a plain white shirt over a pair of grey trousers, Harish sat in front of the desk on an upholstered black leather chair. His legs crossed, his eyes scanning the surroundings. The office, where this meeting took place, seemed more makeshift than a fully formed workspace. Wooden cartons were littered in the corner, some opened, some closed. The walls were freshly painted, but he could see a construction worker's ladder resting against an edge of the wall. That particular edge led to a closed door, from within which he could hear the slow rattle of a hammer hitting against something.

*This place is still under construction,* Harish thought. But he couldn't feel at ease. He crossed and uncrossed his legs repeatedly. The man who sat on the other side of the desk on a large swivelling chair was poring over a sheaf of papers. Harish kept his left hand on the desk but quickly put it on the armrest. A glass of water was placed on the desk.

'Feel free to have the water, Mr Harish,' the man said. Harish nodded, brought himself forward, picked up the glass and took a few quick sips before putting it back.

'Do you need anything more?'

'No, thank you. I am all right,' Harish said.

'Oh, by the way, you don't need your breathing mask here. I know this place is still under construction, and I apologize for the mess, but it's being made ready. And we have installed a few powerful air purifiers—Millennium City tech—it should help you breathe easy.

Harish nodded like an obedient child, removed his mask and placed it on the table. The man was right. The air in here was better. Cleaner. It was like inside the Citadel. He could smell mahogany and paint in the air.

'What do you think?' Harish asked.

The man did not reply and continued reading for a short while.

'Well, the documents are all in order. Was it your father who built the house?'

'It's complicated. The land was bought by my grandfather. He used to work in the mines in those days.'

'Ah, I see. Ancient history . . . he he.'

'Yes. Very much so. So yes, my father built the house, but it wasn't done in one go. Happened over the years.'

'I see. How many live there now?'

'My mother and my young son. That's all, ever since my father died.'

The minute Harish said this, he bit his tongue. He didn't know why it was necessary for him to add those details, which the gentleman in front of him probably wouldn't care about anyway.

'I am sorry to hear that. Well look, we are quite keen on the deal. In fact, when I found out you were looking to sell the place, I knew we could use it for our . . . boss. He wants a house.'

Harish nodded.

'I think we can—'

A few seconds later, Harish realized the man had used the word *sell*. 'Um, just a minute. You see, I am not looking to sell the house. At least not at this moment. I just want to mortgage it. And of course, you can rest assured that as per the terms we would agree upon, I would return the required money in due time.'

The man flinched. 'What I was saying was that as of now, we can go ahead with this. You shall get the money upfront too. In cash. We don't deal with any other kind of transaction. Besides, it's not like this place is Millennium City,' the man said. He ensured that Harish noticed the edge of irritation in his voice and the fact that he had conveniently ignored everything Harish had just pointed out.

Harish could feel his face redden.

'Look,' the man continued, 'I know all this must be weird for you. I mean we don't know each other. And here we are sitting across the table, talking about big money and whatnot.'

'How did you find me, and why exactly did *my* house catch your interest?'

'Oh, for that second question, my boss has been looking around for a decent place to stay here and chanced upon your house, I guess. Don't worry, he is a man of . . . How shall I put this so as not to sound indelicate? . . . He's a man of very specific interests. What he likes, he likes. What he hates, he detests. Simple. Your house happened to fall in the former category. He he he he.'

'And the first question? How did you know I was looking to mortgage it? Also I need to stress on this: mortgage. I am not selling my house. So in that way, I don't know how this deal would be of use for your boss.'

'Well, my company . . . Latif Associates . . . We know our way around the Citadel. And word goes around. See this as a game of cards, which I don't know how familiar you're with, but you have to see everything clearly. Observe, observe . . . he he.'

Harish felt as if the chair he was sitting on would collapse any moment and swallow him whole. And perhaps that fate would have been acceptable to him. It meant his suspicions were correct. Word was indeed out in the Citadel about his impending financial crisis. How would he ever go back there, face the same people?

Latif Associates . . . *Latif* . . . the name brought back strange memories. Where had he heard that name? . . . More than being familiar, it carried with it a taste of the lost world. But what kind of a world it was, Harish couldn't make out. If he hadn't filled his days with incessant drinking, then maybe things wouldn't have been so hazy. But no. This wasn't

a haze born out of drunkenness. It was more wilful. As if
Harish *chose* to forget the name and what it meant. And now
it wouldn't come back.

'Mr Harish?'

Harish snapped back into reality and just managed to nod.

'Are we clear then? Look, if you're worried about the
money, don't be. Wait a minute.' The man pushed his chair
back, walked towards a freshly painted mahogany cupboard,
brought out a black bag and placed it on the desk in front
of Harish.

'Here's all the money. Hard cash. And it's in Millennium
City currency. Not your shitty Old City ones.'

Harish looked at the bag askance. He couldn't move his
hands to touch it. His eyes darted back and forth from the
bag to the man.

'Oh, don't be shy. It's yours. All yours. Do we have a deal
then?' The man opened the bag and lay down the money in
front of Harish.

'Yes, we have a deal. What do I need to do?'

'Oh, just sign these house papers here. And you're free to
take the money.'

Harish nodded.

'Yes, now we have a deal.'

■ ■ ■

That evening, as the sun went down and darkness wrapped
itself around Old City, Haksh walked inside the makeshift
office of Latif Associates. Umesh would come in any
minute. The balls Haksh had been juggling in the air were
slowly coming down, each in its spot. Standing in the glass

balcony, he peered out at the city. Oh, how he hated this place. If he had enough explosives, he would have turned the place and everyone in it into dust. A place like this did not deserve to exist on the face of the earth. And yet, here it is. Teeming with people living and dreaming inside their immensely empty lives. As if everything was okay. Normal. Peaceful.

The door, which Haksh had kept ajar, cracked fully open.

'Are you there, boss?'

'Yes, please come. Did you get the papers?'

'Oh yes. Fresh with the goat's signature . . . he he he.'

'Show me.'

Umesh fumbled around in his briefcase, removed the sheaf of papers from it and handed them to Haksh.

Haksh glanced through them quickly. At each place where the word 'signature' was written in bold letters, Haksh saw the word 'Harish' scribbled in elongated letters. He ran his fingers over the paper, feeling the ink.

'It seems I wasn't wrong about you, Umesh.'

'Of course. You see, Hardik isn't a good boss. Plus pays in peanuts. Not many in Old City pay in good MC currency.'

'In fact,' Umesh continued, 'the goat was so dumb, he did not even read the papers carefully. I think he missed out that crucial detail, boss, the difference between Old City currency and the ones from MC. What a master stroke. With this brain of yours, by God, you will be unstoppable!'

There was not a hint of remorse on Haksh's face. He knew currency from Millennium City, given its greater value, was regulated here in Old City. And a large stash of money from there would be enough to put you in trouble, with eyebrows being raised about its point of origin. In other words, people from Old City did not just *get* Millennium City money.

'Oh, here are the house papers I got from the goat.' Umesh said.

'Call him Harish, please,' Haksh said coldly. Flinching a little, Umesh swallowed hard and nodded.

'You kept your money?'

'Oh yes, I have,' Umesh said.

'Then you can leave. If I need something, I know where to find you.'

'Sure, boss. I need to head off to Hardik's boss's house anyway. It seems his wife—that poor thing—has taken a turn for the worse.'

Haksh stared at Umesh, who could now feel his steely eyes peering into his soul.

'What happened?'

'Didn't I tell you before . . . the cough . . . It has become worse. So I have to swing by for a bit.'

Haksh paused. And just when Umesh was about to leave, he called him back.

'Umesh, I need you to do something. And nothing I say comes for free. You already know I can be generous, if I choose to be.'

■ ■ ■

When Umesh arrived at Hardik's house, he was greeted with silence. Hardik sat on the same sofa where Umesh had found him on the morning before the party. The lights were dim.

'Is everything all right, boss?'

Hardik did not say anything but motioned to him to take a seat.

'She's resting. The doctor from the Citadel had come. I don't know . . . I don't know what to do, Umesh.'

Umesh could see that Hardik could burst into tears any moment. That he was holding them back with great effort. He felt embarrassed and immediately regretted his decision to come. But then, the visual of the MC currency wads floated through his mind. And he could see his dream of not being this errand boy, becoming independent, starting his own business, making his way into the Citadel, and from there on, endless success. Working for Hardik, and many others before, right from the age of eighteen, he had begun to understand the subtle changing nuances of the Citadel. Though he was still far away from getting to know the inner workings of that place, he believed that by making the right moves—and more importantly, money, lots of money—it wasn't impossible.

'What did the doctor say?' Umesh asked.

'Nothing. It's the cough. There's nothing he can do. It seems it had gone worse because Chhaya must have gone out and forgotten to wear her breathing mask. Or some such thing. But he isn't sure.'

'How are you coping?'

'Fucked is the word. I have barely slept in the last few days, business has gone for a toss and this Citadel tender will have to wait, man.'

Umesh nodded in agreement.

'You should go to bed, boss. If you need anything, I'm here.'

'No, no. I can't sleep. The doctor has told me to sleep in another room. Chhaya needs total rest. I can't sleep.'

'But you have to rest. Look at your eyes, I have never seen you in this state before, boss.'

It took Umesh a combination of small talk, feigned empathy and sweet pious platitudes to convince Hardik to hit the bed. When he finally did, Umesh sat on the sofa in the darkened room, alone with his thoughts. He looked around. The door to Chhaya's room was ajar. No sound came from there. Only the quiet footsteps of the darkness treading evermore softly in this doomed place. Umesh knew it would take only a miracle to snatch Chhaya away from the clutches of that cough. The dust and ash would have descended into the deeper recesses of her lungs. There was no escape. The inevitable had to be accepted. But in the midst of it all, what he really found surprising was his new boss's interest in this dying woman. What's the story? Umesh could have looked into it—he knew very well how to. But it did not interest him. Umesh saw himself as a thorough professional. If paid well, he would do anything without asking. Unnecessary questions and curiosities only stymied work, stopped you from growing. It was important to ask the right questions, at the right time. And according to Umesh, his new boss's interest in this dying woman did not qualify as 'the right question'. Who cares why he was interested? He was paying him handsomely, and so, Umesh was happy to oblige.

When he realized that the house had quietened down, and that there was no danger of Hardik, or his sister or anyone walking in and catching him in the act, he tiptoed towards the door, opened it further and stepped inside Chhaya's room. He quietly closed the door behind him.

The room, contrary to what he was expecting, wasn't really dark inside. A bedside lamp that diffused thin yellow rays of light illuminated the room—helping Umesh see where Chhaya lay asleep. Umesh hesitated a little but knew there was no choice. He walked towards her cautiously and stood near the lamp. He touched Chhaya's forehead. She was running a high fever, Umesh realized. He slowly tried to wake her up. It did not take much effort. Chhaya was a light sleeper. When she opened her eyes, Umesh could see the confusion on her face. He put his finger up to his lips, motioning her to be quiet. He bent down and whispered, 'Please be quiet. Someone is waiting for you outside, in the garden. He wants to meet you.'

Chhaya got up. She did not need any further direction. She knew who was waiting. The angel of her death.

■ ■ ■

Cicadas groaned in the darkness. And in their invisible presence, Haksh felt oddly comforted. He didn't need to hide. The darkness was enough to envelop him in its embrace.

Footsteps on the grass. Muffled. For anybody else, the sound of those footsteps would have been anonymous—bereft of bodies and face. Unknown. Strange. But Haksh knew whose footsteps those were. More than that, it was as if he could feel it. Its sensation coursed through his body.

He saw her. In the hazy darkness. Frail. Bony. A whisper and she could melt away like a cloud of mist, acquire another shape and become something else.

'I knew you'd come,' Chhaya said.

'I had to.'

'Don't try to pretend now and say you've come to inquire about my health. It'll just make me laugh, and you'll feel bad.'

'I don't need to ask you anything. I see everything. Nothing escapes me.'

'Oh really? What do you see then? Death?'

Haksh didn't say anything.

She stepped closer. The leaves of the tall banyan tree swayed gently.

'Once upon a time, there was a girl . . . Do you know how that story goes?'

'No,' Haksh said.

'Once upon a time, there was a girl, and once upon a time, there was a boy, and they lived happily ever after. Isn't that what every story seeks to be? Strange how they turn out.'

Haksh glared at her. As if his eyes could pervade her deepest secrets and leave nothing in its wake.

'I don't know what you're up to. But leave Harish out of it. He isn't responsible for anything that happened to you in the past,' Chhaya said after a long pause. Partially turned away from Haksh, she didn't seem to be looking at anything in particular, just staring into the distance, as if she was inside a dream.

Haksh walked towards her. He held her arms and drew her towards himself. It didn't require much effort. She turned to face him.

'Leave Harish out,' she repeated. This time in a whisper.

'Why? Why should I spare him or anyone else for that matter? I will take everything that was mine.'

'*Leave.* Do you not see what you've become? Your eyes, your all-seeing eyes, how you forget nothing—turn your gaze on yourself and marvel at your emptiness.'

'Come with me. There are better doctors in Millennium City. You'll be better. We'll be kids again. Laugh. Love. Just as it was yesterday, before it was snatched away from us.'

'This is my place. I lived here. I'll die here. It's my choice, and I have made it.'

'What about everything?'

'Everything? There never was everything. The past that you hold so dear inside you, the past that nurtures your hatred, it's over. You have a choice, just like Easwaran— the one who brought you into this world—had a choice. Live, Haksh.'

'The more you exhort me, the more resolute I become.'

'Yes. Because your hatred is not towards Harish. Or the Citadel. Or this entire godforsaken place. Your hatred is towards *me*. This crazy idea of avenging the past, you're not avenging any past. You're avenging me. We were kids, Haksh. What do you think we could have done?'

'Come with me. We can run away now. No one will find us. And you'll be happy. We'll live again.'

'No. I can't. I just can't.'

'You tell me to "live", but have you lived yourself? All these years? We're the same. We've always been the same.'

'I have to go. I can't talk more. If I cough here, it'll just wake everyone up.'

She took a long, hard look at Haksh and allowed her fingers to graze his hair.

'Will I see you again?' Haksh asked.

'Soon,' Chhaya replied.

■ ■ ■

The morning in Hardik's household, much to his surprise, seemed rather pleasant. Chhaya woke up early and prepared breakfast.

At first, Hardik met this new reality not with disbelief, but rather with fear. Chhaya hadn't coughed since the morning. She was filled with a new kind of energy. During breakfast, which Hardik ate after fervently protesting about Chhaya wanting to work when she shouldn't, he could see his wife's paleness lessen. A hint of reddish hue flushed her cheeks. She smiled. Asked Ishita about the party scene in the neighbourhood and promised her she would turn up at the next one.

Ishita and Hardik exchanged unquiet glances.

But as the day wore on, so did the disquiet. Chhaya's energy did not lessen. She chattered enthusiastically. Asked him about his new tender from the Citadel, even commented on the fact that he had been losing weight and ought to eat more. She inquired about lunch, and although she offered to cook, Hardik flatly vetoed it.

By afternoon, with things more or less normal, a new kind of assurance began to seep into Hardik.

Maybe things will get better. That in order to get better, they have to first get worse, and perhaps, the worst was in the past for them. Maybe it was finally time to renew things. Start from scratch, maybe.

He was sitting opposite Chhaya. She was sitting on the sofa and gazing at the garden outside the window. He got up and sat right next to her. She moved an inch to make space for him. She could feel the warmth of his eyes resting upon her.

'Listen, I know things haven't been great between us of late. And this cough gave us both a mighty scare. Although,

you would have to get a check-up done tomorrow . . .'
Hardik said.

'I'll go to the doctor, don't worry. But I think I'm
fine. In fact, I've never felt better,' Chhaya said with
a smile.

'That's good,' Hardik said and nodded, his eyes still on
her. 'But, here's the thing, I think we have to start looking
towards the future.'

'What do you have in mind?'

'Nothing elaborate, really. But I was thinking, just as a
symbolic gesture, let us renew our marriage vows,' Hardik
said. The moment he saw Chhaya open her mouth to speak,
he added, 'I know, I know.' He placed his hands in hers.

She could see the earnestness of his words reflect in his
eyes. That it meant something for him. After a long pause,
Chhaya nodded in agreement.

He was elated. And Chhaya could see that he was.

'I think I am going to go to bed and lie down for a bit,'
Chhaya said, 'and if you want, you can go to the office, get
some work done. You've been here far too long.'

'No, I am staying right here with you.'

'Ha ha, no. You go and work. I can take care of myself.'

Hardik could sense the resolution in Chhaya's voice.
Maybe she wanted some space. But she was right; ever since
her cough had worsened, Hardik had almost stalled work.
There was a lot of work that needed to be done on the tender.
Umesh, too, hadn't been very regular, and since he had a
tendency to slacken off, Hardik needed to keep him on a leash.

He relented, got ready and left. Ishita had also left. It
seemed as if the sudden silence in the house rushed towards
Chhaya in order to claim her as its own.

She sat there on the sofa for a long time, gazing at the garden. It would be safe to assume that in that silence, her thoughts might have wandered to the events of the previous day. To Haksh's arrival, the two meeting. But it wasn't so. Nothing played on her mind. She felt, perhaps for the first time, at ease.

The sunlight had started to grow dim, making the levitating ash invisible. Soon it would be night. The cycle of life would continue.

Chhaya got up from the sofa and walked into her room. She brought a stool from under her bed and sat in front of the dressing table. She took out a comb from a drawer and let her long, curly hair flow freely. She stared at her reflection as she began combing her hair. The deafening silence in the house seemed to be all-consuming. Everything was still.

Chhaya placed the comb on the table and opened another drawer. She could feel the touch of cold metal brush against her clammy skin. She brought the revolver out in the open. Embossed on the handle in bold black letters was the word 'Hardik'. Chhaya looked at herself in the mirror, holding the gun. She then saw herself bring the nozzle close to her head, touching her right temple. An inch of skin near the exposed temple shrunk just a bit.

The silence in the house was soon disturbed by the loud noise of a gunshot. A few seconds later, the silence returned to reclaim its reign over the doomed house.

# EPILOGUE

## Interstate

What was the song they used to listen to when they were kids? Haksh tried to remember. But, for the first time, nothing came to him.

The evening had draped itself over the vast stretches of the Interstate. There was still a long way to go. Haksh kept walking.

The days spent in Old City were now a blur. As if they were all some part of a dream. As if he himself was some part of a dream—a lost phantom trying to wake up.

*Is it we who dream, or are we somehow parts of someone else's dream?* thought Haksh.

The empty soulless land stared back at him but offered no answer.

Haksh put his hands in his pockets and felt the rough edges of crumpled paper. He took them out. Currency notes—both from Old City and Millennium City.

And yet, such a vast difference lay between these two. Difference of value. Difference of meaning.

*Like him and Chhaya together*, he thought.

Her curly, black hair flowing away as she walked, in that sombre night outside her house. Haksh replayed the memory in his mind and reminisced about how she looked. The last thing she said to him.

*Soon.*

The word rung like an explosion in his ears.

Around him, darkness had begun to gather. Like a pack of beasts so common in these parts.

*In some ways, was he one too?* Haksh thought.

As always, no answer was forthcoming.

Without her, there was no point to it at all. No point to love. No point to hate.

Chhaya knew that.

*Soon.*

Soon, the Interstate, with no definition, with no loyalty to belong anywhere, would glimmer in the thick darkness of the night. The beasts would be out. Looking for their next victim. And Haksh's questions that never got answered would waft here forever.

Haksh walked. In front of him, the darklands, like his questions, stretched for eternity.

# ACKNOWLEDGEMENTS

A host of people were responsible for this book.

Anupam Kant Verma, during his time at Penguin, envisioned and championed it, and saw the book through its initial stages. My dearest friend, this adventure started because of you.

Arpita Nath, for taking over the book. An extraordinary editor, it was she who read the book minutely and gave some amazing suggestions. More than anything else, for being patient with me. Writers can be difficult people to deal with—and I, in particular—but she was always available—even in the dark of the night—to go through the various editorial changes with me.

Aditi Batra, for diligently and patiently going through the entire manuscript with a keen and watchful eye, removing errors as they cropped up. If the book is better, it's because of her.

Kanishka Gupta of Writer's Side, my agent; though the word 'agent' is grossly inadequate to define the friendship we have shared over the years, we have always been bound by our shared love for books.

The staff at Penguin are someone I have forged a bond with, and it all started with this book. Hemali Sodhi, Sohini Mitra, Ahlawat Gunjan, to name a few.

To Nandini Sundar, for being an early champion of the book and for all the support. Also to N. Kalyan Raman, who started off as my teacher and then became a lifelong mentor and friend. Gratitude also to Veejay Sai, one of the first friends I made in this journey.

Anees Salim, for being an early reader and for generously agreeing to give me a quote.

The book owes a wealth of gratitude to my friends and family—in particular, Mom, Dad, Shreya, Rituparna and Ritwika—for their unwavering love and support, for being there through thick and thin and for teaching me the value of love, a lesson I don't think I've fully learnt yet.

My grandfather, my two aunts.

To Pratichi, Avipsha, Maitryee.

Also, Supriyo, Jay, Vipul—friends for all time.

Two ex-colleagues and now comrades-in-arms: Khemta and Sahal.

Pallavi, Astha, Shraddha, Pranay, Esha Verma.

Pallavi Pundir, for being a friend and for lending a patient ear to my pitches, first for the *Indian Express* and then for *Vice*.

Martand Kaushik for the love at the *Caravan*, Arunava Sinha for giving me an open platform to write for Scroll, Aditya Mani Jha, Tanuj Solanki and many, many more.

If I've missed someone, the fault is mine. But that in no way means I'm not indebted to you.